With unflinching honesty and heart, *To Have and to Hold* offers an achingly beautiful yet hope-filled portrait of one woman's journey to motherhood. Brown writes with a rare tenderness and courage, shedding light on a subject often kept in the shadows. Readers will feel deeply seen within these pages and will be reminded of the fierce and enduring strength of a mother's love—even before the first lullaby is sung.

—Janine Rosche, Selah Award-winning author of *The Road before Us*

Christian fiction author Deb Brown's debut novel, "To Have and To Hold," is a stunning, poignant novel about a loving couple experiencing the most exquisitely personal of human dramas—the longing for a child while facing the agonizing highs and lows of infertility. Deb Brown's crisp writing is smart and poignant, painting powerful images and complex characters we cheer for and cry with. Most laudable is the masterful way she handles this delicate topic, with painful honesty, empathy, humor, and faith.

—Laurie (L.C.) Lewis, author of Whitney Award's Novel of the Year,
*The Letter Carrier*

In "To Have and to Hold," Deb Brown paints a sensitive and oh-so-real portrait of the rollercoaster that is infertility, pregnancy loss, and adoption. Those who have experienced any of these realities will recognize themselves in Amelia and Melvin: the stress, the conflict, the need for grace and forgiveness in marriage, the raging at God, and the difficulty of discerning how much to tell and to whom. Women who have gone through these experiences know that no matter what you tell or don't tell others, the responses will always cause you further pain. This book should be required reading for all people of good will who have not walked this road. Perhaps it can bear fruit in a community of people better able to understand and support those who weather some of life's most difficult journeys.

—Kathleen Basi, Author of *A Song For The Road*, traveling story-teller/musician, and composer of "Come, All You Thirsty," ACP's 2022 Song of the Year

# *To* HAVE *and to* HOLD

DEB L. BROWN

PESHINA
PUBLISHING

I waited patiently for the Lord; and he inclined unto me, and heard my cry.

Psalm 40:1 KJV

But they that wait upon the Lord shall renew *their* strength; they shall mount up with wings as eagles; they shall run, and not be weary; *and* they shall walk, and not faint.

Isaiah 40:31 KJV

To all those who are waiting upon the Lord for answers to their prayers, I testify that He hears you. May you feel His Holy Spirit guiding you in this season of waiting.

# Chapter 1

A t what point do you cross the line from tenacity to insanity?

My thumb hovers over the screen as I scroll through social media. *The definition of insanity is doing the same thing over and over and expecting different results.* The graphic quote shouts at me from my phone.

A piercing alarm interrupts my thoughts, and I swipe my finger to silence it. I close my eyes to compose myself. I won't cry. *Pull it together, Amelia.* I remind myself that I can handle this. After all, this is how I spend my lunch hour every day—running home for my ovulation test. My mind counts the months I have been going through this routine with nothing to show for it. Maybe I *am* crazy.

Most women test first thing in the morning, but I have done a *lot* of research. The hormone surge won't show up in my urine until four hours after waking up. And after ovulation, I only have a twelve-to twenty-four-hour window to get pregnant. Testing twice a day doubles my chances of getting it right. I don't want to take the test at work. Fortunately, I live close enough to run home, take the pee test, eat lunch while I wait for the results, and then rush back to work without drawing any attention.

The process was fun and exciting when Melvin and I first started trying for kids. Private moments together. Each month, anticipating new life. But after six months with no results, I did what I always do when something isn't working. I searched for solutions. My attention shifted from playing the game to analyzing the game plan. I changed my diet, started taking prenatal vitamins, and scheduled baby-making on the most optimal days. It was like playing a team sport instead of pickup ball at the park. We had a game scheduled, and we showed up. Without fail. You can count on us. Team Greathouse. But my playbook needs some tweaks. It's been another six months, and we haven't won.

As I push back from the kitchen counter, the barstool scrapes on the wood floor. I abandon my lunch and slip to the bathroom to check the ovulation test stick. Negative again. I don't know why I expected anything different. My blue-gray eyes stare back at me through the mirror. I run my fingers through my long blonde hair. A couple of squirts of hairspray to tame the frizzy spots. A fresh coat of lip gloss. I eye the clock. Time to get back to the office. I can't seem to plan my pregnancy, so I'll stick with planning events. At least I know I'm good at that.

I dash into the office as the staff meeting is about to start. Proceeding straight to the conference room, I grab an ice-cold bottle of water and twist into the soft black seat. A whoosh of air escapes the chair. I browse the agenda on the table. The smell of coffee floods the room from the steaming cups in front of each of my coworkers. I peer around the room and smile at the four other members of the team.

Margot is the owner of Turn of Events. There are three employees, plus our intern. She's been running this business for over 20 years. She trusted me to take charge of an event next month, and I'm eager to show her what I can do. I scan through my checklist, anticipating every possibility before I begin so I can execute it with perfection.

"Our customer appreciation event for Prosperity Capital is a month away. They wanted an art theme, and I kind of have an 'in.'" I smile and wink. Melvin is a curator at the art museum. "We have the place reserved for the evening. As guests arrive, the photographer will greet them at the front entryway and take pictures." I turn my attention to the intern. "Hailey, did you find a photographer yet?"

"Yeah. My sister does photography, and she said she could do it cheap. I thought it would help with the budget." Her brown eyes blink over the rims of her glasses.

The muscles in my shoulders tense. "I'm sure your sister is great, Hailey. But we have a list of vetted photographers we use. If she wants to go through the process, we can use her in the future. But for now, we need to stick with our approved vendors." I smile politely. "Don't worry about it. I'll book the photographer. I was talking to one the other day, and she owes me a favor."

No one owes me any favors.

I turn my attention to the other side of the table. "Theresa, do you have the catering menu confirmed?"

"Yes. They have five different appetizers for the reception." Theresa tucks her long, light brown hair behind her ear, consulting her notes. "And at the end of the night, they will serve fruit tartlets for dessert."

"Are we covering our bases with gluten-free and vegan options? I'm a bit concerned about the tartlets." My fingers adjust the paper, squaring it with the edge of the table.

"I verified it. They will have a crustless option for the tartlets. The rest of the menu items cover our dietary needs."

My shoulders relax, and I place a checkmark next to the food tasks. "Perfect. Could you email me the menu so I have it on file?"

Theresa nods, and I move on, reviewing the details for the scavenger hunt activity that Melvin helped me plan.

"It sounds like everything is on track, Amelia. This will be a memorable event." Margot smiles, and a sense of pride swells in my chest. Perhaps she does notice how hard I work.

The moment the meeting is over, I hurry to my desk and send inquiries to photographers we have worked with in the past. If you want something done right, you have to do it yourself.

Turn of Events focuses on corporate gatherings, but I secretly love children's birthday parties. And I can't wait to have my own children so I can celebrate with them every year. Corporate events bring people together, but a birthday celebrates a life, an individual. And children's parties are full of fun and whimsy. Kind of like Melvin. I suppose that's why I was drawn to him.

After dinner that night, I take my nightly ovulation test. I hover over the stick lying on the glossy white granite counter and wait. The first pale line appears, telling me it's working. Wait. Is that another line? Am I imagining things? No. The line gets darker like an ink stain in a shirt pocket, spreading across the strip as hope spreads through my heart. When my alarm goes off, I'm sure. It's positive! Even though I've been persistent about testing for ovulation, I've never been able to pinpoint it before now. I practically skip out to Melvin, who is watching TV in the living room, reclining on the grey couch, his legs propped up on the footstool.

"Look who's positive!" I wave the stick with a smile.

"Really?" His eyes dart from the TV, and a grin spreads over his face.

"I'm *positive*!" I emphasize with a laugh.

"Get over here!" He holds out his arms.

I cross the room, and he pulls me onto his lap.

"Are you ready to make a baby?" he asks, kissing me behind my ear, waves of his hair tickling my cheek.

"Not so fast, Romeo." I place my hand on his chest and push away slightly. "I've studied this. Your swimmers are best in the morning. Let's save the romance until then."

"In the morning? We have work tomorrow." He pulls me close and whispers in my ear. "How are we going to squeeze that in?"

"Oh, don't worry. I think I can squeeze you in." I wink and pull away. "If you get up half an hour early, I'll make it worth your while." I place a lingering kiss on his lips and gently stroke his jaw. "And imagine how it will put a spring in your step for the day." I run my hands down his muscular biceps. "But that means we need to get to bed earlier tonight. So…" I rest my forehead on his. "Goodnight."

He chuckles, bouncing me on his lap. "All right. I'll be up in a bit." Melvin plants a kiss on my cheek, and I dance my way down the hall, my insides swirling with excitement. We're finally on the right track.

\*\*\*

The high-pitched beep of my alarm wakes me. I turn it off and smile. This could be the day I get pregnant. The anticipation kept me from falling asleep last night. I roll over and nuzzle up to Melvin, sliding my arm underneath the sheets and around his chest. I deliver a trail of gentle kisses on his shoulder and run my fingers through his wavy brown hair. It's wild and unruly in the morning. "Good morning, sweetheart. It's game time."

Melvin rolls on top of me, enveloping me in his arms. We connect with new purpose and hope. Team Greathouse plays a strong game. We won't know for another couple of weeks if we won the championship, but we relish knowing we played our best.

"Ready to hit the showers?" Melvin turns for the bathroom.

"I need to lie down for another fifteen minutes. They say it helps increase the odds." I blow him a kiss. "Good game, hon. I'd say you hit a home run."

I rest my hands on my pudgy abdomen. Is it possible? Could there already be a little Greathouse starting life inside of me? My heart flutters with the possibility. Although I love being an event planner, the job title I want most of all is "Mom." I've always wanted to raise a family. And I know how much Melvin wants it, too. He wants to be a better dad than the one he grew up with. I twirl my wedding ring on my finger, imagining our future. This could be the start of our family.

***

The buzzer on my phone echoes through my ears, just barely exceeding the volume of my anxious heart. I don't know if I'm more afraid to look or more afraid not to. Bad news might be waiting on the other side of that pregnancy test - a single line could destroy the confidence I've built inside me since Melvin and I were last together.

The plan is going well so far. I have the symptoms—lack of a period, mood swings, and a few cravings.

But I've read that those things could all be psychosomatic, and I may be fooling myself.

I blow out a long puff, my fingers touching the cool edge of the counter. *Think positively.* I've done everything right. *We've* done everything right. This is the one. It will be the one.

I swallow hard and pinch my eyes shut. The test flips in my hand, and after a few more calming breaths, I peek one eye open.

One line.

One dreaded pink line. Not a glimpse of another in sight.

My hope and my heart fly from me like a balloon, careening around the room as it loses all its air. My knees give out, and I stumble to my bed, flopping on my back and staring at the ceiling.

Tears gather in the corners of my eyes, and my arms don't have the strength to wipe them away. They slowly slide down my face, pooling in my ears. If we can't get a win by doing everything right, then how can we?

***

Melvin greets me with a hug when I get home from work. "Hey, Melly. How was your day?"

"I'm not pregnant," I say without any preamble. "Again." I rest my head on his collarbone and exhale slowly, finally allowing the sadness I have been holding back all day at work to slip out. He's only slightly taller than me, but those few inches make me feel watched over and protected.

"I saw the test." He tucks my blonde hair behind my ears. "I know you're heartbroken. But this isn't a dead end; it's just a detour." He cups my face with his hands, his thumbs brushing the tears from my cheeks. "I've been praying about it a lot—probably annoying God at this point—and I really believe we're supposed to be parents. He's just taking us on the scenic path." A crooked smile spreads across his face. "And when we get there, you will be the most amazing mother. The kind who has the route planned out, the reservations made, and remembers all our favorite road trip snacks."

I lean back against the counter, fixating on my feet. The weight of the negative test crushes in on my chest. Merely hearing the word *mother* triggers a wave of disappointment that rolls through my stomach. "I wish I had your conviction. Right now, I sure don't think of myself as amazing." My throat tightens. I want to make Melvin a dad. What if I can't? I swallow the lump and continue in a low voice. "I'm beginning to think I'm broken. This is what my body was created to do. Why can't mine do it?" I turn away, ignoring the ache in my heart, and busy myself gathering ingredients for dinner.

He takes a step toward me, his eyebrows drawn together. "Amelia, it's not your fault. We're doing everything right. Why don't you make an appointment and find out what the doctor says?"

"You're right. It's just that I hate those doctors. I feel exposed. Literally." The back of my neck bristles, and my abdomen tightens as I struggle to peel back the outer layers of the onion. *What if the doctor delivers more disappointing news?* "From what I've learned, they won't do anything for you until you've been trying for at least a year. It doesn't make sense to pay for the doctor to tell me, 'just keep trying,' or worse, to hear what's wrong with me. All of our friends are getting pregnant. Why can't we?"

Melvin leans against the counter next to me, slowly shaking his head, his lips pulled together. "We've been trying for *over* a year. Let's get some help. Make the appointment, and I'll take off work and go with you." He rubs my back, hesitating. "We don't know. It could be a simple solution. Give the doctor a chance."

I slice through the onion, and hot tears bite at the backs of my eyes. I'll blame it on dinner, even though my aching heart begs to differ. Gulping, I bring the knife down over and over, while I gather myself.

"Okay," I agree with my always-optimistic husband. "After dinner, I'll go online and schedule an appointment."

He grins, the lines creasing his cheeks, then places a kiss on my forehead. Even though my faith isn't as strong as his, *I'm* strong, and I've got this.

*** 

Melvin and I sit in the waiting room. His leg bounces next to me. The little basketballs on his socks seem like they're dribbling down the court. His short, wiry frame appears ready to pounce. I cross my legs and flip through a magazine, noticing every sound around me. Papers shuffle at the receptionist's desk. Footsteps echo down the hall. A door creaks open.

"Amelia Greathouse?"

We startle at my name and stand up, following the nurse. Some bloodwork. A urine sample. An exam. Anxiously awaiting a verdict. *Just give it to me straight.*

The doctor finishes the exam and helps me sit up on the exam table, with a paper cloth across my lap. "I'm glad you came in today. I know it can be frustrating when you're trying to get pregnant, and it doesn't happen. This is more common than you realize."

I give a skeptical glance to Melvin across the cold, sterile exam room. His kind brown eyes focus back at me. Everyone I know is announcing their pregnancy on Instagram. Except me.

"You've been doing all the right things. The next step is to try medication to stimulate ovulation. Sometimes our bodies need a little extra help." She writes the prescription. "Let's give this a try and see you in six months if it isn't successful. It may still take a few cycles, but for many women, this is all the help they need." A jolt of optimism zips through my body. Maybe she's right. Maybe this is all we need.

We thank her, and she leaves. I shimmy off the table, and Melvin hands me my clothes. We silently process her words. Hand in hand, we exit the building, my insides quivering.

"Want to grab some sushi before we head to work?" Melvin asks. He knows it's my favorite. My mind races to find the right words.

"I'm taking myself off raw fish. It says online that pregnant women shouldn't eat it. I'm trying to be more careful about my diet. It might be part of the problem."

He crinkles his eyebrows and purses his lips. "I guess I hadn't realized that." We caravan to our favorite sub sandwich shop instead. I order a salad because lunch meat is also a no-no.

"What do you think about what the doctor said?" Melvin unwraps his sandwich.

"I'm all over the place. I want to trust that the fertility meds will do the trick." My stomach flutters with the possibility. "But I'm also disappointed we can't do this on our own." I bite my lip and concentrate on opening my bag of chips. "If having babies is a natural thing, then why isn't it coming naturally for us?" I pop a whole-grain chip into my mouth, crunching into its salty ridges.

Melvin examines his food. "What if it's my fault?"

My heart plummets at the expression on his face, usually so upbeat and positive. A line forms above the bridge of his nose, his straw forming endless circles in his drink.

I place my hand on his, pausing his circling. "I'm not searching for blame...only answers."

Melvin drops the straw and intertwines his fingers with mine. "The fertility drugs could be the answer to our prayers. I mean... we've done our part," he pauses and winks at me. A warm smile spreads across my face. "God often answers prayers through other people. Maybe this is our answer."

"You're right." I release the air in my lungs and press my palm to my heart. "I need to keep my hope in Christ. He knows our problems, and He has our solutions."

After lunch, we both walk to our cars. He embraces me and gives me a quick peck on the cheek. "After dinner. Tonight?" He raises his eyebrows and dips his chin. "Practice makes perfect."

I let a giggle slip from my lips. I don't mind the practice, and I try to be perfect, but in this one area of my life, I'm falling short.

# Chapter 2

I don't know why Melvin can't get ready according to schedule. I pull the door open and step over the threshold. The car is loaded and ready to go. Gifts. Food. Decorations. *Check. Check. Check.* We should be leaving for the gender reveal party right now, so I can help set up. All he had to do was get dressed, and here I am... *waiting*. I focus on the mirror by the front door and check my outfit. The flowy blue blouse hangs long over my navy pants and disguises my imperfect middle. My long blonde hair hangs in perfect loose curls, just past my collarbone. I check my makeup. It brings out the blue in my eyes. My heart is engaged in a tug of war. I'm excited for Allie and Powers, but also a little jealous. I open my fertility app on my phone and scroll through the data. The charts and graphs are proof of our efforts over the last six months. I have been meticulous about every detail. But we still have nothing to show for it. Time to get my game face on. *I can do this. I'm ready.* Checking the clock, I straighten the pictures on the entry table and let out a deep sigh.

Melvin bounds out from the hallway with a swagger in his step. He places one hand on his hip and the other behind his head. "How do I look?"

As I turn and take him in from head to toe, a chuckle slips out of my lips. "So, you're team girl, then?"

Pale pink board shorts fall slightly above his knees, and the matching pink Hawaiian shirt with little black flamingo silhouettes fits snugly across his chest. He slips on a pair of sunglasses, runs his hand through the curls on top of his head, and takes a bow. My heart and frustrations melt at his adorable silliness.

"Yeah. I totally envision them as girl parents. I mean, can you imagine Powers with a little princess? He'll be a great girl dad." His voice swells with excitement.

"I don't know. I can picture him tossing the baseball to a little boy. Besides, Allie would be the mom to raise a perfect gentleman." I hold my arms out, giving him a good view of my navy top and blue jeans. My lips press tightly into a half smile; and I blow out a puff through my nose.

He pulls me into his arms, dips me, and raises his eyebrows. "We can do this. Let's leave our troubles behind and enjoy ourselves." He kisses my cheek, lifts me back up, and grips my hand.

My smile spreads, and I pull him out the door, shaking my head. He lets go of my hand, bows, and offers his elbow. "M'lady?" I slip my hand through his arm, and he escorts me to the car, opening the door for me. We drive in silence, both of us happy to see friends and celebrate, but dreading the inevitable. It seems that no matter where we go, people insist on asking *the* question. *"So... are you guys ready to have kids yet?"* or *"When are you going to start a family?"* I know people mean well, but it's none of their business.

We pull up in front of their white bungalow and walk to the backyard. I inhale the scent of the rose bushes growing alongside the house. There are round tables scattered across the yard, covered in white linens, and a food buffet near the sliding glass door.

Allie waves from across the lawn. She is adorable. Absolutely glowing, as they say. Her clingy white dress accentuates her cute little pregnancy bump. I love her, but right now? It hurts. I can't stop thinking about the fact that she has what I want. I smooth my blouse over my stomach, the emptiness crawling to my heart and stinging my eyes. Fingers crossed that someday soon, I'll be greeting guests in a flowing white sundress with my belly poking out.

"Hey, Allie. You look amazing, as always." I say, and she pulls me into a hug, her growing torso pressing against my empty one. I pull back and stretch out my arms. "Team boy, here! But Mr. Hollywood is all in for team girl." I point my thumb over my shoulder and roll my eyes in Melvin's direction.

"You two are the best." She pauses, nibbling her bottom lip before leaning in close. "I'm sure we'll have one of these parties for you soon." She settles her arm around my shoulder. She understands. Best friends. We hoped we would do everything together. But so far, not this.

The sun shines through the trees on this beautiful early autumn day. There is a light, shifting breeze, making it pleasant for an outdoor party. I bring my tortilla pinwheels to the food table and rearrange everything in a logical order. Plates first, then appetizers and vegetables, cookies, candy pacifiers, cups, and lemon water.

*That's better.*

Allie had already brought the food out, but it was a little helter-skelter. Even though I'm not officially "on duty," I can't help myself. The event planner part of me knows how to organize and arrange things for maximum efficiency. And it drives me crazy when things are out of sequence. I drag a slice of orange sweet pepper through the ranch dip for a quick taste test. Cool. Creamy. Delicious.

I move on to the 'guess' station, placing the sign with instructions next to the basket. As guests enter the backyard, they sign their names on either a pink or blue piece of paper and place it in the basket. If everyone dresses in pink or blue, do they really need to enter their guess?

The thought flees from my mind, and I look up to see Allie's sister, Claire, walking into the backyard in a lovely orange sundress. It's adorable, but you would think the sister of the guest of honor would read the invitation.

"Amelia!" she squeals. "This is so exciting! I can't wait to be an auntie! When are you and Melvin going to have a baby? Wouldn't it be fun for you and Allie to be moms together?"

*And so it begins.*

I let out a nervous laugh. "We're enjoying our freedom right now. I need sleep too much to give it up for a crying baby." Sarcasm. Deflection. I've learned it's the best way to handle these comments.

As the guests trickle in, I play hostess and make sure everyone follows the rules and registers their vote before directing them to the food. Helping out is part of the unspoken rhythm of our friendship. Allie doesn't have to ask. She knows I will jump in and make sure things run smoothly. Soon, the yard is buzzing with conversation and excitement.

"All right, everyone. Gather around!" Allie waves, holding a giant opaque white balloon. "Thank you for coming. Let's empty the ballot box and count your guesses. Amelia, will you do the honors?"

"A lot of you are dressed in blue." I pause and sort the cards. "But it seems like more of you voted for a girl than for a boy. There are thirteen votes for girl and eleven for boy."

Powers slides his arm around Allie's shoulder. "On the count of three, we'll pop the balloon," his deep voice booms to the crowd.

"One... two..." everyone chants in unison. Allie and Powers adjust their pins to pop the balloon, and a gust of wind whooshes through the yard. The string slips from Allie's hand, and it blows sideways, around the house. Allie's eyes grow wide as she grasps at the string.

"Guess we'll find out when the baby is born." Powers shrugs, chuckling.

"We are *not* waiting until the baby is born!" Allie throws her hands up, fighting tears.

"I've got it," Melvin says. "Don't worry."

We all shift, making small talk while he takes off toward the front yard, his Hawaiian shirt fluttering as he runs around the corner of the house. After a few moments, my phone dings with a text.

Melvin

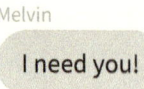
I need you!

I walk casually to the front, picking up speed as I go. What's wrong? Is he okay? As I round the corner, my heart plummets. Shredded pink confetti clings to the grass while deflated remnants of the balloon litter the yard.

"What in the world happened?" I ask.

"It hit a branch and popped. What are we going to do?" He runs his hands through his hair, pacing back and forth.

I go into full rescue mode and think as fast as I can. "Give me the car keys." I can't let Allie down.

"Are you *leaving*?" He freezes, his eyes widening.

"No. Give me the keys." He hands them over, and I rifle through the trunk. I grab a reusable grocery bag and return to his side. "We can still salvage this. We'll shove the confetti in the bag and toss it at them. It will have almost the same effect."

We're on our hands and knees, picking up tiny pieces of pink paper and shoving them in the bag, when Allie, Powers, and the guests meander around the side of the house.

"Dude, what happened?" asks Powers.

I cautiously stand and brush off pieces of pink confetti from my blue jeans. "Surprise! It's a girl!" I cheer, holding out my arms.

"Sorry, man. I tried. The balloon hit the tree." Melvin rises, his shoulders rounded in defeat.

"We're having a girl?" Powers pulls Allie in for a hug.

"We're having a girl!" Allie bounces on her toes and kisses him.

Standing next to me, Melvin's hand finds mine. My heart thuds inside my chest. What would it be like if we were expecting a daughter?

Melvin pumps my hand once and releases it, striding over to Powers. "Congratulations, man. This is awesome. Why don't you two stand over there and I'll snap some photos for you?" My handsome photographer husband takes over, giving directions.

Allie and Powers stand surrounded by the mess. Melvin tells the guests to throw handfuls of confetti, and everyone wanders to the backyard to continue the celebration. I clasp Melvin's hand and lean my head on his shoulder, following the guests. If only I had attached a weight to the balloon. I hate that Allie's reveal didn't go as planned, and on the ride home, I hate myself even more for the jealousy twisting around my insides during the party.

"Can you believe that?" Melvin asks. "What an anticlimactic failure."

A staccato giggle bubbles up from my throat, and my brow furrows. "Honestly, these gender reveal parties are getting a little over the top. If we ever have a kid—" My voice falters, an unexpected wave of disappointment hitting me like being rear-ended at a stoplight. I swallow hard and cough lightly. "Let's skip the gender reveal and find out at the ultrasound like normal human beings." The words crackle as they leave my mouth, and I sniffle, my heart dropping into my stomach.

He takes my hand. "*When* we have a kid. We'll have a house full of them. We haven't been trying for long." He traces circles across my knuckles.

"It's been a year and a half already. We started the medication six months ago, and the doctor thought that would do the trick. But we're right back where we began."

"Don't worry, Amelia. It will happen. Didn't the doctor say if it wasn't working after six months, you should make another appointment?"

"Yeah. I just feel like such a failure. I was sure this would work, but it hasn't. The next thing might not work either."

"Send a message to the doctor. Find out what she says. We can't give up. God has a plan for us." He pulls my hand to his lips and gently kisses it.

"You're right. I will." With a slow breath, I gaze through the window at the world rushing by. If only it would stop for a minute so I could uncover the answers I've been searching for. God has a solution to every problem, right? So, where is ours?

# Chapter 3

M elvin and I huddle together at the dining room table in front of the laptop for a virtual appointment with our new fertility doctor. I smooth the tablecloth and adjust the angle of the screen. Dr. Larson is supposed to be one of the best. She's gifted in this specialty. I place my hands in my lap and fiddle with my wedding ring, sliding it off and on repeatedly. My heart flip-flops in my chest when the call connects. She appears on the screen, her short brown hair cut in a bob.

Dr. Larson straightens her glasses and begins. "I've reviewed your history, and I'm glad you made this appointment. When the standard methods aren't working, it's time to try something different." Her eyebrows pinch together. Melvin lays his hand on my knee, the calming connection spreading through me to ease my troubled heart. "However, I want you to understand that going through infertility treatments is a big commitment. It's important to talk to each other as you go through the process. There may come a time when the cost of moving forward is too high. It might be a financial burden, but consider the emotional and physical costs." Melvin and I share a meaningful glance. This journey has already taken a toll. "For whatever reason, when the cost is too high, there is nothing wrong with stopping. Growing your family is important, but not if it costs you your health or your relationship. Only you can determine how much you can handle." She smiles warmly and explains the process.

"The next step is to schedule Amelia for the initial tests and get a sample from Melvin for analysis," she says. "You can bring the sample on the same day Amelia has her tests, but the sample needs to arrive within an hour. It needs to stay at body temperature—not too hot, not too cold. The best way we've found is to tuck it under your arm," she puts her hand in her armpit for demonstration, "or hold it between your legs when you're transporting it."

Melvin clears his throat. "No problem." He squirms in his seat, running his hand across the back of his neck. Little beads of sweat emerge on his forehead, and his ears turn red. The last thing he wants to do is discuss his 'sample' with a female doctor.

She goes over more housekeeping details, leaving us with a reminder that the nurse will call to handle scheduling.

Melvin blows out a shaky breath, closing the laptop when the call ends. "Well, that was awkward."

I shrug and push from the table. "It's not a big deal for them. They deal with this literally every day. It's only awkward if you make it awkward." I cross the kitchen and pack my lunch to go to work.

Melvin twists in his chair. "I don't like to talk about my swimmers. They're analyzing my manhood and making me produce it in a way nature never intended." He shivers and covers his face with his hands.

"It's a medical procedure. It's science to them." I fold my arms across my chest and cock my head toward him. Is he serious right now? He's going to have to get over it. "Besides, if I can bear everything on the table over and over again, the least you can do is produce a sample." Glancing across the kitchen, I look at him with my eyes full of pleading.

"I'll produce it, but you need to deliver it. I'm not going to show up holding my vial. Those ladies behind the counter know exactly what I was doing, and they'll probably smirk and giggle when I turn around and walk out the door."

I narrow my eyes. "Do you really think that? No one's smirking or giggling. It's just part of their job." A frustrated breath escapes. "I'll deliver it. My appointment's at the same time, anyway." Honestly, his contribution to our science experiment is far less painful and humiliating than mine. I just want to be a mother. Whatever it takes, I'm all in.

***

It's D-Day.

Delivery day.

Melvin isolates himself in the bathroom to produce a specimen. I check the time, waiting for him to emerge. When I can't wait any longer, I tap on the door. "Can I come in? I need to get ready."

"Fine." Melvin huffs and swings the door open, a towel wrapped around his waist.

"Performance anxiety?" I tip my head at him.

He runs his fingers through his brown hair and studies the floor. "I guess so."

I release a breath. "Let me take care of it." I dial up the heat like a summer day, and quicker than you can turn on the hose, Melvin fills the collection cup like a kiddie pool in the backyard.

"See? That wasn't so hard, was it, sweetheart?" I smile up at him.

The side of his mouth quirks up. "Couldn't have done it without you."

I finish getting ready after he leaves for work. The clock is ticking as I rush out the door. I put the collection cup in a brown paper lunch bag to be a bit more discreet and nestle it between my legs for the drive to the clinic.

Every traffic light is red on my route. When the upcoming light goes yellow, I speed up slightly and sneak through. Red and blue lights flash in my rearview mirror.

*Dang.*

I pull over and rifle through the glove box for insurance papers.

The officer approaches. "Excuse me, ma'am. Do you know why I pulled you over?"

"The light was orange?" I smile sweetly.

He doesn't crack a grin. "I need to see your license and registration." He eyes the paper bag between my legs. "Can I ask what you have in your sack there? Do you have an open container?"

My heart jumps into my throat, and I hold up my hands, shaking my head emphatically. "No! No, officer, I swear. It's a sample I'm dropping off at the clinic. I'm on a bit of a time crunch, which is why I pushed my luck when the light turned yellow. I'm so sorry."

"What sort of sample?"

"It's my husband's semen specimen," I blurt out. "It's supposed to stay at body temperature, which is why I put it between my legs. See?" I shove the vial at him.

His eyes bug out, and he takes it between his thumb and pointer finger, inspecting it at arm's length as though he might catch a disease if he gets too close to it. "Okay. This is a first for me." He passes it back through the car window and adjusts his belt, clearing his throat. "Hang on a minute. I'll be back with your license and registration." I watch him amble to his squad car in my mirror and let out a sigh. He takes what seems like *for-ev-er* to process everything. Not wanting to be late, I nervously check the clock. I can't put Melvin through this again.

The officer hands me my license and registration, and a slip of paper. "I'm going to let you off with a warning today, ma'am. But please be more careful. And for the record... our traffic lights are red, yellow, and green. There is no orange in the future, got it?"

"Got it. Thank you, officer." He walks to his vehicle, and I consider the time. Ten minutes. I desperately want to peel out of here, but it's probably not a good idea with a police car directly behind me.

I merge into traffic and make it to the clinic with minutes to spare.

# Chapter 4

Sunday evening, I call my mom to catch up while I clean the kitchen. Mom and I have always been close, and I look forward to our weekly calls. She's one of the kindest and most compassionate people I know.

"How's work been going for you?" she asks.

"We're in the middle of planning for the Restaurant Convention. Margot put me in charge of the classes and cooking demonstrations, but she asked me to work with our intern, Hailey." I flip the dishwasher shut with a click. "Last time I worked with her, I ended up having to do it all myself. I can't let her inexperience reflect badly on me." I toss the dishcloth onto the sink and wander into the living room.

"Oh, honey. That's hard. But sometimes you have to let people do their jobs. You can't do everything yourself. Learn to let other people help you. You are capable, but you aren't Superwoman."

"I realize that, Mom, but I'm the only person I can depend on. It's easier this way. I want to impress Margot and show her what I'm capable of."

"Sometimes people will step up, and you'll be pleasantly surprised. Give them a chance to help you once in a while."

"I will, Mom." I toss her well-meaning advice aside like junk mail into the recycling bin. It's a good idea in theory, but it never works for me.

***

As the fall days grow shorter, I begin my preparations for the holidays. Today is our annual Christmas crafting day. We've been doing it since college. Allie and I each choose a craft we can make in bulk to give away as gifts and spend a Saturday in early November working on them. I arrange all the ingredients for soup mixes on the counter in order: lentils, pasta, and seasonings. The doorbell rings, and I usher Allie, along with her bags of supplies, into the dining room.

"Is that everything?" I ask.

"Yeah. There's a lot, but I couldn't decide between bath bombs or shower steamers, so I brought enough to make both." She searches through her bag and pulls out a giant container of baking soda.

We settle into a rhythm, assembling dried soup mixes in canning jars.

"How's everything going with the pregnancy?" I ask.

"It's been going really well. I'm almost to my third trimester." She gazes down and slides her hands over her belly. "That's when I pack on the pounds and get uncomfortable."

"Well, you look amazing." I share my most sincere smile.

"How are things coming for you in the baby department?" Beans rattle against the glass as she tips a scoop into a jar.

My heart clenches in my chest, and I blow out a breath. "We keep trying and failing. The infertility drugs didn't work. I've been poked and prodded, tested, and evaluated—and Melvin has too."

"I bet he loved that."

"You have no idea." I tilt my head and raise my eyebrows at her. "The latest disappointment was IUI. I was so sure that it would work. We're getting ready to try IVF—the holy grail of infertility treatments, and also the most expensive. I could still be pregnant before the end of the year, but I'm not getting my hopes up. Otherwise, the disappointment is too devastating."

"I'm sorry. It must be rough." Allie folds me in her arms, and I relax. I don't have to pretend with her like I do with other people in my life.

"Thanks. I've spent a lot of time on my knees, and I'm trying to trust that God is in charge." I straighten, pulling in air through my nose and huffing it back out. "But enough about my medical procedures. Let's get these soup jars made." I wave my hands along the counter, doing my best game show host imitation.

\*\*\*

Weeks later, we leave our quiet Minnesota home and make the trek to Ohio for the holiday to be with Melvin's family.

"Happy Thanksgiving!" My mother-in-law, Brenda, greets us at her door. We take off our coats and hand out hugs and handshakes like raffle tickets at a school carnival.

"How's our favorite starving artist?" Melvin's dad, Marcus, booms, enveloping him in a hug. Although barely a few inches taller than Melvin, his imposing stature and deep voice demand respect.

Melvin and I share a silent exchange. Marcus tries to be funny, but I understand how much those jabs hurt him. He badgered Melvin incessantly when he was an undergrad to choose a major with more income potential. In the end, Melvin followed his heart, but part of him still wants to prove to his dad that he can be a good provider.

Melvin pulls back from the hug. "Still not starving, Dad."

"You definitely won't be today. Your mom's been cooking up a storm." Marcus moves down the hall, the light reflecting off his bald head.

I breathe in the smell of the turkey roasting in the oven. We haul in our luggage and make our way into the kitchen to nibble on some snacks. There is a spread of veggies and dip and adorable little Pilgrim hats made from a fudge stripe cookie and a marshmallow arranged on the island. Brenda is the queen of cookies, and her round figure is proof that she has sampled her work. I pick one up and take a bite. My teeth crack through the chocolate coating and sink into the soft marshmallow underneath.

Melvin wanders into the family room to watch the game with the guys, and I offer my help in the kitchen. Small talk halts when Brenda says not-so-casually, "So... does anyone have any big announcements for the family this year?" Her eyes dart to my belly with a rather obvious wink, then she turns and pulls the turkey out of the oven to baste it. Melvin's sisters, Celeste and Elise, pause from their kitchen tasks to look at me. Yeah, I've put on weight. Bloating is a side effect of the fertility drugs. We are in the middle of a cycle of injections to stimulate my ovaries.

"Not me. How about you, Celeste?" Heat blossoms from the inside out, and I break out in a hot flash. Impeccable timing. Another side effect. I swipe a napkin from the counter and dab my forehead.

Celeste looks at me blankly, rhythmically peeling potatoes, her shoulder-length brown hair pulled back in a ponytail. "Same old, same old with us. Tim started his job in September, but that's not new information."

"How is he liking it?" I ask, attempting to keep the conversation away from me.

The four of us girls bustle around the kitchen for the next hour, mashing potatoes, taking casserole dishes out of the oven, scooping stuffing from the bird, and bringing everything to the dining room.

We take our places at the table. Brenda has a flair for a beautiful tablescape. The gold tablecloth contrasts with the burnt orange napkins. Ceramic pumpkins and candles flank the fall floral centerpiece on either side. Before digging into the food, we go around the table for the Greathouse family Thanksgiving tradition. Everyone shares one thing they are most grateful for and one thing they are hopeful for in the coming year. It's a sweet tradition, but I have been dreading it. The grateful part is simple. It's the hopeful part that ruffles my feathers. Our deepest hope is to become parents, but we've buried our silent struggle where no one can see it.

Brenda goes first, folding her arms under her ample chest and leaning into the table. "I'm grateful to have Paul here and joining our family soon." She smiles at Elise and her fiancé. Elise loops one hand over Paul's biceps and runs the other through his dark auburn hair. They are glowing with excitement about their upcoming nuptials. "I'm hopeful our family will continue to grow, and I will be a grandma next year!" She gawks at Melvin and me, and every part of me wants to melt into a puddle on the floor.

Melvin rubs my leg under the table. "I'm grateful for my dream job at the museum this year. It took a couple of years to work my way up

to it, but I love it. And I'm hopeful we can take an epic trip next year."
He grins.

My turn. Deep breath. "I'm grateful for the new house." Everyone
nods in agreement. "And I'm hopeful no one gets food poisoning at
the Restaurant Convention in January." Chuckles echo around the
table. Phew! Next, please. I lean back in my chair and let out a deep
breath. The attention moves to Celeste, and I barely register what
anyone else shares as they go around the table, each taking their turn.
My true hope prods and pokes at me, but I keep it carefully protected.

Dinner was delicious, and we're all moving slowly and settling into
a food coma. I was cautious about today, but it turned out okay.
The women retire to the living room while the men return to the
family room with another football game. I sit at one end of the couch
with Celeste at the other. Brenda and Elise are across from us on the
loveseat.

Brenda turns to me. "I loved what you said at dinner. It's wonderful
that you guys have a house. Now that you've put roots down and
Melvin has his dream job, you can finally have a family."

A strangling feeling grips my neck, as if someone shoved me on stage
with a spotlight blazing, everyone waiting for me to speak when I have
no idea what to say. I search my mind for the script I've memorized,
mixing it with a bit of improv. "We'll have kids… eventually. Don't
want to intrude on Melvin's epic vacation," I quip.

"Well, there will always be excuses. It's never going to be the perfect
time. Sometimes it requires a leap of faith," she says.

I swallow, searching for the right response. She has no clue how
much the last few years have stretched and tested our faith. I already
worry about not being able to make Melvin a father. But I would be
letting down Brenda, too. My eyes sting, but I push through with a
pleasant smile. "That's true. There's a lot to consider."

"Oh, Mom! Don't worry about becoming a grandma. We have a wedding to plan this year!" Elise stretches her lean, toned arm across the loveseat and rests it on Brenda's shoulders.

"You're right. My baby is getting married! How are the wedding plans coming?"

"Pretty good. Paul and I are trying to keep it simple." She flips her long brown hair over her shoulders. "We want an elegant, vintage-themed wedding with an outdoor garden reception."

"Well, let me help." I lean forward toward her, resting my arms on my knees. "I love a party."

"That means a lot. We can use your expertise," Elise says. We continue chatting about their upcoming wedding and discussing the menu and décor.

Melvin appears. "I'm heading to bed, Mom," he says. I take my cue. Rising from my spot, I turn toward him. "I think I'll join you."

"So soon? We were hoping to watch a movie together."

"I get it, Mom. But we've had two days of travel, and we're tired."

The truth is, it's time for my IVF injection. Our new nightly routine. It has the best success rate, but also the biggest price tag. I didn't want to draw any attention to our plight, so I made Melvin promise to pull me away tactfully. We say goodnight and escape upstairs for my injection. Next week—egg retrieval. I could be pregnant by Christmas.

# Chapter 5

"Those are some good eggs!" the doctor exclaims. Kind of a weird compliment, but I suppose she means well.

"What can I say? I'm a good egg." I throw up my hands, my pulse pumping. Today is the big day—transfer day. My stomach flutters as the doctor shows me images of our embryos. I cross and uncross my ankles. My arms and legs buzz with energy.

"Have you decided how many you want to transfer?" Dr. Larson asks.

I clear my throat. "What do you advise?"

"IVF treatments can be expensive, and there is always a risk that one or more embryos won't implant." She folds her hands in her lap and maintains eye contact. "If you can face the possibility of twins, we recommend transferring both. It won't cost more because it's still one procedure, and it increases the odds of pregnancy."

"We are on board with transferring both. Melvin loves a good deal. If we could get a BOGO on babies, we're all for it." A high-pitched laugh escapes my throat. I'm willing to do whatever she suggests. Let's get this over with.

"All righty then. Are you ready to get pregnant?" Dr. Larson slaps her hands on her legs and rises from her stool.

My toes tingle, and I rub my sweaty palms on my medical gown. "You lack somewhat in the romance department, doctor. I was hoping you would woo me before you slipped under the sheet." A giggle bubbles from my lips. We might finally have a baby. Or even twins. Can we handle that?

The doctor sets a hand on her round hip, her brown eyes glinting with amusement. "I can't count how many times people have said that to me."

The transfer procedure continues, and I'm left to lie on the table alone for twenty minutes after the doctor finishes. I never imagined I would get pregnant without my husband in the room. But with Christmas music playing in the background, I realize Mary didn't either. This isn't an immaculate conception by any means, but I can't help reflecting on the irony.

I take the next few days off work to rest and take it easy. They say bed rest isn't necessary, but I'm not taking any chances. It's a perfect time to have a few days at home, watching a Christmas movie while wrapping presents. I chose *Home Alone* to make me laugh. But when Kevin's mom discovers she's left him home alone, I can't stop sobbing. The poor kid! His poor mother! My heart breaks for her. This is supposed to be a light, funny movie, but my hormones are making it a tragedy.

***

The smell of peanut butter fills the kitchen as I roll balls of dough and place them on the pan. Melvin lifts his head slightly from the stack of bills on the table, his nose sniffing out what I've been busy doing all morning. I hide a grin, pleased with my work, and then stir the bubbling chocolate on the stove for dipping. Peanut butter Buckeyes resemble nuts from a Buckeye tree. It's a holiday tradition to honor Melvin's Ohio roots. I guess Brenda's baking is rubbing off on me.

"Amelia, we need to talk," Melvin says from the kitchen table.

"What's up?" My eyes furrow, and I slide the pot of melted chocolate off the warm burner. I walk across the kitchen to him and rest my hand on his shoulder.

"I got the insurance estimate for the IVF treatment. They won't cover much. It will take all our savings and then some." He points at the statement on the computer.

"Holy cow, that's expensive. I expected the insurance to cover more. But really, how can you put a price on having a child?" I pat his shoulder and cross over to the cabinets in search of toothpicks. "If that's what we have to do, then that's what we have to do. The doctor said it's the best option for us. All parents sacrifice for their children. Our sacrifices are simply starting *before* we get the baby."

"I understand how much you want to be a mom, but if this round doesn't work, I'm not certain we can afford to *keep* doing this." He leans back in his chair and bounces his knee. "It's like playing the lottery. We put all this money in, but what are the chances we win the jackpot and get pregnant?"

My heart sinks, and I keep my face hidden in the cupboard to avoid Melvin's watchful gaze. It was already so lonely in that doctor's office without him; I don't want to be alone in pursuing children, too. All the money in the world wouldn't make up for the vacant bedroom down the hall, the fridge standing naked in the kitchen with no children's artwork to clothe it, or my empty arms.

I swallow hard, my fingers fumbling around the box of toothpicks. "I get it," I say, forcing my voice to resemble something normal. "But the doctor said I had good eggs. I'm sure there won't be a problem this time."

I jerk the box out of the cupboard, and toothpicks scatter across the counter. Gathering them up, I pierce the peanut butter balls, one by one.

After a few moments of silence, he twists his fingers into his curly mop of hair and leans over the bills on the table. "I'll pay this bill with our credit card, but we don't have enough credit to cover another round."

The tension around my heart eases, and I stride back over to him. My hands rest on his shoulders, and I lean in and kiss his stubbly cheek. "We won't need another round. We've got this."

***

Two weeks of waiting have me on the edge of my seat when Melvin and I arrive at my follow-up appointment. They warned me I could get a false positive if I took a home pregnancy test because of all the hormone injections. Today's blood test will give us the answer.

I rub my hand on Melvin's thigh, trying to still his bobbling leg. The quiet energy magnifies my senses. The smell of disinfectant lingers in the air. Bright lights. Clean surfaces. Muffled sounds come from the hall. A gentle knock on the door, and the doctor finally enters. I search her face for clues.

She smiles.

That's a good sign, right?

She shuts the door behind her and takes a seat, crossing her legs.

No... it's bad news. She's delaying it.

"It's good to see both of you again. As you know, we transferred two embryos two weeks ago," she begins. I draw a deep breath in and press my lips together. I slide my hand into Melvin's for support. She continues, "Hormone injections can throw off home pregnancy tests, but the numbers from your blood test confirm you are definitely pregnant."

My heart stops and then races forward as my brain struggles to process the information. *Definitely pregnant.* Is this for real? "Wait. Really? I'm pregnant?" Melvin tightens his grip on my hand, and I lean into him, tears of relief streaming down my face. He gives me a tender kiss on the top of my head.

*I'm going to be a mother.*

The feelings I've been trying to hold at bay take over. My entire body is vibrating with electricity. My heart swells with joy as I allow myself to celebrate this moment.

"Your next step is to schedule an ultrasound. Then we will verify everything and listen for a heartbeat." She congratulates us and moves on to her next patient.

We linger in the exam room, holding each other in a warm embrace. Melvin pulls away and wipes tears from under his eyes. He reaches behind him and grabs the box of tissues, offering me one first.

He stands and offers me his hand. "You're pregnant." A wide smile spreads across his face.

I stand and rub my hand across my belly. "We're pregnant."

He pulls me close, lifting me off my feet, and swings me in a circle.

We bound out of the office and back to our car. On the drive home, we hold hands, like when we were dating. "We're going to be parents, Melvin! Can you believe it?"

"A Christmas miracle."

"We should make a special announcement for the grandparents. What do you think?" I glance at him while he drives. I was trying not to get too emotionally invested, but I have a secret Pinterest board with fun ways to announce a pregnancy. We should be able to pull something off for the holidays.

"That's a great idea. My mom is going to lose her mind." He shakes his head. "Do you want to FaceTime them?"

"Actually, I saw a project online. We could decorate a Christmas ornament with the words, 'Our Christmas Miracle, Baby Greathouse Coming Soon' on it. Want to make it with me?"

"It sounds like a lot of work." He presses my hand. A smirk appears at the corner of his mouth.

"You were an art major, Melvin. You could probably do this in your sleep." I let go of his hand and swat his shoulder. "I've got everything we need at home. We can work on it tonight after dinner."

"Deal."

A flutter of excitement bubbles up inside me like foam overflowing on freshly poured root beer. I lean my head back and close my eyes, allowing gratitude to swell in my heart. The doctor's announcement washed away all the moments of doubt over the years we've been trying. It was all worth it. We are finally going to be parents. God answered my prayers.

# Chapter 6

December has been a whirlwind between doctors' appointments and preparing for the holidays. We arrived at my parents' yesterday, and I can finally relax. The fire sputters and crackles, warming my back. Melvin has one arm around me, and the other rests on my knee. The Christmas tree stands centered on my parents' wall of windows. I admire the snow-covered Colorado Rockies and breathe in the steam from my frothy mug of cocoa. It's a picture-perfect Christmas Eve.

The whole family is here. Mom is in the kitchen cleaning up after dinner with my dad at her side. They have always been an example of a marriage that works as a team, supporting and helping each other. My younger brother, Henry, stretches out in the recliner, eyes locked on his phone. He's home from college for Christmas break.

My older sister, Audrey, and her husband, Clement, live close by, so they're here for the evening. They sit snuggled on the loveseat, keeping an eye on their two kids. I've always looked up to her, and despite our childhood squabbles, we've become good friends. But I can never seem to keep up with her. She's two years older than I am. When she and Clement got married, I caught the bouquet and married Melvin a year later. We waited until he was done with grad school to try to have kids. Obviously, Audrey has been more successful in that department. But after our announcement tonight, I will join her in the mom club. And then we can bond on a whole new level.

Mom enters from the kitchen, her hands on her hips. "Is everyone ready to open presents?"

Dad steps up beside her, rubbing his hands together, his eyes wide with excitement. "We better hurry so Lucy and Noah can get home and get to bed before Santa comes!" Lucy squeals with delight and runs to Papa, wrapping her arms around his legs.

I catch Melvin's eye, and he winks at me. He jumps up and grabs three gift bags.

"We got a little crafty and made something for each of you." He hands one to Mom and Dad, another to Audrey and Clement, and the last to my little brother, Henry. "You can open them all at once."

Two-year-old Noah mounts his latest attack on the tree, and Clement jumps up, scoops him in his arms, and flies him around the room like an airplane. Big sister Lucy hovers over Audrey. "I want to open it, Mommy!" Audrey tucks her long blonde hair behind her ear, holds the bag open to her preschooler, and lets Lucy pull at the tissue paper. She finds the ornament at the bottom of the bag and grasps it with her pudgy hands.

"It's just an ornament." She sets it on the ottoman and skips toward the Christmas tree. "I want to open *my* presents!"

Mom examines the angel on her ornament. Warmth spreads through my chest as I watch her flip it over and read the words aloud. "Our Christmas Miracle." She gasps and rises from her seat. "Oh, honey. This is wonderful news!"

Audrey scrambles to retrieve her ornament and exclaims, "Amelia! Why didn't you tell me?"

Mom and Audrey cross the room and sweep me into their arms. Congratulations and tears flow like a brook down the mountainside, gaining momentum before it settles peacefully at the bottom.

Lucy pulls on Audrey's sweater. "Why are you crying, Mommy?"

"It's happy tears, sweetie. Auntie Amelia and Uncle Melvin are having a baby." She pulls away and kneels beside her daughter, brushing away the tears. "You're going to have a new cousin."

Lucy tips her head up at me. "Where's the baby now? When do I get to see it?"

I place my hands on my stomach. "It's growing in my tummy. You can see it after your birthday in September."

Everyone settles back into their seats. "I can't believe you kept this a secret. When is the baby due?" Audrey cleans up the tissue paper from the package.

"It's still very new. Not until late September."

Mom looks up from the gifts she's organizing under the tree. "Are you feeling okay? Any morning sickness?"

I shrug. "A little. Nothing a little ginger ale and saltines can't handle."

Dad turns toward us. "And how about you, Melvin? You feeling okay?" He lets out a laugh.

"I'm feeling great, Ed. I think I'm getting a craving for some Christmas pie, though." Melvin plays along.

"Presents first. Then pie." My mom hands Lucy a package. "Give this one to Uncle Henry."

***

On Christmas morning, I wake up next to Melvin. "Merry Christmas, sweetheart," he says. "Stay right here. I have something for you." He climbs out of bed and returns with a gift.

I pull out a maternity t-shirt that says, 'Not a Food Baby.' Laughter bubbles up from my chest.

"I realize it's early, but I couldn't resist." He snuggles in close to me.

"I love it." I sink back into my pillow, clutching it to my chest.

He rubs his hand across my belly. He leans his face over my stomach, lifting my pajama shirt to expose my skin. "Hey, baby. It's your daddy. I can't wait to meet you in September."

My mind flies ahead, making plans. "I can most likely work right up to the due date." I twist and roll onto my side, propping my head on my hand to get a better view of Melvin. "Although it could be twins. If that's the case, I'll probably deliver early—maybe in August." Melvin listens politely, a smile tugging at the corners of his mouth. I mentally run through scenarios. "What if I have to go on bed rest? How much paternity leave do you get?"

A low rumble emits from Melvin. He scoops his arms around me and pushes me back into my pillow, hovering over me. "Slow down, Amelia. We've got plenty of time to plan everything out." He dives in for a deep kiss. I release my mental gymnastics and return his affection. I love this guy. What a beautiful life we are creating together.

Later in the day, we have a video call with Melvin's family in Ohio. We told everyone to wait to open their gifts until we connected virtually so we could see their reaction to our big announcement. "We made something for everyone. You can all open it at once," I say.

Elise opens her ornament first and quickly catches on. "Are you serious?" she asks.

"Wait, what do you mean?" Brenda unwraps her gift, reads it, and jumps out of her seat, just like my mom and sister did last night. "'Baby Greathouse Coming Soon?' I'm going to be a grandma? Really?"

I stare at the screen, my arm looped through Melvin's. He grins broadly. "Yeah, Mom. You're going to be a grandma."

"When are you due? How long have you been keeping this from me? Were you already expecting at Thanksgiving?" My heart beats a little faster, seeing their excitement. Brenda has wanted this almost as long as we have.

"The baby's due in September. We were not pregnant at Thanksgiving. This is very new." I wipe the moisture from my cheeks, so glad we get to make not only our dreams come true, but hers, too.

"I'm glad to hear you're not shooting blanks, son. Gotta keep the Greathouse name alive." Marcus's shiny bald head bobs on the screen. My stomach tightens, and so does my hand around Melvin's arm. Does his dad have no filter?

Melvin lowers his eyes and shakes his head. "We're all good in that department, Dad."

Celeste and Elise discuss a summer baby shower in Ohio. Excitement swirls inside me, feeling connected to my sisters-in-law. "That sounds fun. I would love that."

"Our first official responsibility as aunts." Celeste high-fives Elise, and they giggle in delight.

"Do you need me to find someone else to help with the wedding planning? Will that be too much?" Elise's eyes narrow in concern.

"I should be fine. But I'll let you know."

After logging off the call, Melvin grasps my hands in his and rests his forehead on mine. "Everyone seems to share our excitement."

"The first grandbaby—or babies—on your side of the family. Everything is going to change in the next nine months."

Melvin kisses the tip of my nose and wraps his arm over my shoulders, pulling me back onto the couch. "I can't wait."

# Chapter 7

The click of Sue's pen interrupts my thoughts, and I glance across the table at her. The first weekly staff meeting of the year is about to begin. I look over the agenda, noting the upcoming Restaurant Convention and a few smaller networking events in the coming months.

Margot breezes in and slides into her seat at the head of the conference table. "Good morning. I hope everyone had a fantastic holiday. It's good to be back." Her warm smile fills her face, and the lines next to her eyes crinkle with joy. "Before we dive into planning, I want to share some big-picture items for Turn of Events. I started this company when I was thirty years old. That was twenty-five years ago. You can do the math." She winks at us. "Every year on January first, I spend some time evaluating the past year and planning for what is next. As I reflected last week, I concluded that it's time for me to plan my exit strategy."

I suck in my breath, my eyes locked on Margot. Is she shutting the business down? What does this mean for my job?

She holds up her hands. "You all look panicked right now. Don't worry. This is a good thing. Over the next year, I will look for someone to buy the business." Her gaze sweeps the room. "I hope it might be one of you. Give it some thought and let me know in the next couple of weeks if you want to be considered. I will evaluate candidates based on their performance over the next year. In December, I will make my decision. I'll spend the following year mentoring and advising my successor as she takes the reins."

My heart leaps within me. This is my chance. I can prove myself and earn her approval. This is the perfect time in my life to have my own business, and I won't have to start it from scratch. Everything is coming together—growing my family, advancing my career.

***

I wake up and race to the bathroom. Even though I'm not very far along, I swear I need to pee more already. My heart sinks when I discover I'm spotting. From what I've read, it happens in the first trimester, but I panic. After I get ready for the day, I call the nurse line, and they make an appointment for me for tomorrow.

The next morning at the doctor's office, they do the usual routine screening and get me in for an ultrasound. Melvin is in the middle of a project at work, but I told him I would be fine on my own. It's probably no big deal. We already had the blood test and ultrasound to reassure us. I'm barely over seven weeks.

Dr. Larson furrows her brow and squints at the screen. Her silence shouts a warning at me. She tucks her sleek brown hair behind her ear and continues probing. My heart dips and twirls in rhythm with the ultrasound wand. Something must be wrong. We implanted two embryos. What if only one of them made it? A weight spreads across my chest. I brace for what she will say. I blink at the screen, searching for something that will give me hope.

She turns from the machine and grasps my arm. "I'm sorry, Amelia. It appears the embryos didn't make it. This happens sometimes, but it doesn't mean you can't have a baby. It may take a few tries."

I freeze, tears welling up in my eyes, and suck in a shaky breath. "Neither of them?" I squeak out.

She shakes her head, never letting go of me. Clasping my hands in front of me, I stare straight up at the ceiling tiles. I swallow and wet my lips. "I understand."

She explains the next steps and turns to go. The moment the door clicks behind her, I tremble uncontrollably. The crisp lines of the sterile room blur through my tears. *Why did I tell Melvin he didn't have to be here?* I lie there for several minutes, my hands pressed on my vacant abdomen. My body feels weighed down, like I'm buried under the sand at the beach, and I can't escape the approaching waves.

I was positive it would work. Now what do we do?

Footsteps echo in the hall, prodding me back to the present. I unearth myself from the exam table and go through the motions of dressing and gathering my things. My feet carry me forward, finding their way to the car, the icy wind penetrating my coat and chilling the deepest parts of me. I sink into the driver's seat and text my boss to inform her I won't be coming in. My finger hovers over the button on my phone to call Melvin with the news. An ache spreads across my chest as I lean my head on the steering wheel and repeat Dr. Larson's words to him. He offers to come home, but I assure him I will be fine.

I'm not fine.

At home, I burrow under blankets, and my bed slowly transforms into a nest of tissues. Sleep evades me, and I stare into the stillness of the room, wishing the doctor were wrong.

Barely an hour later, the sound of the garage door opening stutters through the silence. Steps quicken up the stairs, and Melvin pushes the bedroom door open, holding a bouquet by his side.

"Hey," he says softly, like he's afraid I might break if he speaks too loudly. "How are you feeling? Are you hurting?"

Just hearing his voice cracks something open inside me.

He came home.

"Physically, no," I whisper, barely able to speak. "Emotionally, I'm a mess. We lost our baby. Our babies." I curl into a ball and clutch the pillow, trying to hold it all together. My voice cracks. "We had a positive test. We were already making plans."

He crosses the room in two quick strides and drops to his knees next to the bed, placing the flowers on the nightstand. He takes my face in his hands, his eyes squeeze shut, and a tear trickles out, forming a rivulet down his cheek. "I know." He pauses, pulling air into his lungs. "I wanted them so much. I was already envisioning us as a family of four. Two tiny babies and two clueless parents figuring it out together."

He climbs over me to his side of the bed and pulls me close. Rolling over, I curl into him. His chest rises and falls unevenly—his hand trembles against my back. "I would've given anything," he murmurs into my hair. "Anything to keep them safe. To keep *you* safe. I wish I could take it away. To make it different. And I hate that there's nothing I can say that makes it better."

His grief wraps around mine, and suddenly I'm not alone in the dark. I fall into his arms with a sob, and he holds me tighter, like if he holds on hard enough, he can keep me from slipping away too. I'm afraid that I'm letting him down. We put the date on the calendar and told our families. We started planning our lives around this life—these lives. It was going to make us a family. And it was our last hope. Melvin doesn't want to pour more money into my broken body. It's not worth it.

I'm not worth it.

\*\*\*

Saturday afternoon, Allie shows up at my door with face masks and chocolate. "I thought you could use a little girl time." She pulls me into a hug that undoes me.

"Thanks," I choke out, the word catching in my throat.

"I'm sorry, Melly. This sucks." She continues to hold me until I run out of tears. I open the bag of truffles, and we both indulge. We spend the afternoon watching a chick flick, looking ridiculous in our face masks.

"How long do you have to wait before you can try IVF again?" We peel off our masks in the bathroom.

"I'm not sure if we'll try again. Melvin doesn't believe we can afford another round. It was our one shot." The backs of my eyes sting. I can't cry again. That's all I've been doing for days.

"That's tough." She peers at me through the mirror, washing her hands and grabbing the towel from the rack. "Are you considering adoption?"

I take the cloth from her and wipe my hands. "Not really. My plan has always been to get married and have kids. It never occurred to me we wouldn't be able to have children of our own."

"I get it. But it might be a way to have a family." She shrugs.

"I'm not ready to think about it yet. The wounds are too raw right now."

Allie enfolds me in a hug. "Then don't. Just focus on recovering. You've been through a lot."

I lean my head on her shoulder and whisper, "Thanks." Our future seemed so clear a week ago, but now everything is out of focus.

# Chapter 8

Sunday morning. We always go to church, but it's especially ago-nizing today. After this failed pregnancy, I need God more than ever. But it seems like He has abandoned me. All that time praying, trying, searching for answers... my heart is bursting with love for a child He won't bless us with. Two children I'll never get to meet. It's so easy for everyone else, but ridiculously difficult for me. Melvin rests his arm around my shoulders. I lean in and try to pay attention.

During the service, I observe families with small children every-where. A few rows in front of us, a toddler peeks over his mother's shoulder with an impish grin. Somewhere behind me, an infant cries while the mother shushes to calm him. Across the aisle, I notice Wendy with her new baby. This is their fourth. Her kids are holy terrors. They show up a mess—shirts untucked, hair rumpled. They're loud and disruptive. While she bounces the baby, her preschool-aged son crawls under the pew and pops out in the aisle. Before she detects a thing, he races down the aisle, and her husband scrambles to catch him. She can't keep control of them. And yet she has another.

The more I watch her and her chaotic family, the harder it is for me to breathe. I fake a cough and get up, pulling away from Melvin. His eyes follow me before refocusing on the meeting. I proceed out the doors of the church and keep walking. I stride straight out to the parking lot and flee to the car. In my rush, I wobble on my heels and wipe out on the pavement, the contents of my purse spilling everywhere. I sit up and inspect my wounds. A scraped knee and hands, but I'm okay.

I lean my head and arms on my knees, the tears silently spilling out. The sting of my scraped skin is sharp, but the ache in my pride hurts more. Crouched on the pavement, I wipe my eyes and collect my strewn belongings, shoving them back into my bag. My chapstick rolled under the car, just beyond my grasp. I have a clear view, but I can't quite reach it. If only my arms were longer. My shoulders shudder, and my chest heaves. It's just a stupid tube of lip balm. Why am I crying? I should leave it and go home, but I'm determined to reclaim it. I can't walk away from my goal. My eyes settle on a stray pen. Wrapping my fingers around it, I use it to reach the cylinder and roll it toward me.

I push myself to my feet, checking my surroundings. Thank goodness no one saw me make a fool out of myself. I open the car door and slip inside, leaning my head back against the seat and shutting my eyes. Why do I keep coming to church when the one blessing I desire is still out of reach? I've worked and prayed for this. Does He even hear me? I slam my hands against the steering wheel, the horn piercing the quiet parking lot. I glance around, my heart pounding, hoping no one heard. Perhaps I'm kidding myself to believe in a higher power. I was always taught that God hears and answers prayers, but He doesn't appear to be answering mine. God is supposed to help us make sense of the world, but right now, my world doesn't make any sense. A buzz interrupts my ruminations. I dig through the contents of my purse, landing on my phone and plucking it out. The screen turns on, and I see a text notification.

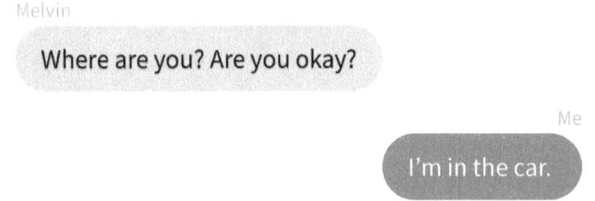

Melvin

**Where are you? Are you okay?**

Me

**I'm in the car.**

I can't say any more. He doesn't get it. To him, it wasn't meant to be. I can't picture anything else I *am* meant to be.

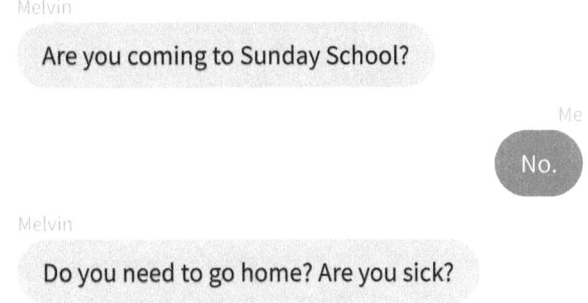

Melvin

**Are you coming to Sunday School?**

Me

**No.**

Melvin

**Do you need to go home? Are you sick?**

I grasp for the right response. I can't sit through Sunday School with all the perfect families.

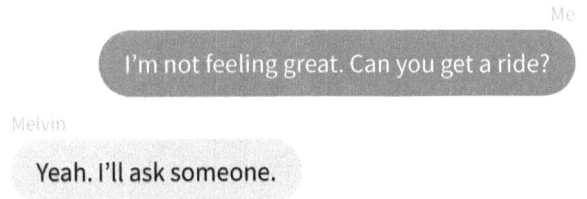

Me

**I'm not feeling great. Can you get a ride?**

Melvin

**Yeah. I'll ask someone.**

I start the car and peel out of the parking lot. Is he clueless? Melvin should rush to my side. He should take me home, hold me, and cry *with* me. We are supposed to be partners. Doesn't this ache hit him the same way it overtakes me? Right now, I feel so alone.

Back home, I gingerly get on my scraped knees out of habit. I've been doing it since I was a young girl, and I give it one last shot, despite my wavering faith. Usually, I pray silently, but since I'm alone, I speak my mind out loud to the Lord.

"I'm hurting right now. I desperately want to have a baby. You know that. Why won't you give it to me? I go to church every week, pray, and spend time in daily devotion. My parents taught me to do what is right—be honest and hardworking. Aren't we supposed to be rewarded for the good we do? I understand I'm supposed to count my blessings, and I have a lot to be thankful for. Melvin... my job... my family." I pause and draw in a breath. "But it's all so empty without children. What am I missing? Everywhere I go, people are having babies. The church is full of families with children. And why Wendy, Lord? She has four kids. All I want is one. You delivered it to the wrong person. It was supposed to be me." I gaze up at the ceiling. Tears stream down my face. "Are you aware I am here? Do you listen to what I am asking for? Show me you are conscious of me. Help me comprehend that you care about me and are mindful of my struggles. Give me what I'm begging you for."

I stay there on my knees, listening for an answer. After a few minutes, I push myself up and turn to sit on the bed. Grabbing tissues from the nightstand, I dab at my eyes and blow my nose. Deep breath in. I grab a chocolate from the drawer and allow the silky smoothness to comfort me. Melvin will be home soon. I stand and straighten my black pencil skirt. My feet guide me to the kitchen automatically, where I work on lunch for us.

Melvin shows up shortly after noon, the front door clicking gently shut behind him. I hear his footsteps before I see him, then he appears in the doorway of the kitchen.

"Hey, Melly. How are you doing?" His lavender bow tie hangs loose around his neck, and he has already unbuttoned the matching vest.

"Okay... I guess." I lift my shoulders and let them fall. "It was too much to sit through church, with all the babies and families." I swallow the lump in my throat. "I had to get out of there."

Without saying a word, he crosses the room and gathers me into his arms. He holds me firm and steady like a clamp that's keeping broken pieces of a vase together until the glue dries. "I'm sorry. You should have said something."

"I was trying not to make it a thing," I say into his chest. "I'm trying to be strong. Trying to handle it."

He pulls back slightly, just enough to look me in the eye, but he keeps his hands on my shoulders.

"You *are* strong," he says gently, "but you don't have to do this alone. Don't try to carry everything just to protect me."

I wipe the tears from my eyes and sniffle, forcing my face into a smile. "Want some lunch?" I gesture toward the counter.

His eyes linger on me for a moment. "Yeah. This looks great." But he doesn't reach for the food yet. Instead, he grasps my hand, holding it tight for a few seconds longer.

"How was Sunday School?" I take a bite of my sandwich, piled high with ham, cheese, and lettuce. The salty ham and tangy mustard roll around on my taste buds. It tastes so good after avoiding lunch meat for the past year. Changing my diet didn't actually make a difference.

"It was good. We were discussing Samuel. It reminded me of us."

"Why's that?" I set my sandwich down.

"Well, Hannah wanted a child desperately. Her husband's other wife had a bunch of kids, but she had none."

"Do you have another wife with a bunch of kids I should know about?" I quirk my eyebrow at him.

"Obviously, you are my one and only." He glances at me with a twinkle in his eyes, grasps my hand, and weaves our fingers together. "Anyway, she was praying desperately to have a child, and the priest observed her and assumed she was drunk or crazy or something."

"So I'm crazy?" My eyes jerk toward him.

"No!" He holds up his hands and shakes his head in innocence. "But God blessed her with a son, and she dedicated him to the Lord. She gave him to the priest when he was big enough. She had a baby, and she gave it away!"

"I had two babies, and they were *taken* away." I huff and glare at my sandwich.

He takes my hand again. "I realize that. But the point is, we're not alone. Others have struggled to have children. And she put God's will before hers. I want to have kids, too, but what if God's plan is different than we expected? Sometimes we arrive at the best solutions by seeing things from another perspective." He puts his head on the table and peeps up at me with a grin to make his point.

Biting into my sandwich, I try to imagine another plan. I've held this in my heart for as long as I can remember. Maybe I *am* crazy, like the priest concluded about Hannah. I'm supposed to trust God, but how can I when I don't believe He listens to me?

\*\*\*

The doorbell rings later in the afternoon. I answer it and am shocked to find an older woman from church at my door. "Hi, Louise. What are you doing here?"

"Did a little baking today—thought I'd try something new. I found a magazine clipping with this recipe for white chocolate and craisin cookies. It's just me at home, and I can't eat all of them." She extends a plate full of cookies out to me, the plastic wrap crinkling under her fingers. "Your name came to mind, and I brought you some. I hope you like them."

I accept her offering. "Believe it or not, it's my favorite kind of cookie. How did you know?"

"Really?" She considers me with a satisfied grin. "I had no idea. But I have learned to listen to the whispers of the Holy Spirit, so I'm not surprised." She winks and turns to leave.

"Thank you, Louise," I call after her. "This was thoughtful. I will definitely enjoy these."

"You're welcome, my dear. See you next Sunday." She waves and shuffles to her car.

I shut the door, lean my back against it, and dive into the cookies. One bite tells me this is no coincidence. I can taste the two things setting this cookie apart: orange peel and almond extract. Not every recipe has these ingredients, but it's the way I like it. A whisper of a voice enters my mind. *I'm* aware *of you. I care about you. I am conscious of your struggles.* My chest swells, and tears sting my eyes. God listened to me. I stare up at the ceiling.

*Message received, Lord.* He used Louise as an instrument. My eyes shut as I savor the cookie, a calm settling over me. The tartness of the craisins and the sweetness of the white chocolate chips rest on my taste buds like a comforting blanket. The Spirit wraps me in a warm embrace, and I allow the impressions and the message to calm my heart.

Before bed, I pick up the Old Testament to read what I missed in church today from 1 Samuel chapter one.

*And she was in bitterness of soul, and prayed unto the Lord, and wept sore.*

That describes exactly what I'm experiencing—bitterness of soul. As I continue reading, I see she promised that if the Lord gave her a son, she would give him to the Lord for the rest of his life.

How could she promise to give her child up if she finally had one? I couldn't do it. I finish chapter one and continue into the next chapter.

*And the Lord visited Hannah, so that she conceived, and bare three sons and two daughters. And the child Samuel grew before the Lord.*

The Lord blessed her with even more children. If I knew I would have more kids, it would be easier, but I'm afraid I lost my chance to be a mother.

But still. This story brings me more peace. Hannah found a way through her pain. She put God's will before her own. I remember the impression I had when Louise brought me the cookies, and trust that God is mindful of my concerns. *Okay, God. I'm sorry for the unkind thoughts I had in my heart toward the mothers at church. Even though things aren't going according to* my *plan, I will trust yours.*

# Chapter 9

With the Restaurant Convention right around the corner, I arranged a meeting to finalize the details. Now that Margot has made her announcement, there's even more on the line. As I pull open the door, I'm immediately greeted by a tall, lanky, blonde man standing behind the host podium. "Welcome to Yuzu. How can I help you?"

"Is Chef Lee here? I have an appointment."

"You must be Amelia Greathouse. I'm Chef Lee. Nice to meet you." He steps out from behind the stand and extends his arm, shaking my hand. His appearance takes me by surprise. I realize I was stereotyping, but I expected a short Asian man to be the head chef at an Asian restaurant.

After an awkward moment of silence, I gather myself and respond, "Yes. I'm Amelia. Nice to meet you in person."

"Let me guess. You were expecting an Asian guy, right?" he says with a warm smile.

Heat blossoms through my cheeks. "Honestly, yeah. How did you become an Asian expert? It doesn't seem you had family recipes handed down to you."

"It's true. The name Lee is from Robert E. Lee. I am a descendant of a famous Southerner, not an Asian by birth. My wife and I adopted our kids from Asia. As a chef, one way I can honor their heritage is through food. I threw myself into learning all I could about Asian cuisine. After studying and experimenting, I evolved. Ten years ago, I opened this place." He holds his arms out in a flourish.

"That makes sense. What countries are your kids from?"

"Our oldest is from China. And our two youngest are Korean. We are well-rounded Asians in our house," he boasts. "Say, have you had lunch yet? I'd love to make you up a plate to enjoy while we discuss everything."

"That would be great."

I follow him through the dining room, rows of square tables lined up like dancers ready to take the stage, each one ornamented with costumes of white linens resembling tutus and perfectly placed utensils and glasses. We leave the calm and enter the kitchen, where everyone moves in their own choreography, like ballerinas warming up backstage. The practiced movement of knives chopping vegetables provides a background rhythm. Arms twirl over pots. Cooks glide from one end of the kitchen to the other. Each member of the team practices their part to prepare for the evening meal. But when Chef Lee enters, there is a hush of respect and anticipation.

He fills two plates, nods at the staff, and we leave the chaos of the kitchen to sit down in the empty dining room.

"You'll have to explain to me what each of these is," I say.

Using a chopstick as a pointer, he directs my attention to a row of three potstickers nestled together. "From Japan, you have gyoza.

That's the dumpling." Moving to a miniature pyramid, he continues. "This is zongzi. It is a rice dumpling wrapped in bamboo leaves, typically served in China during their Dragon Boat Festival." He gestures to the bowl, explaining, "And finally, from Korea, kimchi. I hope you like it."

"It smells wonderful," I say, piercing the gyoza with my fork. After biting into the crisp outer layer, the juicy filling explodes on my tongue. I hold my hand over my mouth to keep it from spilling over. "Mmm. That's delicious!"

Chef Lee's eyes crinkle in a smile. "I'm glad you like it." He expertly picks one up with his chopsticks and pops it in his mouth.

I wipe my mouth with a white linen napkin and lean over, rifling through my bag. "First, I want to thank you for being willing to do a cooking demonstration at the conference." I hand him a packet of papers. "I have a checklist and a schedule here for you. It shows where you need to be and when, as well as what we need from you before the event. My number is here at the bottom. I will be on site for the entire conference. Text me if you run into any problems. There's nothing I can't handle."

"I'm grateful to be in such capable hands. I'm excited to showcase authentic Asian cuisine."

We confirm the details for the convention and finish our lunch.

"Do you mind if I ask about your family?" I finger the napkin in my lap.

"Of course not. What can I answer for you?"

"Well... you mentioned your kids were all adopted. What made you decide to adopt? If it's not too personal."

"Oh gosh, no. I'm an open book." He places his napkin on the table and leans in. "My wife and I always wanted a family, but it wasn't happening for us. It was a tough time. We did a lot of soul-searching.

Ultimately, we realized there's more than one way to create a family, and there are orphans who desperately need parents. We felt called to go out and search for our children and bring them home."

"What a beautiful way to view it. I bet it was quite the journey."

"The amazing thing is, you hear about the immediate love parents have at the birth of their children. We experienced the same thing the moment we viewed our children's pictures on their profiles. It's hard to explain, but something about them drew us in. We felt they were always meant to be in our family." He shares a bit about his children and their home countries before we finish up. My heart swells at his story. His words echo in my mind—*there is more than one way to have a family.*

"Thanks again for the food. This is way better than picking up chow mein or even grocery store sushi. I'll have to bring my husband sometime for dinner."

"Definitely! Tell me when you're coming, and I'll take good care of you." We part ways, and I drive back to the office, physically full and mentally reassured that Chef Lee will handle everything expected of him.

But there is also an intriguing whisper in my mind about adoption that I can't quite capture. It's not as though I've never heard of adoption before. Even Allie mentioned it to me. But I guess I've never fully considered it.

When I return to the office, I spend a few minutes researching adoption online. There are so many options. It's not a quick process, but there are children who need families out there. I tuck the idea away and return to my work responsibilities.

Back at home that evening, we settle into our nightly routine. Melvin is at one end of the couch. I'm on the other. Although we share the same space, it feels like we are strangers in a waiting room. He watches TV and draws in his sketchbook. I open my laptop to research favors for Elise and Paul's wedding.

A distance has been growing between us in the weeks since the miscarriage. Melvin has been quiet and withdrawn. An ache has permanently settled in my chest. It takes all my effort to function each day, and by the evening, I have nothing left to give. Melvin seems to have moved on. I try to be strong as I silently process the light of our dreams being snuffed out. I feel like I'm letting Melvin down. What if I can't make him a dad? He might be better off with someone else.

After narrowing down ideas for wedding favors and sending Elise the top three to choose from, I close my laptop and say goodnight. My feet plod up the stairs, and I go through the motions of preparing for bed. I collapse onto the mattress, alone in the darkness, with a gaping hole in my chest where my heart once was. The physical ache is real. Sleep is an escape, but each morning, I awake to a cloud that follows me through my day.

# Chapter 10

"Hey Melly, want to go out for dinner tonight?" Melvin asks as we get ready for work. He ties his Van Gogh Starry Night necktie over a deep blue button-down shirt. "Let's get out and celebrate your making it through the conference."

"That sounds nice. Where should we go?"

"What about Yuzu? Ever since you told me about it, I've been craving Asian food. Do you need to make a reservation?"

"You'll love it. I'll call Chef Lee and check."

That evening we arrive at the restaurant, inhaling the combination of ginger, garlic, and soy sauce. The hostess guides us to our table, handing us our menus. We browse through the dishes until Chef Lee stops by to greet us.

"Welcome to Yuzu!" he says.

"Hello, Curtis, thank you so much for accommodating us. This is my husband, Melvin. Melvin, this is Chef Curtis Lee."

"I hope you're hungry. What are you in the mood for?" he asks.

"I am a sushi fanatic, and I didn't get to try any the last time I was here." I fold up my menu. Melvin inspects me with a wrinkled brow.

"Perfect. And what can I get for you, Melvin?" asks Curtis.

"Actually, Amelia was telling me about some Japanese dumplings. What was it?"

"Gyoza. You will love it. Anything else?"

"That's all. Thanks," says Melvin.

Once Curtis walks away, Melvin studies me. "Aren't you avoiding raw fish in case you get pregnant?" he says in a hushed tone.

"Well, it obviously didn't help, did it? I figure, what the heck? I'm not pregnant, so I might as well enjoy myself."

He tips his head at me and then looks down, straightening his silverware on the table. "I guess so. We haven't talked about things since the miscarriage. What are you thinking?"

I straighten my spine and pierce him with my eyes. "I'll never get pregnant. That's what I'm thinking." My heart constricts in my chest. I pull my napkin onto my lap and smooth it out. "We've tried everything. We're good people. This is what God wants married couples to do. I mean, he told Adam and Eve to multiply and replenish the earth. Why can't we?" I view him with pleading in my eyes.

"I get it, Amelia. I'm frustrated, too—"

"Yeah. But you're only frustrated about how much it costs."

He rubs his hand down his face and sighs. "Of course, I worry about the money, Amelia. It doesn't grow on trees." He glances down, resting his hands on the table. "I'm aware artists don't make a lot of money—my dad reminds me every time I see him—but I still want to support my family."

He takes a sip of his water. "Once we have kids, I want you to stay home with them if that's what you want. Which will mean our income will go down. I want to provide for our family, and we'll never be able to survive on my salary if we rack up a bunch of debt to have a baby."

Melvin fiddles with his silverware. "But I *do* want kids. We've talked and dreamed about having a family together since we got engaged. I want to be the dad who coaches soccer for my son or goes to dance recitals for my daughter. You make me sound heartless."

My shoulders slump, and I take in the space on the table in front of me. Exactly like my life right now—empty. I can't grasp why this is so important to me, but it is. Maybe I need to face reality.

"I don't think you're heartless, but you can't put a price on having a family," I whisper. My head moves from side to side, attempting to clear my thoughts. "Let's not get into this here. We're supposed to be having a nice evening."

"I'm not trying to ruin it, Amelia," he says, his voice low. "Having a child we created together–that will deepen my love for you. And I'm trying to balance our dreams with reality. But we need to talk about this and decide what to do next."

Before I can respond, the server brings our food. Conversation dies. Our knives and forks scrape across our plates, punctuating the dead air between us. I can't talk about this here and now, or I'm going to have a breakdown in the middle of the restaurant. Flashes of doubt about our future rush through my mind.

Tension charges the air in the car on the ride home. We ride in silence like travelers on an airplane—close enough to touch, but with an unspoken rule of solitude. Will someone start a conversation, or will we each pretend to be preoccupied?

Back at home, he takes the first tentative step. "Amelia, can we talk?"

My throat tightens as I squeak out my response. "I'm at a loss for words, Melvin. You've made your opinion perfectly clear."

"I wonder if we should take a break from worrying about having kids right now. It might not be God's timing yet."

"If you want." My hands hang at my sides, and I drop my gaze. I can't keep fighting. We bounce around each other like bumper cars for the rest of the night. Never fully connecting, simply trying to avoid getting hit. We slip into bed, and the silence screams of the differences between us. I listen for his breathing to fall into the gentle rhythm of sleep, allowing me to be safe from confrontation.

It's 1:00 am, and I'm still tossing and turning while Melvin dozes beside me. I get up and shuffle to the kitchen to scrounge up a snack. I grab a bag of chocolate chips and wander to the living room. Mindlessly flipping through channels, I arrive at the Broadway musical channel. Perhaps a song and dance, and an uplifting story will pick up my spirits.

Annie is playing. One of my favorites. I hope 'the sun'll come out tomorrow.' I need brightness and hope after the gray evening I had.

Spunky Annie and her positive attitude warm my heart. My edginess from last night softens. When Daddy Warbucks and Annie sing, *I Don't Need Anything But You,* a jolt of love for Melvin pierces my heart. That's how we started. When we got married, we promised to have and to hold each other through anything. A few hours ago, I didn't even want him to touch me, let alone hold me. But now I remember the connection we had as newlyweds. I knew the two of us could take on the world. We need to rediscover our connection. It's there somewhere.

\*\*\*

I wake up the next morning to the scent of bacon wafting from the kitchen. I pause on my knees to pray before investigating the smell. *Dear God, help us through this. Please guide us to find common ground and learn your will for us amid this trial. Allow us to have a baby. I promise I will teach a child to love you.*

As I make my way downstairs, the smoke alarm goes off. I hurry to the kitchen, my feet slapping the hardwood floors. Smoke streams from the frying pan, and Melvin rescues the remaining charred pieces of meat.

I rush to turn on the fan and slide open the door to the deck, the acrid smell filling my nose. "How's it going?" I tilt my head at him, hands on my hips.

"Want some breakfast?" He shrugs, looking sheepish.

I narrow my eyes. "Are you trying to butter me up?"

"I was up early this morning, so I ran to the grocery store and got some donuts and juice. Then I thought, what goes with everything? Bacon." He jabs his fingers into his hair, waves of brown poking up. "The first couple of batches were fine, but all of a sudden, everything was smoking."

Laughter rumbles up from my chest. "I'll give you an 'A' for effort, but next time leave the cooking to me." We clean up the kitchen, setting the blackened grease outside.

Melvin holds my chair out for me. "Madame?"

We tuck into the table with donuts, juice, and some slightly burnt bacon. After a prayer, he grasps my hand and looks into my eyes. "Last night didn't go the way I'd planned. Can we push the reset button and try again?"

"Of course."

"I love you, Amelia. That's the bottom line. If it's just the two of us, you are enough for me. I *do* want to have kids. I've always wanted to be a dad." His thumb strokes circles on the back of my hand. "Every disappointment along this journey has been disappointing to me, too. I'm not disappointed *in* you; I'm disappointed *with* you. This has been harder on you than it has been on me. What you've had to put your body through is crazy." His head moves from side to side, a look of empathy in his eyes. "I hate it when we fight. It's not what I want. I just wonder if God has a different path for us." He releases my hand and takes a sip of juice.

Crunching into a piece of bacon that didn't burn, I savor the smoky flavor and swallow it with a gulp. "I love you too, Melvin. I really do. Sometimes, it seems like you don't understand me and how important this is to me. I know God has more than one path, but I won't be complete if I'm not a mother." I regard him cautiously. "We can try again, but it'll cost money, and you've made your opinion clear about the cost."

"Do you remember what I said a while back about seeing things from a different perspective?" He smiles, puts his head on the table, and peers up at me to reinforce his point.

I grin and let a quiet snort slip through my nostrils. "Yes. Why?"

"Would you ever consider adoption, Amelia?" He swallows and wets his lips. "I had a dream last night that we adopted a little girl. What if the reason we haven't gotten pregnant is because God wants us to give a home to someone else's baby?" He takes a bite of a jelly-filled donut, the jelly oozing out of the corner of his mouth. He quickly wipes it away with his napkin.

"It has crossed my mind, but... I wonder if I would feel like an actual mother if I didn't get to grow my infant in my womb and experience it moving within me." I rub my hand across my stomach. "I can't imagine falling in love with a stranger's child and calling it our own." Pausing, I recall my conversation with Curtis the day I met him. "But

Chef Lee said that's exactly what happened for them from the first time they saw their children's pictures online."

He holds still, surveying my eyes. "We don't have to rush into any decisions. But it's a way to grow our family."

"You realize adoption is expensive, too, right? It's probably not any cheaper than IVF."

"That could be true. But there's more of a guarantee. If we spend all the money on another round of IVF, it's like rolling the dice. At least this way, we're investing in becoming parents. Just consider it."

"I will." My heart lifts a little, a hint of hope finding its way back in.

"Okay. Let's finish breakfast and get ready for the day. I have something fun planned for us." He rubs his hands together and gives a mysterious smile.

# Chapter 11

I hop into the car with Melvin. A few brown curls peek out from under his tweed newsboy cap. I have no idea where we're going, but I'm excited. This is what I need—a carefree Saturday to have fun together.

"Where are you taking me, Mr. Greathouse?"

"You'll see."

After about thirty minutes of driving, he pulls into the parking lot at the sculpture garden. I smile. Of course. There is nothing my spontaneous, art-loving husband would love more than hanging out with sculptures for the morning.

Melvin grabs his camera and tripod from the backseat, and we crunch our way through the fresh snow. The sun reflects off the blanket of white covering the ground, and I'm glad I have my sunglasses. We walk up to a sculpture of two oversized figures reclining in the middle of an open area. Melvin hops down on one knee and gathers up snow.

"What are you doing?" I take a step back. "No snowball fights today, *please.*"

"Do you wanna build a snowman?" He squints up at me with raised eyebrows.

I laugh. "We could have done this at home, you know."

He rolls the first ball and places it next to the sculpture. We roll the next two balls together and stack them up. Melvin whips a hat, scarf, carrot, and rocks out of his pockets and decorates our creation.

"You had this planned all along, didn't you?" I give him a gentle shove, and he wobbles for a moment before returning to our creation.

"Maybe..." He smiles and shrugs. We snap photos of our sculpture. He takes the cap and scarf with him, but we leave the snowman with its carrot nose. We walk along to the next sculpture. He puts the hat and scarf on the walking man and poses next to it with his arm around the figure.

"Take my picture, Amelia!" he says. I snap a couple of shots of him staring off in a pensive pose.

We continue walking around, adding ourselves and the winter gear to different sculptures in different ways, and always taking a picture. After about an hour, my toes grow cold, and Melvin's nose is bright red. We lumber back to the car, and he navigates to a coffee shop for a cup of cocoa.

"That was fun. Thanks for getting me out of the house, honey." I loop my arm through his as we wait in line.

"We needed some downtime." The corners of his eyes crinkle in a smile.

After warming up in front of the fire at the coffee shop with our hot chocolate, we stop for groceries and ride home, fingers intertwined. I sigh, filled with a new sensation of lightness. The world outside sparkles in the sunlight. One thing I love about Melvin is his playfulness. Today was just what I needed.

Back at home, we unload the groceries. "Melly, toss me those apples," Melvin calls across the kitchen.

"All of them?"

"One at a time." He smiles, a sparkle in his eyes. I toss green apples his way. Instead of placing them in the fruit bowl, he turns it into a juggling routine. He ends with all the apples in the bowl except one, which he holds high above his head. With a flourish, he takes a bite and then a bow.

I applaud and cross the room, where he holds out the apple to share. It crunches under my teeth, and my lips pucker at the sour taste. "You're such a clown sometimes."

"And that's why you love me." He leans down and presses a kiss to my lips.

After the groceries, I plan the food for Elise and Paul's wedding. Brenda has a caterer that she has used in the past. The menu will feature finger sandwiches, deviled eggs, and mini quiches, along with fruit, veggies, and cheese and crackers. I send the menu to the caterer and move to folding laundry.

As I methodically put away the clothes, I find the shirt Melvin got me for Christmas.

Not a Food Baby.

My chest tightens. I sink into the bed, and tears escape from the corners of my eyes. A food baby is probably the only kind I will ever have.

*Where are my answers, Lord? Can't you see I'm trying? All we want is a child. Is that too much to ask?*

Melvin pokes into the room and sees me curled up on the bed. "Are you okay?" He raises a brow.

I hold up the t-shirt I've been using to blow my nose.

Melvin nods and slides onto the bed next to me, cradling me in his arms.

\*\*\*

A few weeks later, at church, I hear that Wendy's entire family has picked up a nasty bug that's going around. The leader of our women's group approaches me later and asks if I could bring dinner to their family to help while they are recovering.

"Of course," I say instinctively, immediately second-guessing my-self. How do I show up with a loving heart to the woman who has everything I want?

At home, I plan a menu that will be good for healing and still kid-friendly. I decide on Lemon Chicken Orzo Soup, some rolls, and a side of fruit salad. Plus, my from-scratch brownies. Chocolate heals everything.

Melvin and I bring the dinner over the next night. Wendy's hus-band, Will, opens the door holding their youngest and lets us in. I glance around at toys and Legos strewn across the living room floor. We carefully step around the obstacle course and bring the food to the kitchen, placing it on the counter. A crying kid down the hall calls for Will. "Can you hold her for me?" he asks, thrusting the child into my arms and turning toward the sounds of distress.

My stomach lurches. "I can't do this," I whisper to Melvin, handing him the baby. He tries to calm her as we return to the living room. I breathe deeply and swallow back the stinging in my eyes. Wendy appears in her pink fuzzy robe and slippers.

"I'm sorry. I can take her." She takes the baby from Melvin, and the little girl instantly stops crying. "It's been quite a week here." She pushes the hair out of her face. "Thanks for bringing dinner."

I nod, noticing the piles of laundry on the sofa, and listening to the continued cries down the hall. "We'd better get going so you can eat. Hope everyone gets well soon."

As the door shuts behind us, I suck in air through clenched teeth. Even though Wendy's house was chaotic, right now I would trade my well-organized life for a bit of disorder. In the car, I grab some tissues and blow my nose. Even the simple act of holding someone else's infant is enough to set me off. My babies died in my womb, and I'm left with empty arms. I silently pray, squinting out the car window. *Heavenly Father, do you even realize my babies died? Do you even care? I'm here waiting to become a mother. I want to raise children to believe in you. Why are you keeping this from me? I believe you are a God of miracles. I have seen it in the Bible. Lots of women struggled to get pregnant, and you intervened. Why won't you intervene for me?*

Back home, we quietly eat some of the soup I set aside for us. After dinner and cleaning up, we cuddle next to each other and read together from the Old Testament. Melvin opens the Book of Esther. I love her story and her strength. We take turns reading chapters. As we read, I notice something I hadn't before.

"I knew Mordecai was Esther's uncle, but I guess I forgot he had raised her. Her parents had died. Mordecai was close to her because he was a father to her." We finish the beautiful story of Esther. She was hesitant, but she rallied and saved her people. The words of Mordecai ring in my mind. *"...who knoweth whether thou art* come *to the kingdom for such a time as this?"* She was an orphan. Her life must not have been easy. But God led her to do great things. It's such an inspiring story.

Throughout the night, I toss and turn. I wake up with inspiration from Hannah, who wanted a son so badly that she was willing to give him up and dedicate him to the Lord. Eli, the priest, adopted him. I ponder Esther, the orphan, and the great things she did. Mordecai, her uncle, adopted her. I remember Daddy Warbucks adopting Orphan Annie. The song "Something Was Missing" from *Annie* rings out in my brain. Adoption completed them in the story. Chef Curtis' adopting his children influenced his entire career.

When my alarm goes off at 6:00 am, I have a calm sense of certainty. We're supposed to adopt a child.

I sit up on the bed, rubbing my hands over my upper arms. Can I fully love a stranger's child? Does this mean we will never have children of our own? I slide my palms across my stomach. I want to feel life fluttering inside me. Tiny kicks and prods from a human that Melvin and I created together. But somewhere in the night, God placed it on my heart to adopt.

Perhaps God has been preparing us for this exact thing. Melvin brought it up weeks ago, but I'm convinced of it now. That's what we're supposed to do.

I ease through my morning routine, feeling lighter than I have for a long time. There are a lot of details to figure out, but I'm willing to try. As we waltz around each other, I bounce up on my toes and give Melvin a peck on the cheek. "Good morning, sweetheart!"

"Someone is in a good mood this morning. Did you sleep well?"

"Actually, no. I tossed and turned all night. But I got an answer to my prayers." I reach up and brush Melvin's wavy hair off his face. "I'm ready to talk about adoption."

# Chapter 12

All day long, questions fill my brain. How will it work? How long will it take? I didn't want to consider adoption, but now I feel it in my bones. We can bless someone's life who needs parents. Like the Pharaoh's daughter did for Moses, Eli did for Samuel, Mordecai did for Esther, and yes, even Daddy Warbucks did for Annie. Even if I can't give birth, God can still provide a way for me to be a mother.

After work, we move about the kitchen, preparing for dinner. I fill a pot with rice and water and turn on the burner.

"I've been thinking all day about adoption. There are so many possibilities! We could adopt an infant or an older child. Domestic or foreign. Have you thought about it at all?"

Melvin pulls the plates out of the cupboard. "A little. I know it's harder for older children to get adopted, but I kind of want us to have a baby—even though we're not 'having a baby.'"

I turn to him and smile. "Me too. I've wanted that for so long. I can't imagine skipping newborn cuddles and pudgy little fingers and toes." As excited as I am about the possibility of adoption, I still mourn for the life I thought we were going to have.

"Domestic or foreign?" Melvin tips his head toward me.

"It was amazing to hear about Chef Lee's experience with international adoption, but it seems way more complicated. Thoughts?"

"I'm with you. There are babies who need families right here in the good old U.S. of A." He nudges me with his shoulder before opening the silverware drawer.

It's going to be expensive. It may take a long time. But we're in. And we're united.

As we proceed toward adoption, I realize this is what I was made for. I'm organized and great at getting things done. I do what I always do and make a checklist. We identify an agency and start preparing the paperwork. Then, a social worker will evaluate our home and us to determine if we are worthy of adopting. It's crazy the hoops you have to jump through—anyone can give birth, but they make it so hard to adopt a baby.

I diligently organize birth certificates, social security cards, and employment verification, my pulse quickening every time I check off another item on the list. Now, I need to ask for reference letters. We need several, and they can't be from family members. This step will also mean telling people we haven't been able to get pregnant and answering lots of personal questions. Allie and Powers are an obvious choice.

I emailed our pastor to ask for a letter and a suggestion of one more person. Who else could we ask? A friend? A neighbor? Someone who has been associated with us for a while.

I see Pastor Matthew's email response and share it with Melvin as we curl up together after dinner.

"Look at this. Pastor Matthew is so excited for us." My heart warms with his support and praise. As I continue reading, my stomach drops. "As for another letter of reference, have you considered Wendy and Will? They are faithful members of our congregation, and I believe they know you well enough to verify your suitability as parents." I turn to Melvin, biting my lower lip. "What do you think?"

He puts his feet up on the ottoman, crossing them at the ankles. The light from the TV casts a glow in the dim room.

"We've been going to church with them for years. I mean, you brought dinner to them. Surely, they could vouch for us."

"I guess so. I have mixed feelings. Every time I'm around her, I feel almost... mad. She's got everything I want, and I don't think she appreciates how lucky she is. I might fall apart if I have to open up about our struggles."

"Amelia, no one is going to judge you for wanting to adopt."

Sitting up, I face him. "I'm aware people won't judge me, but it's like publicly proclaiming, 'I'm a failure!'" I hold my hands up. "Everyone will realize that my body doesn't work, and I can't have kids."

"People adopt for lots of reasons, Amelia. And this may have been God's plan for us all along." He places his hands on my upper arms. "It's not about what you can't do. It's about what you *can* do. We need to find God's path for our lives. It may be different from what we imagined. But it will be okay."

Tension melts from my body at Melvin's words. Can I believe people will rally around me rather than judge me? "You're right. I need to get over it and connect with Wendy."

"I love you, Amelia." He pulls me into his arms. "You've got this. We've got this. Exciting things are in store for us. I'm certain of it."

***

The next day, I muster up the courage to approach Wendy. I call and hear screaming kids in the background.

"Hello?"

"Hi, Wendy. It's Amelia." My voice is too cheery, too unlike me. I take a calming breath. "I'm calling to ask a favor of you."

"Of course. What do you need? I've got some extra kids I can loan you!" She laughs.

My heart clenches. Ouch. "That's actually not a bad offer. I might have to take you up on it." Trying to keep my voice steady, I continue. "I was wondering if you could write a referral letter for us. Melvin and I decided to adopt, so we need several letters of recommendation from people who know us but aren't related to us."

"Oh!" A beat of silence hangs in the air. "You really *would* like one of my kids, wouldn't you? I had no clue you wanted children. You guys are so happy and have such amazing careers. I thought you were enjoying the freedom I wish I had."

"Yeah. We're living the dream." I scoff, tossing my gaze up toward the ceiling and biting my lip. "Honestly, your life is pretty appealing to us. We've been trying for years, and it isn't in the cards for us." I pace back and forth in the kitchen like a caged animal. The pounding of my heart echoes in my ears, and my hands tremble. I grab a dishcloth and scrub my already-clean counters.

"Well, truthfully, we would give anything for a quiet house with no interruptions. I guess you always want what you don't have." She pauses, and if she takes any longer to answer me, the grout will peel under my washrag. "I can work on a letter for you. When do you need it by?"

I straighten and release my grip on the towel. She said yes. Just like that. I scramble to let my words catch up with my brain. "The quicker, the better. Would a week give you enough time?"

"I can manage it. Do you have any ideas about what I should write? I've never done anything like this before."

"I'll send you a template you can use as a jumping-off point." Pausing with my heart full of gratitude, I continue. "Wendy? Thank you. I really appreciate it."

The phone call ends, and I soften against the counter. The bubbling anxiety that I had built up in my head releases like a newly opened can of pop, spritzing me with relief. My imagined fears were unwarranted. And I gained unexpected insight into her life.

# Chapter 13

O n Sunday afternoon, I get an SOS text from Allie.

Allie

> My sister is planning a shower for me, and it's falling apart. I need my best friend/event planner to save it. Do you have time?

Me

> Of course!

Immediately, my phone rings.

"Oh, Amelia! You are a lifesaver. Claire is a complete disaster. You get how she is. She said she would throw this party, but it's supposed to be in two weeks, and she hasn't even sent out invitations. I doubt she has considered a theme, food, or activities. Do you have enough time to rescue everything?" Allie asks.

"I can probably pull something off. What's your dream baby shower?" I shift my phone to the other ear and open my laptop.

"I don't care at this point. Make it fun and festive. You're good at that."

"I can run with that. What should we do about Claire?"

"Well, I don't want to offend her..." Her words trail off as she considers the situation. "It can't appear that I was meddling. I'm not sure how to handle it."

"How about if I call her and say I asked you about a shower, and you told me she was planning it? Then I can beg her to let me help."

"Perfect! Tell me how it goes," Allie says. As soon as we end the call, I search for inspiration online. Half an hour later, I have ideas for invitations, decorations, and food. Now to contact Claire and weasel my way into this event. I send her a text.

Me

> Hey, Claire. I heard you're having a baby shower for Allie. I love throwing parties. Do you mind if I help?

Claire

> That would be awesome. It's in 2 weeks, on Saturday.

Me

> What do you have planned so far?

Claire

> Not much. I was trying to think of a theme. Got any ideas?

Me

> I saw an idea online. 'About to POP!' With the fiasco from the gender reveal, it would be appropriate.

Claire

I like it. What do I need to do?

Me

Send me the guest list, and I'll send out
an email to invite everyone. I can send you
some food ideas. I'll handle the decorations
and games.

Claire

You're amazing, Amelia. This is going to be
so much fun!

Before dinner, I race through the tasks, efficiency fueled by the vision I have for this event. The chance to celebrate my best friend fills me with a hum of excitement. My shoulders droop for a moment, remembering the due date I had on the calendar and imagining Allie planning a baby shower for me. I push aside the weight and throw myself back into planning. This party will be 'popping.'

\*\*\*

Two weeks pass in a flash, and we are gathering for Allie's baby shower. The guys took Powers out for lunch and a superhero movie. This afternoon, it's girl time.

Claire's apartment overflows with pink and white balloons. She executed the refreshments perfectly. There are cake pops, popcorn, Pop Rocks, and fizzy punch arranged on the counter. After the guests arrive and fill their plates, I call for their attention.

"Thanks for coming, everyone. We're so excited for Allie to welcome a new little girl. If you remember her gender reveal, the balloon popped a little prematurely." I wink at Allie, and she drops her head, shaking it slightly. "Today, we're going to give you all a chance to pop a balloon. I have a basket filled with diaper pins. Take one and pass it on. When it's your turn, choose a balloon and pop it. Inside, you'll find a question to ask Allie. Who wants to go first?"

Claire's hand shoots up. "I will." She grabs a pink balloon, pops it, and unfolds the paper. "What was your strangest pregnancy craving?"

Allie grins. "Mustard. Normally, I'm not a fan, but one day, all I wanted was a mustard sandwich. Nothing else."

The guests chuckle and take turns reading their questions for Allie. We learn how she found out they were expecting and how she broke the news to Powers. I reflect on the moment we found out we were expecting—and the moment I found out we weren't. The phone call when I told Melvin replays in my head, and my heart clenches. Our pregnancy turned out so differently from Allie's.

After the games, we ooh and ahh as she opens adorable outfits and blankets. Each one is a reminder of the nursery we never created, the cute baby clothes I yearn for. Yet, with our plans for adoption moving ahead, there is hope that we might do all these things, too. Just not in the way I had planned. After the party winds up, I clean the kitchen while Allie visits and accepts well-wishes from everyone.

She's at the front door saying goodbye to the last of the guests when I hear her shriek. I bound out from the kitchen to see what's happened.

"What's wrong?" Claire asks.

"I popped!" As if on cue, water drips down her leg, and a puddle forms on the foyer floor.

Claire, the hot mess express, rushes around, panicking. "You aren't due for another week. What do you need? Let me grab some towels. Stay right there. I can't mess up my carpet. I'm renting."

Allie takes a deep breath. "Calm down, Claire. Let me call Powers and have him take me to the hospital."

Powers doesn't answer his phone, but the guys are probably still at the movie. Claire offers to drive her to the hospital, and Allie throws me a pleading glance.

"I can do it, Claire," I say, grabbing my keys. "I mean, you have all this to clean up from the shower. And I wouldn't want you to get your new car messed up."

"Honestly, we can probably wait a bit," says Allie. "These things take hours, and some women get turned away if they arrive at the hospital and their contractions aren't close enough together. If you give me a towel, I will sit in the kitchen so I don't mess up your carpet. I left a message for Powers. He'll see it and call when the movie is over."

An hour passes, and still no Powers. Allie searches her phone, watching the time and hoping for a message. She shifts and breathes through her contractions. I try to distract her with small talk, but the conversation is going nowhere. She fidgets with her hands and picks at her nails, barely glancing at me. She's calm on the outside, but I sense her growing concern at not hearing from Powers. Claire, on the other hand, hasn't left DEFCON 1. She mops up the mess at the front entryway. She tries to feed Allie, but Allie says she can't eat while in labor. Claire nervously paces, asking every thirty seconds, "Does it hurt? Are you okay? Should we get you to the hospital?"

After ninety minutes, Allie calls Powers again, and it goes straight to voicemail. She leaves a message, "Call me as soon as you can, honey. I think we're having a baby today." Her cheerful voice trembles slightly.

I finally take things into my own hands and text Melvin.

Me

How was the movie? Are you home yet?

Melvin

Yeah. It was good. I dropped off Powers at home about half an hour ago. When will you be home?

Me

Half an hour ago? We've been trying to reach him, but he's not answering. Allie is in labor!

My phone rings right away. I get up and walk into the other room to answer it.

"She's in labor? Where are you? At the hospital?"

"No. We're hanging out at Claire's place right now, waiting to hear from Powers." I stand at the picture window and peer out at the street.

"Do you want me to go get him? I can run over to their place."

"Would you? Bring him to Claire's house, and he can take Allie from here."

Allie sits up straighter and rubs her hands over her belly. She closes her eyes and takes a deep breath.

"Another contraction?" I place my hand on her leg. She nods and continues to breathe deeply until it passes.

"How far apart are they?"

"About ten minutes. But they say not to come to the hospital until they're five minutes apart, so we're fine."

My arms are jittery. I try to keep busy but stay close by. Each time a contraction starts, I return to Allie's side. There's an emptiness in my stomach, realizing I may never experience this for myself. Finally, Melvin calls again.

"Hey, Mel! Did you get him?" I ask.

"He's not there. I rang the doorbell and went to the backyard."

I relay the information to Allie. "Your car is there. Where would he go?"

"Seriously? I'm going to give birth! Maybe he went out for a run. I have no idea." She throws her hands in the air.

I share Allie's thoughts with Melvin and ask him to drive around and try to locate him.

"Of course. I'll call you when I find him."

We try to distract Allie with funny videos, but the contractions get more frequent. She could not be in worse hands. Neither Claire nor I have any clue about having a baby. A tug of war is going on inside me. I could never abandon Allie in her time of need, but I want to escape the reminder of my loss. Twenty minutes later, Melvin calls again.

"I found him. Allie was right. He was out for a run. His phone is dead. He's in the shower right now."

"In the shower? Doesn't he realize his wife is in labor?" I roll my eyes.

"Well, yeah, but he was gross from his run. He guessed Allie wouldn't want to be around him."

"Mel, hurry... please."

Allie interjects, "Ask him to get my bag. It's all packed and by the door."

We continue waiting and watching videos. Allie winces and pulls in a sharp breath, rubbing her hands across her swollen belly. Beads of sweat adorn her forehead. Hours ago, her hair was perfectly curled in loose waves. Now it's piled on her head in a messy bun, with a few loose strands slipping out. "How are you doing, Allie? How far apart are they now?" I ask.

"They're getting intense. They're about four and a half minutes apart now."

"Four and a half?" I slap my hands on the table. "Didn't you need to get to the hospital when they hit five minutes apart?"

"I did, but I keep expecting Powers to get here soon. I can't do this without him."

"Don't worry. He'll be here soon." I stroke her arm.

Allie moans as the next contraction hits her hard. More fluid leaks out, splattering on the floor below her seat.

"Holy cow! It's time to go to the hospital," Claire exclaims. "I'm excited to be an aunt and everything, but I don't want this kid to be born in my apartment."

"But Powers," Allie says after the contraction has subsided, her eyes full of concern.

"Listen. We need to go. Melvin and Powers can meet us at the hospital. Claire is right. You don't want to have your baby here." I stand and search for my purse.

Allie finally agrees, and we gather things up. We make it out to my car with one pause for a contraction. Somehow, we avoid dripping on Claire's carpet.

I send a text to Melvin that we are heading to the hospital.

# Chapter 14

We sign in, and the nurse leads Allie to a room. "You can't leave me until Powers is here," she says, grabbing for my hand.

"I won't. I promise." Supporting her around her waist, I help her waddle down the hall.

The nurse pushes open the door and hands Allie a gown to change into. The room is spacious but sparsely decorated. Next to the bed are screens and wires. The window on the far side of the room overlooks a gravel-covered rooftop. Allie slips into the bathroom to change, and the nurse pulls supplies from cupboards and arranges everything on the counter.

Allie emerges wearing pink grippy socks and what looks like a spacious tent. She eases onto the bed, and the nurse hooks her up to monitors and explains each one.

"This one monitors your contractions." She wraps a belt around her abdomen. "And this tracks the baby's heartbeat." She wraps Allie's arm in a blood pressure cuff and clips an oximeter on her finger. She slips on a pair of gloves and grabs a tube of jelly. "Let's check and see how far you're dilated." She reaches under the blanket briefly, pulls her hand away and pulls off the gloves. "You're at an eight. It won't be long now."

"I'm going to be an auntie," Claire says, bouncing in the chair in the corner. "I can't believe this is happening right now."

"Can you call Melvin again?" Allie asks me, tears pooling in her eyes. "I can't do this alone."

"They're probably almost here. You won't be alone."

I step away and call Melvin to ask how much longer they will be.

"We're in the Chick-fil-A drive-thru. Can we get anything for you guys?"

"You're *where*?" I tilt my head in disbelief.

"At Chick-fil-A. Powers needed to 'power up' before he's trapped at the hospital for hours."

Powers' voice interjects, "Hey, Amelia! We'll be there soon with the nugs!"

"They have food at the hospital." I run my hand through my hair and glance at my shoes.

"Sure. Hospital food. He needed something that tastes good."

"Get. Here. Now. The nurse said Allie is dilated to an eight." I let my hand drop to my side and walk over to Allie.

I reassure her that they are about five minutes away. She nods, eyes closed, breathing slowly as another contraction builds on the monitor.

"You've got this. Keep breathing. Squeeze my hand." She clenches my hand like a vice grip, the pain radiating up my arm. "Okay. That's a bad one. It's almost over." The numbers on the monitor go down, and she takes another deep breath. "Wow! That's quite a grip!" She releases my fingers, and I shake my arm out.

"Sorry. Too hard?" She winces.

"No apology necessary. I'm sure it hurts far less than what you're experiencing. Do you need anything?"

"A cool washcloth?"

Claire hops over to the sink. "I've got it." She wets it down, wrings it out, and presents it to Allie.

Before long, the door opens, and in walk Melvin and Powers... with a tray of chicken nuggets.

"You know what they say. Nugs, not drugs!" Powers exclaims. "You said you wanted to do this naturally, so hey, who wants some chicken nuggets?"

"You can't be serious," Allie snaps. "I can't eat anything until after I have the baby."

"Just because you can't eat doesn't mean the rest of us have to starve," says Claire, grabbing the gallon of lemonade Melvin is carrying.

Allie lets out a moan, and takes a deep, cleansing breath.

Powers hands off the nuggets to me and rushes to her side. "Oh, my gosh. Are you okay?" He pushes her hair from her face and grabs her hand. She transitions to short, shallow breaths and Powers whispers words of encouragement to her. The contraction passes, and she takes another deep, cleansing breath.

"Oh, honey. I'm so sorry I wasn't here sooner. The birthing class said it takes forever. I figured we had time." He holds her head in his hands and places a gentle kiss on her lips.

Allie focuses on him with tears in her eyes. "You're here now. That's what matters."

The nurse walks in. "Are we having a party in here?"

"A *birthday* party," Claire exclaims. Allie and I exchange glances.

The nurse discreetly checks Allie under the blanket. "You, my dear, are at a ten. It's time to push. Do you want an audience, or should we take the party down the hall?"

"They can take the party elsewhere." Allie breathes through another contraction.

I give her a quick hug. "Good luck." I hold the nugs in the air. "We'll save you some."

***

I must admit the chicken nuggets and lemonade were delicious. We set the extra food aside, and Melvin holds my hand while we sit in the hard vinyl chairs. Claire wanders off to explore. I drop my head onto Melvin's shoulder.

"It's been quite a day, hasn't it? How are you doing with all of this, Melly?" Melvin rubs the back of my hand.

"Of course I'm happy for them, and I'm glad I could be here for Allie, but it's been a constant reminder of what we lost. I had already imagined a baby shower for myself and what it would be like to go into labor. But that dream stopped as soon as it began."

"I know. I wonder if they realize how lucky they are. Powers took his time getting ready. I think he was a little nervous, so he kept taking these detours. I was thinking, *Hurry up! You're going to be a dad today.* I wish it were us in there right now."

Claire returns with a bag of mini chocolate chip cookies from the vending machine. She offers us some and then paces around the room.

After about an hour, Powers enters the family waiting area, his face beaming.

"It's a girl!" he says, even though we already knew. "Seven pounds, thirteen ounces, nineteen inches long. Would you like to meet her?"

We maul him with hugs and congratulations. Claire is the first to slip away. "I've got to see my niece, people. Watch out!"

My heart pulls in two directions. It freezes in place at the remembrance of my loss, but soars with happiness for Allie. Melvin and I walk down the hall. I slide my arm around his waist and lean into him for support. Pushing open the door, my insides vibrate like a hummingbird suspended in flight. There is a calm hush here, even with Claire bouncing in the middle of everything.

"Congratulations." I swallow hard and hug Allie. "How are you doing?" She looks exhausted but happy. Damp strands of hair stick to the side of her face. Her swollen stomach is slightly deflated. A quiet, overwhelming peace emanates from her eyes.

"Next time my philosophy will be drugs, not nugs." She watches Claire, who is already holding the baby.

"Does she have a name yet?" My mind races to the list of names I compiled that I may never use.

"Yes, meet Ruby Allison Hill."

"How sweet." I rub my hands against my empty abdomen.

"Her initials are R, A, H?" Claire asks. "She'll be a great cheerleader someday. Rah, rah, rah-rah-rah!" she cheers.

"That never crossed our minds." Allie shakes her head and chuckles.

"Do you want to hold Rah Rah?" Claire approaches me.

"Of course." I press my arm up to hers, and we carefully roll Ruby from Claire's arms to mine.

I gaze at her round face and breathe in the fresh baby scent. The white blanket with pink and blue stripes swaddles her. A striped cap covers her puffy head. My heart expands at the awe of this being, fresh from heaven. My eyes fill with tears. Oh, how I wish for one of my own. She wriggles for a moment and then settles into a comfortable sleep. My heart pushes up into my throat, making it hard to get out the words. "She's beautiful. You are a very lucky momma."

We visit for another ten minutes before the nurse enters the room to kick us out. I hand off Ruby to Allie and give her a one-armed hug.

"Goodnight, Rah Rah! Auntie Claire loves you." Claire kisses the top of Ruby's head.

Claire jabbers the entire ride back to her place about babies and how she wants ten of her own. I smile and nod along. Relief washes over me when we pull up to her apartment. She calls out goodbye and bounds toward her door. Melvin and I glance at each other.

"Claire was a lot," he says. "Does she ever stop talking?"

"Not really."

The ride is silent after Claire is gone. *Allie had a baby. A beautiful, perfect child.* I smile at the mental image of Allie holding the tightly wrapped bundle. I steer through town to pick up Melvin's car at Allie and Powers' place. My heart pokes me as I wonder if we will ever welcome a newborn into our family.

"Do you think it will ever be our turn?"

He reaches across and rests his hand on my thigh. "I know it will. It might not be in the way we imagined it, but it will."

Perhaps somewhere out there, a birth mother is wrestling with a life-changing decision. I try to imagine us with our own precious child. The newness and excitement, and hope, all wrapped up in a blanket. That's what I want for us. I clasp my hand over his. He pulls my hand up to his lips and touches them softly to the back of my hand. Someday. In God's timing.

# Chapter 15

I scoop a package off the front step when I arrive home from work. It's addressed to Melvin, so I set it on the counter and sort through the mail. A few minutes later, Melvin bursts through the door like a ray of sunshine in his bright yellow shirt. He loosens his necktie, designed to mimic Mondrian's work with its bold squares of blue, yellow, and red.

"Ooh, awesome. My package came."

"What did you order?"

"It's a new lens for my camera. This will be great for shooting Elise's wedding reception." He opens the box and carefully pulls out a huge zoom lens from the form-fitting foam surrounding it.

I quirk an eyebrow at him, his grin wide and childlike over the fragile thing. "Don't you have enough lenses?" I tease.

He points his finger out. "Different lenses, different purposes." He playfully pokes my side, and I jerk away from him with a laugh. "Can't do a good job without the right equipment."

I take the empty box and put it next to the recycling bin in the kitchen. "And how is this lens the *right* equipment?"

He straightens, his eyes sparkling. "You really asking? Or are you razzing me?"

I roll my eyes and tip my head toward him. "A little bit of both."

He chuckles, easing to my side. He wraps an arm around my shoulders, tucking me in close enough to experience his comforting warmth. "This is a telephoto lens," he says, reverently running his fingers over the edges. "It will allow me to capture moments from across the room."

"Hmm," I say, continuing to tease. "Pretty sure you said that about a few of those other lenses in that bag of yours."

He knocks his nose against mine. "Nothing like this. Plus... I got an amazing deal."

"Oh no. It was the clearance tag that did you in, was it?"

His body shakes against mine with his amusement. "Fifteen-hundred, Melly. A steal."

I grow rigid, my heart dropping straight into my stomach. "What?"

"Amazing, right?" His arm falls from my shoulders, and the icy coldness seeping into my bones has nothing to do with his sudden lack of touch.

Fifteen hundred dollars. For a lens. For something he has a million of. Something he doesn't even *need*.

My mind flashes to the stack of bills he shuffled through. To his words about IVF, the panic in his eyes. Something wraps around my throat, suffocating me, the anger rushing through my heart and begging to be released. But it can't seem to find its way to my tongue.

Melvin bounces around the kitchen, oblivious to the thunderstorm brewing within me. My vision blurs, my heart pounding in my ears.

I swallow hard around that suffocating grip, forcing my voice to make an appearance.

"How... how could you spend that much? You said we were struggling."

"It was a good deal." He frowns, setting the lens gently on the counter. "I didn't think you'd mind."

My jaw clenches, the ache in my stomach growing with every second that passes. "We... You said..." My words tangle around each other, bouncing back and forth between accusatory and broken. "What about IVF?"

His shoulders drop, a long breath puffing from his lips. "Amelia... IVF is way more than this lens."

"Obviously." I snap, folding my arms across my chest. "But we could have put the money in the bank to save toward another round or put it toward adoption. That's expensive too."

"I didn't figure there was going to be another round, so I didn't suppose it mattered. Besides, I can use this to *make* money." He raises the lens in the air like a trophy. "I can pick up some more wedding gigs, and this will pay for itself."

My head drops in silence as I walk past him to the bedroom. If it is so easy for him to make more money, why didn't he suggest that so we could try another round of IVF? I peel off my work clothes and shove myself into a pair of joggers and a sweatshirt. I rest on the edge of the bed, holding myself, my eyes glazing over. The heaviness settling on my body crushes my spirit. I flop back on the bed and watch the ceiling fan slowly spinning but getting nowhere, just like our attempts to get pregnant.

***

Our forks clink against our dinner plates, the sound echoing in the room's silence. Across the kitchen, Melvin's new lens taunts me. The chair grinds against the floor as I push away from the table to clean up after dinner. We orbit each other like planets in their assigned rotations, never getting too close.

"You want to work on the adoption paperwork tonight?" Melvin's voice pierces my thoughts, my hands deep in bubbly water.

"I don't know if we can afford it after that new lens you bought." The words slice through the tension like a sword used to defend me.

"Is that what this is about? I told you it's for Elise's wedding." He crosses his arms over his chest, his eyes blazing into me.

Abandoning the dishes, I turn to fully face him, drying my hands on the towel. "I get it. I love your sister, and I want the best for her. But don't you think it would have been possible to do the job with the equipment you already have so that money could go toward growing our family?"

Melvin shifts, leaning back against the counter. "We can have both, you know. A camera lens and a family."

My throat constricts. "But you already have plenty of them. What we don't have is a baby."

"So I'm never supposed to buy anything again until we have a child?"

"That's not what I said." I shut my eyes and gather my thoughts for a moment. "But I wish you would have talked with me about it first."

Melvin pokes his fingers through his hair and softens his gaze, taking a step toward me. "You're right. It was a big purchase, and I should have run it past you. When I saw the sale price, I didn't want to miss out. I'm sorry."

The armor I built around my heart loosens, and I let my defenses down. Melvin is a good guy. His impulsiveness got away from him, but it's one quality I love about him. "I forgive you. Sorry about the overreaction. I know how you get when it comes to new equipment." I inch closer to him and give him a playful jab on his arm.

He grabs my hand and pulls me in, resting his forehead on mine. "We good?"

"We're good." I kiss him squarely on his lips. "Now, how about that paperwork?"

We sit close, feet propped on the footstool, with my laptop and attack the questionnaire. We scroll through options for sex, race, hair, and eye color.

"I can't believe they let you make these kinds of choices. We're adopting a baby, not ordering a custom car! It's like playing God. It's not right," I say.

"I agree. If we truly believe God is in charge, shouldn't we leave the options up to Him?" He turns to me for approval, and I nod.

I show Melvin my adoption checklist. "Here's everything we need for our application. Why don't we divide and conquer? Can you handle pay stubs, taxes, and insurance?" My finger points out those items on the paper. "I can follow up on the reference letters and verify they have everything for the background checks and clearances. I've already copied our important documents from the safe and organized them in a file."

"Sounds like a plan."

"Perfect. The quicker we get everything in, the quicker we will be parents." My eyes twinkle at him, a smile spreading across my face.

"I can't wait." He holds me in his arms. I slide my hands around his waist, tuck into him, and breathe in his musky scent. Soon, our arms will wrap around a little one as well.

# Chapter 16

A couple of weeks later, I update Melvin as we unwind on the couch after dinner. "I got one out of three reference letters back. I texted Allie, and she promised to get to it. She's probably overwhelmed by motherhood." I smile at him. "I texted Wendy, too, but I haven't gotten a response. She's probably busy too, but I told her a week, and now it's been two. I'm not sure what to do to encourage her without being a pest."

Melvin glances up from his phone, his mop of hair on the top of his head bouncing. "She's probably overwhelmed with motherhood, too. We still have loads of other paperwork to gather. We've got plenty of time."

I tuck my leg under me. "I get that, but I want to move this along as quickly as possible. And if she doesn't even text me back, it concerns me. Do you think I should ask someone else?"

"Don't worry about it. Give her a couple more days and then contact her again. It's no big deal."

"You're probably right." I grab two blue M&M's from the bowl and ease up, and wander to the office. As I flip through the file, I cross-reference documents with my checklist. I place the letter from Pastor Matthew in the manila folder and search online for an infant CPR and first aid class. There is one in two weeks.

***

We arrive at the community center for our class. Certification isn't required, but it is highly encouraged and can make a difference with birth parents when they are choosing adoptive parents. I don't want to give them any reason to question our ability or to choose someone else over us.

We proceed through the hallway covered in grey industrial carpet until we find our room. Our instructor checks us in and hands us a packet of papers. The chairs in the room form a semicircle. Melvin takes my hand and leads me to two empty seats closest to the wall. There are four other couples in our class. Each couple sits close to each other, avoiding eye contact with the others. Finally, our instructor enters.

"Welcome, everyone, to Infant CPR and First Aid. I'm Tammy, and I'll be your instructor. Let's go around the room and introduce ourselves before we begin. Tell us your names and why you signed up for the class."

Goosebumps crawl up my arms when we learn that one of the other couples is also preparing for adoption. Suddenly, I don't feel so alone on this journey.

Tammy continues, "First is instruction; then we will practice on a dummy." We watch from our perches while she demonstrates breathing and compressions on the fake infant. Two by two, couples take their turns. When it's our chance, Melvin goes first, then we do it together before I do it on my own. Watching him, I catch myself holding my breath and tensing my muscles in concentration.

Finally, I scoot forward to pass off the required task. Kneeling over the model, I give thirty compressions, followed by two breaths. Rinse and repeat. I've got this. I hear the beat of my heart echoing in my ears as I silently count out the compressions. My lungs fill with air, and I carefully breathe over the doll's nose and mouth. Gasping for more air to deliver my next breath, I feel a little lightheaded. That won't stop me from passing the test. The sounds in the room fade into the background. I continue with thirty more compressions and two more breaths. The third time around, I attempt to focus my vision on the task at hand, and everything else disappears. My skin prickles with beads of sweat, but I push through. The room spins. My eyes blink closed to reset myself, and everything fades to black.

"Amelia, are you okay?"

My eyes flutter open. "Yeah. What happened?"

"You passed out."

Our instructor reassures us, "Don't worry. This is the perfect place to do it. We got to have a real-life example." In the time I was out, they checked my pulse and breathing and discovered I was still alive. Right now, I would rather crawl under the table and die. "This happens sometimes," she continues. "When you are taking care of others, it's important to take care of yourself. Being on your knees for too long can limit blood flow, and sometimes people concentrate intently on breathing into the mannequin, and they forget to breathe for themselves."

After a few minutes of lying on the floor and taking deep breaths, I'm back to normal, and Melvin helps me up. "Does this mean I failed the class?" I ask, my eyebrows puckering in concern.

"Not on my watch," Tammy proclaims. "We'll give you a few more minutes while your classmates take their turn, then you can try again. Why don't you sit in a chair and drink some water until you're ready?"

Melvin brings me a bottle of water. I follow instructions and make sure I'm getting good blood flow—no crossing my legs. I concentrate on slow, deep breaths. On my second try, everything goes as expected. We walk out two hours later, carrying our certificates.

"You doing okay, honey?" Melvin opens the car door for me. "Want to stop and grab some food before we go home?"

"Nothing more than a bruised ego. How embarrassing. Physically, I'm fine, but I would never say no to a milkshake. I mean, my blood sugar might have been too low." I wink at him as he shuts the car door.

Melvin steers us to the Dairy Queen drive-thru. He gets a strawberry blizzard, and I go for cookies and cream. The sweet, creamy ice cream melts in my mouth. I crunch the chocolatey cookie pieces, my overstuffed stomach expanding.

Focusing on our to-do list, I turn to Melvin. "Our adoption file is almost complete. How are you coming on your end of things?"

"I'll get to it this afternoon. I promise." He sneaks a look my way.

"We can't let our paperwork hold us up."

"You still don't have all the reference letters, do you? I'm not the one holding us up," he huffs, his taut arms gripping the steering wheel.

His words pierce my core. I freeze, searching for the right words. It's not my fault either. "Yeah. Still waiting for Wendy. It may have been a bad idea to ask a mother of four to write a letter. Should I ask someone else?"

"Nah, she'll get to it. We could volunteer to babysit so she can get it done," Melvin jokes, relaxing a little. But actually, helping her with the kids might be what it takes to get her to follow through. We'll simply go over and entertain the kids long enough for her to pound out the letter. It shouldn't be too hard.

# Chapter 17

Melvin and I fly in from our home in Minnesota to Ohio the weekend before his sister's wedding. On Monday morning, I'm up and ready to go. We have final meetings with the caterer, florist, and bakery. Elise, Paul, and I confirm with each of the vendors that everything is in order. They are happy with all the details, and I am confident that things will go according to my plan.

Thursday evening, we recruit the extended family to put together the favors for the wedding guests at Brenda and Marcus's house. We gather around the dining room table, forming an assembly line. One-by-one we grab bottle openers that resemble vintage skeleton keys, and attach tags with white satin ribbon. The house fills with laughter as we surround the table. With everyone's help, we quickly assemble all one hundred fifty of them, and people gradually disperse to the backyard for a bonfire. I stay behind, checking each one. The message on the label came out perfectly: 'Thank you for being a key part of our lives. Elise and Paul.' Taking the time to adjust each bow, I arrange them in a box to take to the venue.

When I finally emerge from the dining room, Brenda is in the kitchen, gathering supplies for s'mores.

"Do you need any help?"

"Thanks." Brenda hands me a box of graham crackers. I fan them out across the tray while she unwraps chocolate bars beside me. We settle into a quiet rhythm, punctuated by the snap of square wafers and the rustle of wrappers.

She breaks the silence. "It's been a few months since the miscarriage..." She pauses, choosing her words. "I don't mean to pry, but...is there any chance you guys will make me a grandma this year?" She nudges my shoulder and winks.

My stomach clenches, and I freeze, holding a graham cracker in mid-air. Is she making this about her? I pull in a deep breath and fumble for a response. "Honestly—it's been tough." I place the wafer on the tray, brush off my hands, and clutch my arms around my stomach. "We want a family... but it hasn't worked out for us."

"Have you tried fertility treatments? There's a lot they can do with science these days."

I nod slightly, stripping away the walls I have carefully built to protect me. "True. We have been down that route. Our miscarriage was a pregnancy by IVF. But it's expensive."

"I had no idea." Brenda sets the chocolate down and eyes me. "Melvin never said anything."

"We've kept things quiet because it's such a sensitive topic. And we were trying to avoid extra questions. But we've decided to adopt, and we're working on the paperwork now."

"What can I do to help?" She rests her hand on my forearm.

"What we need most is compassion and understanding, not pressure to have a baby."

"Of course." She pulls her hand away and smooths her apron. "I guess I've said some insensitive things, but I had no clue you were struggling." She scoops me into a long hug and then gently releases me. "It's so lonely with all the kids grown up. And now Elise is getting married." She wipes away a tear. "I keep hoping that if I have grandkids, there will be someone else to love, someone who needs me."

My heart swells with compassion for my mother-in-law. We both want the same thing—someone to love and care for. "Your kids still need you, Brenda. Just in a different way." I turn to the box of Kleenex. We each pull one out and wipe our tears.

***

Saturday morning, there's a flurry of activity as we prepare for the wedding. I want this day to be amazing for Elise and Paul. Everything is crossed off my checklist. I peek out the window as the 1956 Rolls-Royce Silver Cloud arrives in the driveway. Something old. I look in on Elise. She is gorgeous in her white satin gown overlaid with lace. Something new. Brenda places her own string of pearls around Elise's neck. Something borrowed. And I slip her a hanky with her initials embroidered in blue. Something blue. I have personally verified every detail, and I am confident that this wedding will be flawless.

Classic cars don't have room for many passengers, so Elise and her sister, Celeste, along with their mom, Brenda, get the honor of riding to the church in the car. I'm traveling separately with the other two bridesmaids, and we're meeting them there.

Paul and his groomsmen have secluded themselves in the back room. When I arrive, I confirm the groomsmen and the pastor are ready. It's not ideal to be a bridesmaid and event coordinator for a wedding, but Elise wanted my help, so I'm doing my best. Melvin is also doing double duty as both a groomsman and a second photographer. Guests are being seated, and strains of piano music lilt through the air. The limo waits around the corner until 12:55 so Elise can make her grand entrance.

As the front doors of the church close, the limo turns into the driveway, gravel popping under the tires. The chauffeur opens the door, and Brenda climbs out first, followed by her daughters. I hear the click of the camera when the three of them hold hands with excitement. Standing outside the doors, the music shifts to Pachelbel's Canon in D as the bridesmaids begin the procession. As I advance down the aisle, my eyes lock with Melvin's. He stands dignified, with his hands behind his back, but he winks and raises his eyebrows at me. I dip my head, my cheeks heating. What a guy. I'm glad he's mine. The music changes again to the traditional Wagner Wedding March, and I remember our big day. Our friends and family filled the church. My dad walked me down the aisle, where Melvin waited for me. I glance down the row and share a smile with Melvin. The doors separate, and everyone rises when Elise emerges on her dad's arm.

I listen to the pastor share the traditional vows, "To have and to hold." Melvin and I vowed the same vows. Although we have each other, we both want more. My empty arms long to hold a baby. Hopefully, through this adoption process, they will finally be filled. "From this day forward, for better or worse, for richer or poorer, in sickness and in health, to love and to cherish, until death do us part." Thankfully, it's acceptable to let the tears flow at a wedding. I'm crying because it's beautiful, but also because I'm reminded of our hopes and dreams when we got married. I was confident we would have a family by now. Thankfully, the wedding planning has been a wonderful distraction from the ever-present void. The opportunity to focus on joy—even if it was someone else's—has helped me experience joy, too.

After the ceremony, we cross the green to the tents where hors d'oeuvres are served. I sneak a deviled egg from the food table. The smooth sound of jazz fills the space from the gazebo in the center. The tents are buzzing with the sounds of music, laughter, and conversation. Scanning the room, I notice the cake. The three tiers are leaning toward the wall. I have built enough block towers in my day to comprehend that gravity will not be kind. And the baker is long gone. She dropped off the cake before the ceremony began. Elise and Paul weren't supposed to cut the cake for another hour, but from the looks of it, it had better happen soon. I alert them that we are changing the schedule a bit, but it's nothing to worry about. Then I slip a note to the band asking them to announce it after the next song. Melvin positions himself with his camera, and we are ready to go.

Because the cake is in the corner, I hope most people won't notice how badly it is leaning. We have to get it cut and distributed before there is a disaster. The band invites Paul and Elise to cut the cake, and all eyes turn to the Leaning Tower of Pisa. When they step behind the table for the perfect photo op, they realize what's going on. Elise's eyes widen, looking to me for reassurance. I smile sweetly and nod at her. They pick up the knife and cut into the cake. The gentle pressure from the knife was all it needed. The entire thing falls toward the couple, and they jump to avoid being splattered by frosting. There is an audible gasp from the guests, and my heart tightens in my chest. An utter disaster.

"I guess the Leaning Tower of Pisa cake was a bad idea." Melvin pipes up and diffuses the situation. "How can a building stay like that for hundreds of years, but this cake didn't even last an afternoon?" He laughs toward the crowd. Everyone chuckles, and we invite Paul and Elise to the dance floor for their first dance as husband and wife. Fortunately, the table is large and caught most of the disaster. The caterers salvage enough to feed everyone something, although some of it is more like a scoop of English trifle than a slice of wedding cake.

As the party winds down, the guests grab paper cones filled with dried flowers and form two lines leading to the Rolls-Royce. Colorful paper-thin petals shower Paul and Elise as they rush to the car.

Once everyone is gone except for the family and the wedding party, we pack things up. Melvin and I are gathering centerpieces when Brenda approaches.

"Melvin, Amelia told me you guys are going to adopt."

He turns from the centerpieces to acknowledge his mom and runs his fingers through his hair. "We've started the process. There's still a lot of paperwork before we can submit our application, but we're excited about it."

"Well, my friend Ruth's daughter adopted a baby from China." Brenda pulls him close and lowers her voice. "Are you going to adopt from China?"

"We're planning to stick with the U.S.," I slip my arm around Melvin's lower back. "There are plenty of American children who need homes, too."

"Well, I'm surprised you didn't say something to me. I've been wondering why we haven't heard any news after the miscarriage."

"I'm sorry, Mom. We haven't had any news to share so far." He places his hand on my shoulder.

"Since it wasn't happening for us, we found a different way to have a family. We're thinking outside the box." I wink at Melvin.

"I'm sorry you've been struggling, guys." She hugs both of us. "You can share the good and the bad stuff."

Melvin looks his mom in the eyes. "It's been a lot to process for the two of us. We weren't ready to involve others until we had answers for ourselves."

I tuck into him. "And now we have some answers."

***

Sunday night, Melvin and I fly back home. Soon, Elise and Paul will probably stand at the real Leaning Tower of Pisa, trying to figure out how it stays standing. Honestly, though, years from now, they will have a story to tell. The picture-perfect details all blur together on important days, but the mistakes we can laugh at are what create memories and stories to be told. My mind drifts to Allie and Power's gender reveal, and the corners of my mouth lift in a smile. We'll never forget that mishap.

And, as I'm learning in my life, some things are out of your control. But there is more than one path, whether it's a wedding or starting a family. The important thing is where you end up, not necessarily how you got there. With the wedding over, I'm ready to refocus on the adoption.

# Chapter 18

I shuffle through an empty pew toward Wendy to politely ask *again* about the letter. Her eyes get big when she sees me coming. Before I can even ask, she's babbling, "I'm sorry. I promised you that letter. It has been one thing after another with the kids, and Will has been working late a lot. I can barely get dinner on the table."

Melvin's suggestion to help her out might be the right solution. "What if I made you dinner?" I pause, hoping she will agree. "I can come to the house and feed the kids to give you time to sit down and type it up."

"Oh, you don't have to bother." She shifts the baby to her hip. "You don't know what you would get yourself into. Dinner at our house isn't exactly a Norman Rockwell picture."

"You don't believe I can handle it? Challenge accepted." I extend my arm to shake her hand. "Melvin and I will be there at five tonight. We'll bring dinner and eat with them so you can have time to write the letter. What do the kids like?"

"Seriously, you don't have to do this. But if you really want to, keep it simple. They love mac and cheese."

"Done. We'll see you tonight!"

***

After church, I search my cupboards for mac and cheese. It's not exactly a staple around here. I don't have any, but I remember a from-scratch recipe I've been meaning to try. It's gooey and creamy and covered in breadcrumbs. Gourmet mac and cheese will be perfect. Those kids have probably never had something this good. I round it out with some diced watermelon. It's the perfect summertime treat. I'll make my barbecue baby back ribs for the adults. I have no illusions the kids will be interested, but it will be nice grown-up food for Wendy and Will. They'll probably really appreciate it. My chest swells with pride. I'm going to knock their socks off. I spend the afternoon cooking up a storm. This meal is a masterpiece. It's the least I can do since Wendy is doing me a life-changing favor. The smell of barbecue fills the car on our drive over.

We stand on the doorstep, our arms laden with warm pots and pans. The shrill screams of children reach us before we even ring the doorbell. Will opens the door wearing athletic shorts and a 'Best Dad Ever' t-shirt. "Hey! Wendy mentioned you were bringing dinner. That's incredibly nice of you."

We cautiously enter as a naked three-year-old boy streaks past.

"Potty training," Will explains. "I guess you can take it into the kitchen."

We enter the kitchen and discover a sink full of dishes. Will pushes things aside on the island to make room for the food. They knew we were coming and bringing dinner. I would assume they would clean up a bit. I ask where the dishes are. Will points out the cupboard. When I open it, there are a few mismatched dishes of various sizes that I scrape together.

Wendy enters the kitchen wearing sweatpants, and a rumpled t-shirt, strands of hair coming loose from her ponytail. "It smells delicious. I'm sorry for the mess. I meant to clean up before you got here, but it's been one tantrum after another, and with the potty training, things are kind of out of control here."

"It's okay. You go sequester yourself, and we will handle dinner and the kids. We'll save you some food, or you can take a plate and eat in peace," I suggest.

"Thanks. I'd better run and get your letter written while I can. Food is for the weak!" She raises her finger in the air.

Wendy disappears. Melvin and I set the table while Will rounds up the kids. After Will offers a prayer, I carefully dish up mac and cheese and diced watermelon for each of the kids. I pass the ribs to Will, and he digs in.

"Oh my gosh, these are delicious, Amelia," Will exclaims.

"I'm glad you like them." My heart warms, and I smile.

"What's this?" asks the naked three-year-old boy, Finn.

"Mac and cheese." I put a scoop on his plate. "Your mom said it's your favorite."

He pokes at it and then folds his arms across his chest. "Yuck."

"It's okay, buddy," Will interjects. "Please take a bite. Miss Amelia made it for you."

"I want Mommy."

"Mommy's busy right now. Try some watermelon." Will attempts to distract him.

"There's something weird in my mac and cheese. What's this crunchy stuff?" Their oldest daughter, Olivia, picks at her dinner.

"Those are breadcrumbs." I sit up and smile at her. "This is a special recipe from a fancy restaurant."

"I only like *regular* mac and cheese." She sullenly inspects her plate.

"This is the kind they serve to princesses." I try to make it sound appealing to her. All little girls like that stuff, right?

"I'm too old for princesses," she says, pushing her watermelon around on her plate. "Can I be excused, Dad?"

"Take five bites first," Will instructs. "Unless you want to try some ribs?"

She scrunches her nose at the sauce dripping from her father's fingers. "No thanks. They're too messy."

"I like messy food!" exclaims their five-year-old, Ethan.

"All right, buddy. Do you want some?" Melvin offers him some ribs. He digs in and soon has barbecue sauce all over his face and clothes. At least someone likes something I made. While we were busy with Olivia and Ethan, no one noticed Finn disappear.

"Will?" Wendy calls from down the hall. "Can you come here for a minute?"

"I'll be right back," he says, dashing off.

I catch Melvin's eye and shake my head. This is not going according to plan. With three adults at the table, we should have some sense of order. We finish eating, and Will still hasn't emerged. Melvin and I clear the table and tackle the sink full of dishes when he finally returns.

"Sorry about that. Finn did a number two in the hallway and then disturbed his mom. This potty-training thing is awful. Anyway, we got it all cleaned up, and Wendy is almost done with your letter."

I do a double-take and then nod at Will, my lips stretched in a thin smile. I keep my opinions to myself and continue washing the dishes while Melvin dries them.

"Finished!" Wendy pops into sight, waving a paper in her hand. "I hope you like it." She freezes, taking in the scene that surrounds her. "Oh, gosh, you didn't have to clean the kitchen. I was going to get to that. Probably not until the kids got to bed, but eventually." She lets out a laugh.

"It's no problem. We made part of the mess ourselves. Grab yourself a plate of dinner while I finish this up."

Wendy makes a plate of ribs and mac and cheese and sits at the island while I work. "This is amazing. Did you make this all from scratch?"

"Yeah. I like to cook." I shrug. "Your kids didn't enjoy it very much, though." I turn from the sink, wiping my hands on a towel.

"They don't like anything I make either. But this mac and cheese is divine." She points at her plate with her spoon.

Melvin stacks our empty containers. "We'd better get out of your hair. Thanks for writing the letter. It really helps."

"How long until you're able to adopt?" Wendy studies us.

I swing my arm around Melvin's waist and tuck into him. "We don't know. We are assembling our file. Next will be the home study. Once we get approved, it will still take a while."

"Well, good luck. I'm excited for you!" Wendy smiles broadly and walks us to the door. Right then, Charlotte cries from the bedroom. She has been napping the whole time. "Duty calls. See you later."

"Thank you for doing this, Wendy."

She takes my hand in hers, her nail polish chipped on her thumb. "No, Amelia. Thank *you*. It's been at least six years since I've been able to sit behind a closed door by myself for longer than five minutes."

She shuts the door behind us, and we walk to the car. I realize how much I've judged Wendy. She's handling a lot more than I gave her credit for. One hour in her house showed me that my organizational skills can't solve every problem.

"That was a lot harder than I expected it to be," I say to Melvin.

"No kidding. There's a lot going on at their house. Can you believe he pooped in the hallway?" He laughs.

"I know, gross! Glad I didn't have to clean it up!" But honestly, I would gladly clean up poop if it meant being a mother.

# Chapter 19

With the adoption paperwork complete, it's time to prepare for the home inspection. I pull out my weekend to-do list and start checking items off one by one.

Order baby-proofing supplies. *Check.*

Medicine and knives placed out of reach. *Check.*

Baby gate installed (Melvin's job...) *Check... after nagging him a few times about it.*

Check smoke and CO detectors. *Check.*

What else am I missing? I tap the list on my phone, and with nothing coming to mind, I smile to myself and add: *Impress the home inspector, and get approved for adoption!*

It will be so satisfying to put a little checkmark next to that one.

\*\*\*

The night before our home inspection, I'm cleaning like a madwoman. As I mop the floors, I discover how dusty the baseboards are.

I go around the house on my hands and knees, wiping them down. Melvin walks into the living room, raising a brow.

"What are you doing?"

"Dusting the baseboards."

"Are they going to care if our baseboards are dusty?"

"They might. I don't want her to have any reason to reject our application."

"I get it." He rubs his hand over his hair, messing up his styling attempt. "Is there anything you need me to help with?"

"Could you scrub the grout in the bathroom? Even though we clean it every week, the details are important."

"Sure... but are they going to scrutinize our grout?"

"It's hard to say." I throw my hands in the air. "But if they do, I want it to be clean."

Melvin slinks off to clean the grout while I finish the baseboards. I won't sleep until everything is perfect.

***

The next morning, I allow myself to sleep longer than I would if I were going to work, but not much. I run through my mental checklist.

Shower and get ready. *Check.*

Give the bathroom a once-over. *Check.*

Eat breakfast. *Check.*

Wipe down the counters. Load the dishwasher. Sweep the floor. *Check, check, check.*

I take a deep breath and scan my surroundings. We're ready.

The doorbell rings at exactly 9:00 am, and my stomach does a flip. Good, I like punctuality. I smooth my outfit, straighten Melvin's wavy hair, and peek in the mirror to check my reflection. I pull my fingers down through my hair, smoothing the long, loose curls. Melvin swings the door open to meet our fate.

"Hi, I'm Jessica. It's great to meet you." She clasps a binder and adjusts her purse. Melvin steps aside, and she crosses the threshold. Her golden-brown hair brushes her shoulders, her slightly upturned nose dappled with freckles.

"I'm Melvin, and this is my wife, Amelia." We exchange hand-shakes, and I show her to a chair.

She sets her binder in her lap and addresses us. "You're probably nervous. Most couples are. I want to assure you I'm on your side. I'm not here to pick apart your home and look for things that are wrong. My job is to support you and help you get your home ready. I'm an advocate for you as well as the adoptive child. I'm here to be your ally and facilitate your adoption."

The tension in my shoulders eases slightly, and I rest my hand on my heart, gratitude washing over me. She's very kind and clearly here to help and do her job. I imagined a hypercritical examiner. Someone like Dolores Umbridge from Harry Potter—someone trying to pick us apart. But Jessica doesn't seem like that. She reminds me of Allie—like someone I would like to have as a friend.

As she begins the review, she checks medicine cabinets and kitchen cupboards. She asks about firearms. We have none. She tests the smoke alarms and CO detector. All is well there. She notices the outlet covers and the gate on the stairs, although she said the gate wasn't necessary. Thank goodness. I've been tripping over it all week. It's coming down the moment she leaves. When she asks about fire extinguishers, I gawk at Melvin. I didn't order those. Was he supposed to? How could we let something so crucial fall through the cracks?

"Oh, shoot!" My hand flies to my forehead in frustration. "I knew we forgot something. I'm sorry. Do you want Melvin to run out and grab some right now? How many should we have?"

"Don't worry," she says with a small laugh. "You can easily pick one up at a hardware store. You should probably have two for your house, one in the kitchen and the other in the garage. That's the only thing missing. You can get them over the weekend and send me a picture of them installed."

"We aren't going to fail the home study?" I ask.

"Of course not. This isn't a pass/fail visit. It's a chance to work together to prepare you and your home for a child."

She finishes up and leaves. When the door closes behind her, we give each other a high five, and Melvin embraces me.

"I'm sorry. I should have remembered the fire extinguishers, babe. Why don't I pick them up on my way home today?" Melvin apologizes.

"It's not your fault. I forgot too. But hey, at least the baseboards and the grout are clean!" I pull back and wink at him. "Home Depot is on my way to the office. I'll grab them on my way in."

We close the house and leave for work. One more thing marked off our list. One more step closer to making our duo become a trio. One more step closer to giving us both something to fill our empty arms.

# Chapter 20

T he sun is setting in hues of bright pink and orange as we sit on the back deck sipping glasses of lemonade.

"I told my mom that we submitted our adoption paperwork and it's approved. She's so excited for us."

Melvin reaches across and takes my hand. "I'm excited for us, too. By next summer, we may be playing with a little one here in the backyard."

A sigh escapes my lips. "Can you imagine?" I picture adding a swing set in the far corner along the fence with a slide and a covered tower at the top.

Melvin emits a chortle and waggles his head back and forth. "My mom, of course, went into overdrive. She's ready to pack her bags and have them waiting by the door for an announcement."

I pat his hand. "At least we know she's in favor of our decision."

Melvin tips his head. "As if there were any question about that."

I lean forward in my chair. "I want to celebrate this milestone. And I want to thank everyone who helped us. We should host a cookout back here." Energy pulses through my arms as I envision the gathering.

"I think that would be fun. I can be the grill master."

"Perfect. I'll invite everyone. What should we call it? An Adoption Affair?"

"A Paperwork Party?"

"A Baby Bash?" The words bubble out in a giggle.

"How about...a barbecue?"

"You're right. Let's keep it simple."

***

I step out of the sliding glass door with a large bowl of pasta salad and inhale the smell of burgers on the grill. String lights drop in curves along the fence surrounding the yard. Laughter and conversation float through the air. A red and white checked tablecloth covers the food table. I place the bowl down and am drawn by an invisible force to Melvin's side. He looks up from the grill, and his whole face lights up when he sees me. I curl my hand around his biceps, and he leans down for a kiss. After months of wrestling with adoption paperwork, I feel a peaceful confidence about our next steps. "Shall we get this party started?" I nod at him. He's wearing his blue t-shirt adorned with a camera that says, 'I'm about to snap.' He puts two fingers in his mouth, and I quickly step away and cover my ears. A shrill whistle pierces the atmosphere, and everyone turns their attention to him.

"Hello, everyone. We're so glad you're here." He tips his head toward me.

My insides light up like a jar of fireflies. "We wanted to have you all over to thank you for your part in our adoption process. Today, we are celebrating. The paperwork has been submitted and approved!" I raise my arms over my head in victory. Our guests clap and smile. "It has been a long and challenging journey to this point, but we did it. Although we don't have a baby yet, this is a huge milestone. Thank you for being part of it."

Melvin leads us in prayer, giving thanks not only for the food but also for the people filling our yard who have been such an important part of the journey so far. A chorus of amens fills the air, and everyone lines up to help themselves to dinner. Wendy approaches me, Charlotte on her hip and Finn pulling on her other arm. "Amelia, I'm so excited for you and Melvin. You guys are going to be great parents."

"Thanks, Wendy. That means a lot coming from a mom times four. Let me hold Charlotte for you while you get your food." Wendy heads for the buffet and dishes a plate for herself and one for Finn. I wander to the picnic table, bouncing Charlotte on my hip. Allie is there with Ruby in the stroller. I crouch down and introduce Ruby and Charlotte.

"I'm proud of you, Amelia. This is a big step. I hope it happens quickly for you." Allie hooks her arm around my shoulder.

"I hope so, too. There will still be some waiting, but we've done our part, and now we sit back and get ready for the surprise. It will be amazing."

# Chapter 21

Margot sits at the head of the conference table, reviewing plans for the upcoming Peak Performance Leadership Summit. "Sue, how do the registration numbers look?"

Without checking her notes, Sue responds. "We are at eighty-five percent capacity. There are three more emails to send, but I'm confident we will sell out."

"Wonderful. And the programs and collateral materials?"

Hailey timidly raises her hand. "I'm doing the programs."

Margot turns and acknowledges her. "Do you need any help with that?"

Hailey shakes her head without a word. I have my doubts. I should probably take that off her plate.

"Okay." Margot checks her agenda. "Amelia, you are in charge of Operations and Logistics. Is everything set with the venue?"

"Yep, I've confirmed with them and will give them the final numbers once Sue has those. Vendors and staffing are all finalized."

"Last but not least, the agenda." Margot looks across the table at Theresa.

The caller ID on my phone pops up. It's our social worker, Jessica. My heart skips a beat, my mind racing through scenarios. Could we possibly be getting a child this quickly? I push up from my chair. "Sorry. I have to take this." I wave the phone at my coworkers, and I step out the door to answer it.

"Hi, Jessica. What's up?" I try not to sound too eager, but my whole life is waiting for *the call* right now.

"I wanted to discuss marketing with you. With your application approved, it's important to get your name out there. Often, adoptions happen through people you are already connected with. There are a few websites I recommend where you can set up a profile, but you should also create your own website for expectant mothers to review and get acquainted with you. There are a lot of other things you can do, but an online profile is a good starting point."

I lean against the wall in the hallway, looking down, inspecting my black pumps. "Oh, okay." My heart deflates a little bit. "We can explore those websites. Why don't you email me the links, and we can go from there?"

"Sounds good. I'll send those over, along with a tips sheet for developing your outreach. As you work on it, contact me if you have questions or want me to review anything."

"Sounds good. I'll talk to you later." I hang up and pause to collect myself, picking lint from my skirt. What was going through my mind? Of course, it won't happen this fast.

I slip back into the meeting, but I can't focus on the discussion. Listening to the team plan event marketing, my mind keeps going back to having to market myself to strangers. Am I supposed to broadcast to the world that I am broken? We can't have kids. I'd prefer not to be everyone's pity party while they talk behind our backs about 'the poor Greathouses.' My family and close friends are aware, but I'm not ready to tell everyone.

When the meeting comes to a close, everyone darts back to their desks to complete tasks. Still in a daze, I slowly collect my things.

"Is everything okay, Amelia?"

I hadn't realized Margot was still here. I force a smile and straighten my papers. "Yeah. I'm fine."

"You've been a little distracted since you took that call."

My throat seizes up, searching my mind for how to respond. I guess it's time to be open with her. Pulling in a deep breath, I gather my thoughts. "My husband and I are preparing to adopt. That was our social worker."

"Congratulations! That's wonderful news!"

"Thanks." A warmth in my chest grows, and I gain confidence in sharing.

"Do you have a timeline for when it will happen?"

"No. We turned in all the paperwork. Now it's a waiting game."

She clicks her pen and sets it across her papers. "Does this change your interest in stepping into my role?"

I shake my head. "No. I love my career. And being a mom is also important to me. I'm glad I live at a time where I can be both. Plus, owning the business will give me more flexibility to make my schedule fit my life."

Margot clasps her hands under her chin, her eyes sparkling. "You remind me of myself at your age. Full of ambition and drive. Ready to take on the world."

I straighten in my chair. "Thank you."

She presses her hands together, peering at me. "Are you open to some advice?"

"Of course."

"You absolutely can do it all, but you will always feel pulled in two directions. When I was working, I felt guilty about not being there for my kids. When I was with my kids, I was always thinking about the business. Although being a business owner technically gives you more freedom, it also brings more responsibility. If someone on your team drops the ball, you are the one who has to pick up the pieces. I missed some things in my daughters' lives that I can never get back. And I regret that." She averts her eyes, her voice fading.

Her words burrow into my soul, but she's wrong. I'm a juggler—a multitasker. I thrive when all the balls are in the air. Jutting my chin toward her, I stand and gather my things. "I appreciate your input. I'll consider it."

That night after work, I share Jessica's recommendations for creating an online profile with Melvin.

"What do you think?" I turn to him.

"I suppose. What all goes into it?"

"We need pictures and a bio about ourselves. She emailed some guidelines to me. Basically, you want the birth mom to meet you as if you were in person. Then they get to learn about who would raise their child. They might search for someone with the same values or hobbies as they have. Stuff like that."

"Well, I'm the photographer. I can put together some photos of us. You're probably better at the writing."

"Awesome. Let's work on it this weekend."

Over the next few days, I take a crack at writing our bio. I'm a decent writer, but it's always been harder to write about myself, so I write the most ridiculous things I can think of.

*'Melvin and Amelia Greathouse, from Minnesota, have been married for five years. Melvin is a starving artist, and Amelia is a party*

*girl.'* Ha. No one in their right mind would pick us based on that description.

*'Amelia Greathouse cries easily and has a passion for chocolate. Melvin takes photos of himself at sculpture gardens.'* People would scroll right by and wonder what kind of nut jobs we are.

*'After trying unsuccessfully to have children of their own, the Greathouses want your baby.'* Eww. Creepy.

*'We tried to plan our pregnancy, but it didn't work out. Now, we would like to capitalize on your unplanned pregnancy.'* Completely insensitive.

Obviously, I wouldn't put up any of these, but I'm racking my brain for what to write. What do birth parents want to hear? Why is it easier to write something absurd?

Finally, I land on this:

*Melvin and Amelia Greathouse have been married for five years. They live in a suburb of the Twin Cities in Minnesota. Melvin works as a curator at a local art museum. Amelia is an event planner. They were raised in strong families who valued faith. Melvin's interests include photography and sculpture. Amelia loves cooking and hosting parties.*

*Children have always been a part of their lives, and they want to make kids a part of their family as well.*

I add in our infant CPR training and some details about our neighborhood and church community, then finish with this:

*While no one can predict what the future holds, Melvin and Amelia will face whatever challenges arise with faith, family and the strength of their supportive community. They are grateful for the opportunity to share their story and thank you for taking the time to learn more about them. They wish you, as a birth parent, guidance and inspiration to make decisions that are best for you and your child. If chosen, they would be honored to walk this journey alongside you.*

Over the weekend, we set up a website with pictures and our bio. We peruse the sites Jessica recommended and add our profile to those. Next, we are supposed to share it on social media sites and ask friends to share. It makes logical sense that we should do it, but I'm not ready to watch my troubles made public. Most people count how many likes they can get, but the more views we get, the less private our struggle will be.

# Chapter 22

We ring the doorbell at 4:30 at Allie's place. "Hey, guys, come on in." Powers greets us. We step into their bungalow, hardwood floors stretching across the living room. The couch and two chairs form a seating area surrounding the fireplace.

"Your babysitters are here! Where's our adorable baby Ruby?" I ask, peering over his shoulder.

"Allie's nursing her before we leave. They'll be out in a minute."

"Where are you taking her?" Melvin asks, gripping Powers' hand in greeting.

"I got reservations at Giovanni's." He beams. "It's kind of expensive for us. But it's been months since we got out of the house alone. Allie hates to leave the baby."

"Don't worry, you are in very capable hands. Auntie Amelia is here." I grin.

"Believe me. Allie won't even leave Ruby with her sister. She trusts you."

Allie appears with Ruby and hands her to me. "I fed and changed her. Now I need to change *my* clothes. Powers, can you show them the list?" Allie swishes down the hall as I cradle Ruby in my arms.

"Hello, sweet girl," I coo, running my fingers like a spider over her belly. "Is your tummy full?"

Ruby wriggles and smiles, the cotton of her onesie brushing against my arm. I cuddle her close, breathing in the baby smell—Johnson's baby shampoo, talcum powder, and lots and lots of love.

Melvin peeks from behind me, resting his hand on top of mine on Ruby's belly.

"Isn't she adorable?" I ask him.

He nods, his chin bumping against my shoulder.

Powers leads us to the kitchen and hands us a piece of paper. "Allie made a list of Ruby's schedule for you. She also wrote what she likes and dislikes and how to put her to sleep."

"Oh, I love a good list." Bottles, pacifiers, bouncy seat... My *heart* bounces, excitement bubbling through my stomach. This little four-month-old and I will have the best time. She can't even crawl yet. How much trouble could she be? This will be great practice for our own little one.

Allie enters wearing a sassy red dress and saunters straight to Powers.

His jaw drops, and he gawks at her. "You look amazing." He pulls her into a hug and delivers a kiss to her matching red lips.

"Okay," Allie says, breaking free from Powers's hold. "She's hungry every three to four hours. There is breast milk in the fridge with warming instructions. The stroller is in the garage. I'll leave the car seat just in case. If she gets fussy, she loves her swing. Any questions?"

"Don't worry about a thing." I tip my head to Ruby and am rewarded with a drooly smile. "We'll be fine."

They slip out the door, and we wave as they back out of the garage. We sit close to each other near the window and watch their car pull out of the driveway.

"Can you imagine having one of our own? This could be us before long," I say.

"I can't wait." Melvin tucks me under his arm.

I bounce Ruby on my knee and sing 'This is the Way the Ladies Ride.' Ruby grins enthusiastically. When the song progresses to the 'hobbeldy hoi' of the farmer, she giggles up spit-up into my lap.

"Woah there, Mt. Vesuvius!" Melvin jerks away.

"Can you grab a burp cloth or a washcloth or something? There's probably one in her room."

Melvin sprints down the hall and appears with a bath towel.

"That's a bit of overkill, but I guess it will do." I sop up the pool in my lap, leaving me looking like I wet my pants. "Okay. Lesson learned. Perhaps bouncing right after you've eaten isn't the best idea. What should we do? We could take her for a walk."

"Sure. Nothing like a beautiful summer evening."

We go to the garage and find the stroller tucked into the corner, all folded up. Melvin wrestles it open and presents it to me. I gently set Ruby in and pull the seatbelt out from underneath her. The weight of her body causes the stroller to collapse in on itself. I rescue Ruby and hand her to Melvin. "Here. Hold her. I don't think it locked in place."

Melvin takes Ruby, and I inspect the stroller. "I swear, Amelia, I opened it up."

"I get it, Melvin. But you have to make sure it's locked. Do you hear the 'click '? That means it's secure." I thought setting up the stroller would be a good 'man' job, but I should have done it myself. With the stroller clicked and locked in place, I put Ruby in and fish behind her to pull out the straps and secure her in safely. We open the garage door, and I realize we don't have a way to close it behind us.

"Shoot. I should have asked her to leave the garage door opener. Can you shut the door behind us and then go around and go out the front door?" I ask Melvin.

"Okay." He shuts the door and quickly makes his way around and meets us in the driveway.

"All righty. Want to head to the park?" He claps his hands together.

"That sounds perfect." We stroll along the sidewalk, passing families playing in their yards. The buzz of a lawnmower and the smell of fresh-cut grass greet us as we roam through the neighborhood. At the end of the block, we take a right and amble two more blocks to the park. We sit on a bench and turn the stroller to face us. Fingers intertwined, we soak in the warm summer rays when Ruby fusses.

I search for her pacifier in the crevices of the stroller. "Where's the pacifier? She had it when we left."

"Maybe she lost it on the way over."

I fiddle with the straps and scoop her out. "It's okay, Ruby. I've got you." I rock her, but she continues to fuss.

"Allie said she loves the swing." Melvin nods toward the swing set.

"She doesn't quite sit on her own yet. She might not be ready for these swings at the park."

"How about if I hold her and swing with her?"

I hand Ruby off to Melvin, and we walk over to the swings. There are two together, and we sit and sway back and forth. As Melvin and Ruby go higher and faster, Ruby's tiny face puckers up, and her eyes get wider each time they rise forward into the wind. When they fall back, she gasps for air and whimpers.

"I get the sense that she doesn't like this. Let's try something else." Melvin brings them to a stop. I take Ruby from him and bounce her on my way to the park bench. "What's wrong, sweetheart?" I hold her on my shoulder and gently pat her back. Her cries increase. I shift her onto my lap and rub her tummy as she lies on her back. "Do you have a tummy ache?" With each stroke, she winces and cries louder.

Melvin frowns. "Should we take her h—?"

A loud squirting sound interrupts him, like a bottle of ketchup aimed at a bun. Her cries subside.

Melvin's eyes widen. "I bet she feels better now."

My lap warms. Crap. Literally. "It's time to go. I should have brought the diaper bag." I lift her, showing off the mess to my husband. He jerks his head away and gags, his entire body convulsing.

"Oh, gross. Let's get back home."

The leisurely summer stroll on the way over turns into a race for the finish line as we hasten through the same neighborhoods, the damp brown spot chafing my thighs. At least Ruby isn't fussing as we whisk her home. When we walk into the driveway, Melvin hops up to the front door.

"It's locked. Do you have a key?" he asks.

"Why would I have a key? You locked it?"

"Well, yeah. I didn't think we should leave their house unlocked while we were gone. Do you think they have a key hidden somewhere?"

"I don't know. Go see if the back door is open."

Melvin jogs around back. Ruby cries again now that we're not moving, and she has been sitting in her own filth for the past ten minutes. Who can blame her? I rock the stroller back and forth to calm her, hoping to leave her contained until I have a new diaper and wet wipes at the ready. He circles around to the other side of the house after a couple of minutes.

"No luck?"

He shakes his head. "Everything is locked up tight. Can you text and ask if there is a garage code?"

"I hate to disturb them on their date... Can't you jimmy a lock with a credit card or something?"

"I'm an art curator, not a burglar." He dips his head and rolls his eyes at me.

I send a text to Allie, but it alerts me she has notifications turned off. Which is great. I want her to enjoy an uninterrupted evening. But as a parent, wouldn't she want to be available in case something happens? Something like your babysitter getting locked out of the house after your kid shoots poop up her back? I shift my weight and run my hand through my hair.

"She turned off her notifications. Can you try Powers?"

Melvin texts Powers, and we wait while Ruby's volume increases. Poor thing.

"Did you check under the doormat? Or a rock?" I glance toward the front steps.

Melvin lifts the doormat, rocks, and planters. He shakes his head. "Nothing."

"What about a window? See if one is cracked open just enough."

"I'll check." Melvin circles the house again, studying each window like a detective on a case.

I keep rolling Ruby back and forth in the stroller, but it's not helping–she's still fussing, her cries piercing the quiet neighborhood. I search the corners of the house. Where is he?

With a loud creak, the garage door rises, and he is standing there like a knight in shining armor, coming to rescue the fair maidens. "I found a way in!"

"Great. Let's get this little lady inside. Can you grab the towel?"

Melvin nods and disappears for a moment, returning with a towel. I unbuckle Ruby and wrap her, her cries muffling as I lift her to my shoulder. We slip in the door, shutting the garage door behind us, and scoot to Ruby's bedroom.

I strip her down and gently wipe her off, but parts of her back are crusty.

"She needs a bath." I say more to myself than to him.

Melvin nods. "I'll go fill it up."

"Not too hot!" I holler over my shoulder. "Babies can get burned easily." I hear the bathwater start, and I envelop naked Ruby in the soiled towel and bounce her. "It's okay. We're going to get you all cleaned up. Would you like a nice warm bath?"

I slide into the bathroom and maneuver around Melvin. I turn off the faucet and gently lay her down in the shallow water, my hand supporting her head. Her screams grow louder. The bath is ice cold.

"Melvin! It's freezing!" I pick her up, cuddle her in the messy towel, and hand her to him.

"You said not to make it too hot."

"Yes, but babies like it warm. You wouldn't want an ice bath, would you?"

"I mean, sometimes after a workout it's kind of nice." He raises his eyebrows and lifts the corner of his mouth in a half-smile.

I nudge the water temperature higher, letting it flow over my fingers until it's warm enough. When I ease Ruby back into the bath, she squirms before relaxing into the basin, her cries decreasing to a whimper. I work the liquid soap into bubbles and rinse them off, her wet skin reflecting the bathroom lights.

Melvin hands me a fresh towel, open and ready. I wrap her up quickly, tucking the ends around her in a cozy swaddle. We shuffle across the hall, her cries echoing against the walls. Diapers, lotion, jammies–I move quickly hoping to comfort and settle her.

I rummage through the drawer and wrap my fingers around a spare pacifier. As soon as I place it in her mouth, she spits it out. My heart aches as I sink into the rocking chair, swaying gently.

Melvin hovers nearby, concern on his face. "What can I do?" He scans the room for answers.

My stomach rumbles. "Honestly? I'm starving. Could you grab us some dinner?"

We settle on chow mein from the Asian restaurant in the strip mall down the road. He pulls his keys from his pocket and disappears out the door.

The moment I hear the click of the door, I check the time. She's been like this for at least thirty minutes. I go to the kitchen to consult the list. *Eats every 3-4 hours.* It's only been two hours, so she shouldn't be hungry.

Then I remember. Allie said she *loves* her swing.

I wander into the living room and settle her in the seat. The swing begins its rhythmic, gentle sway. Her cries stutter for a moment before continuing. She spits out the pacifier again. Sighing, I crouch next to her, holding it in her mouth, my arm moving with the swing's motion.

I increase the speed. Nothing. Her round face is red, her tiny fists clenched. I remain beside her, fighting frustration and exhaustion, holding the pacifier close to her lips, hoping she will relax and accept the offering of comfort.

The door finally opens, and the scent of takeout fills the room. Melvin walks in, holding the bag of food. "Still crying?"

I nod.

"Here, you take the dinner, and I'll take a turn with Ruby." He hands me the paper sack, and the bottom rips. White rice sprays across the living room floor like a church sidewalk after a wedding, except this is damp and sticky and interspersed with Subgum Chow Mein.

I take my free hand and run it through my hair. "You're kidding me." I should have grabbed it with two hands, from the bottom. What was I thinking?

"I'm sorry." Melvin gazes at me, his eyebrows pinching together as he stretches toward the swing.

"It's not your fault." I grab a trash can and scoop our dinner into the garbage. Melvin picks up Ruby and paces and bounces. I cleaned up most of the food, but I cannot get all these tiny pieces of rice.

Grabbing the vacuum from the hall closet, I gesture to Melvin. "I'm going to clean the rest of this up. The noise might startle her. You might want to take her to her room or cover her ears or something."

Melvin places her head on his chest and covers her other ear with his hand. I plug in and turn on the vacuum. I quickly suck up the remaining particles of rice and turn it off. Ruby startles and lets out a wail.

"Wait a minute," Melvin says. "She stopped crying while you were vacuuming. Turn it on again."

I flip the power switch and eye her. Like magic, she settles right down. Melvin takes the handle and rocks Ruby back and forth as he goes. She stays calm. It's a miracle.

"What should we do about dinner?" I ask.

"Wanna run out and get a replacement meal?"

"Let me see what I can scrounge up in the kitchen. I need to get food in my belly." I dig around in the cupboards and end up making peanut butter and jelly sandwiches. Melvin has successfully cleaned from the living room to the hallway and has worked his way to Ruby's bedroom. I hold a sandwich up to his mouth, and he takes a bite. Ruby is asleep in his arms. He tilts the carpet sweeper upright but leaves it on. Carefully, he sets her in her crib. Miraculously, she stays asleep.

"What about the vacuum?" I whisper. He quietly backs out of the room with the machine and shuts the door. We continue into the living room before we dare turn it off. A peaceful hush blankets the house, and we breathe a sigh of relief. We silently cheer and high-five each other. He puts the carpet sweeper away, and we go to the kitchen to enjoy our PB&Js.

"Fancy meal. Are you trying to impress me?" Melvin winks.

"Something like that." I bump my shoulder against his and sink my teeth into my sandwich.

After we finish eating, I slip into the bathroom to gather the dirty towels and clean up from bath time. Strands of wind-blown hair stick out wildly in the mirror, accessorized with a few pieces of rice. How in the world did I get rice in my hair? There's a new spot on my shirt, and my pants are poop-stained. *I could pass for Wendy.*

After I pick the rice out of my hair, I pull the elastic band from my wrist and gather my long locks into a high ponytail. I strip out of my clothes and slip on Allie's pink fuzzy robe, pulling the belt tight around me. After throwing everything in the laundry, I meander back to the living room. Melvin lifts the blanket without a word, and I nestle in next to him, his warm body filling me with contentment. He presses play, and the glow of the screen lights up the dim room.

By the time Allie and Powers get home, the laundry is done, and I am back in my clothes as if nothing went wrong this evening.

Allie slips off her heels and drops her purse on the counter. "How did everything go?"

"Great!" Melvin and I say at the same time, a little too enthusiastically. We grin broadly and lock eyes.

Allie's head jerks up, and she narrows her eyes at us. "I can tell by the look on your faces; it was less than great. What happened?"

We downplay the series of mishaps and reassure them that Ruby is the easiest, most cheerful, adorable kid ever born.

Powers pulls Allie in close. "Thanks for handling everything. We really appreciated the night out."

Back at home, I flop on the bed and admit my doubts.

"That was one of the hardest nights of my life. How can a tiny baby create such a disaster?" Feeling the tiredness in my bones, I allow my lids to drop over my eyes and draw in a deep breath. "I was sure I was made to be a mom, but tonight was a major fail. I couldn't pull it off. Not even with a list!"

"Now wait a minute." Melvin hovers over me and tucks a strand of my blonde hair behind my ear. "We got her to sleep, did laundry, and vacuumed the entire house. Sounds like a win to me."

"You're right. It didn't go the way I expected, though." I shoot a skeptical glance, and he chuckles, snuggling me in closer.

"I mean it, Melly. You held her close while her tummy grumbled, bounced her till she laughed so much she puked, washed up her cracks and crevices after that disgusting blowout... And now you're doubting your capabilities, worried you aren't enough. If that doesn't say you're a mother already, I don't know what does."

# Chapter 23

My alarm sounds at 4:00 am. It's much too early to be alert, but today is day one of the Leadership Summit, and it's my turn to shine and show Margot how well I can do at the Operations and Logistics for this event. As the sun peeks over the horizon, the venue is a bustle of activity.

I grab my clipboard and pen and begin scanning the list.

Registration table set up. *Sue is handling that right now. Check.*

I inspect the main ballroom. Tables and chairs ready to go. People move in every direction, each with purpose and speed. "Test. Test. One, two. Test. Test." The AV guy taps the mic and strings cables. The conference center staff dash in and out, delivering water glasses, tablets, and pens to each spot.

Main ballroom setup. *Check.*

As I circle back to the registration table, Sue approaches. "Amelia, we have a problem."

"Okay. What's up?" There is always something.

"There is a major typo on the programs. Everything is plastered with *Peek Performance*. That may not go over well with professionals. We aren't playing peek-a-boo with toddlers here."

"Crap. How did I not catch this? Is it only on the programs? Or is it on the name tags and signs and everything?"

"It's just the cover of the programs. Which is good, I guess. Unless you are going for consistency across the board."

"Do you think we can convince them it was a play on words? Like you're supposed to *peek* at your program to learn more about *peak* performance."

"We can try. It doesn't look good for Hailey, though. She was in charge of all the printed materials, wasn't she?"

I freeze in place. "Technically... yes." I push my golden hair over my shoulder. "But I kind of took it over from her."

Sue tips her head at me. "Ouch. I guess it's your butt on the line, then."

"Grab me when Craig arrives. I'll talk with him and see how he reacts." I bustle off with my checklist to make sure nothing else slips through the cracks. How could I have missed that?

When Craig arrives, Sue finds me, and I hurry over to greet him.

"Good morning, Craig. Are you ready for the conference? We are excited to be here."

"Yeah. I'm all set. Is everything in order?"

"Of course. When guests arrive, they will check in here, where they will get their name badges and conference materials. Let's get yours for you." Sue hands me his name badge and a stack of materials. "Here are the conference materials. I hope you don't mind, but we made a slight play on words in the program. This is where they get their first peek at the schedule, so we called the program '*Peek Performance.*'"

"Interesting word choice. I probably wouldn't have done that, but okay."

Whew. He doesn't love it, but he doesn't suspect a major mistake, either. I'll take it as a win at this point. I show him into the main ballroom and walk him up to the stage to see the podium and mic. Once he's satisfied, I leave him to his staff.

Final review with the conference chair. *Check.*

As guests arrive, the registration process goes relatively smoothly. There are a few last-minute attendees who didn't get into our system, but we quickly adjust and get them added. Craig even opens the event with the new and improved *peek*. The keynote speaker is underway. I make a final pass through each area of the conference.

Breakout rooms set up. *Check.*

Staffing at each location. *Check.*

The morning winds up, and attendees make their way to the lobby to pick up their boxed lunches and then go into the ballroom to eat. I'm sitting at the registration table when a participant approaches.

"Hello," I greet her warmly. "How can we help you?"

"Can you tell me about the lunches? I have a lot of allergies. I believe I put it on my registration."

"Of course. Are you gluten-free? We have a separate section for the gluten-free meals."

"Yes. But I'm also dairy-free. Is there cheese on the sandwiches? I don't want to open them up and poke around."

"Let's go find what you need." I consult with the waitstaff to locate a gluten-free, dairy-free lunch. Once she's settled and on her way to the ballroom, I glance down the hallway–and pause. The lunch line still stretches far down the hall. By now, most of the people should have their food and be seated. Perhaps one of the breakout sessions got out late.

I approach the waitstaff and see if there is a way to get the line moving. Together, we set up a second table on the other side of the hallway and move half the boxes over there. It's chaotic for a few minutes–attendees trying to pick up food while we shuffle boxed lunches back and forth–but eventually the second line picks up and the flow improves. Faces relax. The hallway quiets.

Then, I do a quick headcount—people versus remaining meals. My stomach drops. We're going to run out.

I race to registration, pulling up the information for our caterer as I go. They dropped the food off an hour ago... and left.

"Hey Sue, did anyone count the boxed lunches when they were dropped off? It looks like we will run out."

"I didn't verify anything. They had the numbers a week ago, and I showed them where to set everything up."

I search for the caterer's number and call them.

"This is Amelia with the Peak Performance Leadership Summit. We are short on lunches. Any chance you forgot to unload some of them?"

"Let me see." The phone goes mute for a few minutes before he gets back to me. "Sorry about that. It looks like we had a stack in the cooler that never made it your way. We'll rush them over right now."

"How soon will you be here? I have hungry people with a limited lunch break."

"They are already loading them. We will be there in fifteen minutes."

I rush to the tables–less than a dozen lunches left, and at least thirty people still in line. My stomach knots. I should have been there when the caterer dropped them off to count them and confirm. This never should have happened. But I was across the building, overseeing the breakout sessions. I've memorized this conference inside and out–every detail delineated, every contingency considered. Except this one.

If only the people I rely on could handle their part.

I step to the front of the line, projecting a calm I don't feel. "The caterer inadvertently left some lunches in their cooler. They are on their way and should be here in fifteen minutes. You can wait here, or you can take a moment to visit the vendor tables. I'm sorry for the delay."

There are a few grumbles and annoyed glares. Most of them stay put. I plant myself at the entrance ready to intercept the food delivery the moment it arrives.

When the caterer finally pulls up, I jump in to help, grabbing boxes and speed-walking toward the food tables–until I lose my footing, tripping on a mat.

I go down hard. The boxes fly, splaying all around me. My face burns. A wave of voices surrounds me as people rush in, helping me up and asking if I'm okay.

"I'm fine." I say quickly, brushing myself off. The food all stayed in the boxes, thankfully, but it's probably a bit scrambled. With the help of my new entourage, I stack the boxes and get them set on the table, straightening the row. "No harm done. Again, we're very sorry for the delay."

As soon as the last box is in place, I slip away to the restroom to compose myself. How embarrassing. Not my best moment, for sure. Locking myself in the stall, I lean against the door. After a few deep breaths and a silent pep talk, I emerge, checking myself in the mirror. After smoothing some wispy strands of my blonde hair, and tucking in my blouse, I return to the registration desk, checking that there are no other fires to put out.

"How are things going, Sue?"

"We've had a couple of complaints about one of the vendors."

"What's the problem?"

"It's the supplements guy. They say he's being aggressive in his sales with the attendees."

"I'll take care of it." I march to the vendor area and glance through the displays. Suddenly, this guy advances toward me.

"You seem sluggish. Do you take any vitamins?"

"I'm good. I wanted—"

"You don't take vitamins? That's probably why you are exhausted. We have great supplements with energy-boosting properties. They will help you have more energy, a clearer mind, and achieve more of your goals."

My muscles tighten with each word out of his mouth. "I get it, but—"

"But, nothing! Here, give me your email address, and I will set you up with some free samples. Just wait until you try them. People report a significant change within less than a week."

I jump in when he takes a breath, my hands on my hips. "Listen. I am on the event staff. We are getting complaints about your aggressiveness. You need to back down and give people some space."

"Woah!" He takes a step back and splays his hands out. "I'm only trying to help people. You don't have to get upset."

"I understand you are passionate about your product, but people are here to attend a conference, not to be cornered. Give them their space, or we will ask you to leave."

He stands taller and folds his arms across his chest. "You can't do that. I paid for this spot." His eyes narrow at me.

"I'm aware, but you can't harass the guests."

"I'm not harassing anyone. Just having a conversation." He smiles innocently.

I walk away, making a mental note to screen the vendors better next time. Why is everything going wrong today? First the programs, then the lunches, and now this vendor situation. I was sure I had done a good job planning the event. These things shouldn't be happening. This will probably hurt my chances of taking over for Margot.

# Chapter 24

The beautiful Minnesota summer is easing into cooler fall days already, and it is only the end of August. It's nice to escape the sweltering heat of summer, but I'm dreading the cold, dark days of winter. Melvin and I are spending a day at the Great Minnesota Get Together—the Minnesota State Fair. It's summer's last hurrah. We jostle about like cattle being corralled on our way through the entrance. Melvin grabs my hand and pulls me toward the Skyride. Above the crowd, we take in the view. Back on the ground on the other side, we wander to the butter sculptures arm in arm. The yellow blobs look surprisingly realistic to the fair's royalty.

Ready for a break, we grab a bucket of Sweet Martha's Cookies and wander to the All You Can Drink Milk booth. I fold a warm cookie into my mouth, the chocolate dripping out. Grabbing my cup of milk, I wash it down. My pocket rings and vibrates. It's probably my mom. I haven't talked to her all week. I fish my phone out and set it on the picnic table. The contact that appears on my screen causes my stomach to flip.

"It's Jessica," I say a bit breathlessly.

"Don't jump to any conclusions, Amelia," Melvin warns.

I nod and click on the speakerphone, placing it between us. "Hi, Jessica, how are you?"

"I'm good. Where are you?"

"We're spending the day at the fair. Just soaking in the last days of summer."

"I have some good news for you."

My heart leaps in my chest. I inhale and watch Melvin. Her good news might not be the news we are waiting for, so I brace myself. "Okay... What is it?"

"We have a baby for you!"

My hands tremble, and I lean into Melvin for support. "Seriously? When? What are the details?"

"Well, it's a little girl. She was born yesterday in Wisconsin. The mother is single and has put her up for adoption. Can you guys go to Madison to pick her up on Monday?"

*It's a girl.* My eyes sting with happy tears. "Yes! Of course! Let us know where to go and what time to be there."

"Great. You guys are lucky. It rarely happens this quickly. But this was a last-minute decision by the birth mother. I'm so happy she chose you. I'll email you all the details. Congratulations!"

"Thank you, Jessica. This is the best news of the year. This means so much to us. It's... amazing!" We hang up, and Melvin and I hug each other, crying, oblivious to the crowds of fair goers streaming by us. This changes everything.

"Is this for real?" I lean back and peer up at him, my heart racing. A sudden burst of energy pulses through my veins. "I can't even believe it."

"We are finally going to be parents." He kisses me with urgency. "You're going to be the best mother. I'm excited to meet our daughter."

"The fair has been fun, but we've got to get home." I slap my hands on the picnic table and push myself up. "We have a million things to do and a million people to call."

Melvin grabs what's left of our bucket of cookies in one hand and grasps my hand with the other. My insides feel like balls being tossed around in a lottery machine. We bounce our way to the exit. A smile beams across my face, but I quickly go into planning mode. "I already have a list of essentials we will need. I've been working on it since we submitted our paperwork, but it didn't make sense to buy anything when we didn't know how long it would be. Now I'm regretting that decision. We need *everything*. Diapers, wipes, clothes, a car seat, and a crib... How are we going to get all of this done in less than forty-eight hours?"

"Let's start with the basics. They won't let us bring her home without a car seat. We'll need formula, bottles, and diapers. We can stop at Target on the way home and get the necessities." He looks at me, grinning. "Why don't you call your mom?"

"You're right." I return his smile as he drives us down the freeway, my heart racing at the speed of the car. I call my mom through the car's Bluetooth.

"Hey, honey! How are you?"

"I'm great, Mom. How about you?" My voice jumps with excitement.

"Well, you sound enthusiastic today. What are you up to?"

"Mel and I spent the day at the State Fair, but we're on our way home now." I catch his eye for a moment, and we smirk at each other.

"So soon? You didn't even stay for a show at the Grandstand?"

"Well, we hadn't planned on leaving early, but we got some news."

"Really? What news is that?" She pauses, anticipation strong in her voice.

"We got a call from our social worker. There was a baby girl born yesterday, and she's ours!"

"Oh my gosh, sweetie! That is the *best* news. When do you get her?"

"The day after tomorrow, we'll drive to Madison, Wisconsin, to pick her up."

"Can I come help? Even though you won't be recovering from birth, a newborn is still a lot of work. And I would love to meet my new granddaughter."

"How about in a week? Right now, we're trying to figure out what we need and get everything ready for her."

"Of course. Whatever works best for you is fine with me. Do you want me to call anyone for you? Or would you rather make the calls yourself?"

"Call everyone. Shout it from the mountaintops!"

"Of course. Audrey will be thrilled. Henry will be excited to be an uncle again, too. I'll let you go so you can make the rest of your phone calls. I'll work on travel plans."

"Thanks, Mom."

"I love you and Melvin and can't wait to meet your daughter."

We hang up, and I smile and sigh. "Pinch me, Melvin. Is this for real?"

"I don't know, is it?" He pinches my thigh.

"Ouch!" I jerk away.

"Hey, you asked me to," he says with a grin.

I smile back, rubbing the spot where he tweaked me. My head rests on the back of the seat, and I breathe out a contented sigh. God *does* answer prayers. My hopes and dreams are becoming reality.

Melvin connects his phone and calls his mom while I open the list on my notes app and begin adding to it.

"Hi, Melvin. What's new?"

"Not much. I'm leaving the fair with Amelia. How about you?" He winks at me. Brenda launches into a soliloquy of every errand and chore they accomplished for the day. Finally, she draws a breath. "How was the fair?"

"It was the best trip of my life. We could never top this one."

"Really?" She sounds intrigued. "What happened?"

"While we were there, we got a phone call. We are going to be parents!"

She gasps. "Oh my gosh, you're kidding me. Why did you let me go on and on when you had such big news? How soon?"

"Well, she was born yesterday, and we get to pick her up in Madison on Monday."

"We could get in the car tomorrow and meet you in Madison. I have been buying baby clothes. There's a nice stash of adorable girl clothes in the spare bedroom. I can bring them out and stay for as long as you want me to help."

Glancing at Melvin, I slowly move my head back and forth. He returns my look with a nod. "We haven't decided how soon we want visitors. Give us time to plan things out. For the first week, we might want a chance to adjust by ourselves to being parents."

We end the phone call by giving her permission to call Melvin's sisters and share the good news. She is going to be in her element making all those phone calls. I'm sure she won't wait to call her best friends. She's not one to keep a secret for long. And everyone is aware she has been dying to be a grandma.

"Okay. I have bottles, formula, diapers, wipes, onesies, a car seat, and a pack-and-play. We can buy a crib later, but this will get us through the first few days, at least."

Back at home, we haul supplies up the stairs and drop them in the spare bedroom. It's time to transform it into our daughter's room. I empty the dresser drawers of odds and ends and fill them with tiny things. Diapers the size of my hand. Little white t-shirts with snaps at the bottom. I carefully arrange supplies, breathing in the scent of baby powder. Will she really be this small? Does she have hair or a bald head? Are her cheeks round like little chipmunks? Melvin works behind me, taking down the computer desk and setting up the pack-and-play. I turn and face him, leaning against the dresser. He's already such a wonderful dad, preparing everything for her arrival.

Melvin and I fall into bed at the end of the day, exhausted and happy. "Can we handle this?" My voice echoes in the darkness.

"I probably have no clue what we're getting into, but I'm excited. We're having a baby, Amelia! And together, we can handle anything."

"I love you, Melvin. I can't wait to bring her home."

We snuggle into each other's arms and drift off to sleep.

# Chapter 25

Melvin rests his arm on the back of the pew around my shoulders. I nestle into him and allow gratitude to flow through my body. God is so good. He is answering our prayers. When they ask for celebrations and concerns during the worship service, Melvin and I raise our hands. We stand together.

I curl my hand around Melvin's arm and gaze up at him as he shares our good news. "We found out yesterday we are adopting a baby tomorrow."

The people near us quickly congratulate us when we sit down. After the service, we inch our way to Sunday School, stopping every few feet for a new conversation with members of our church family. Although we never make it to class, we hear the language of love in every encounter.

After church, we share lunch at the kitchen counter.

"I was thinking we could leave around 7:30 tomorrow." Melvin takes a bite of his sandwich.

I pull up the map on my phone and calculate our route. "GPS says it will take four hours, but there might be traffic in the morning." The doorbell rings. I tip my head toward Melvin. "Are you expecting anyone?"

"No, probably some high school fundraiser. I'll get it and let them down easy." Melvin rises and goes to the door. "Of course, step right in," his voice echoes through the house. "Amelia, we have a visitor!"

I walk around the corner from the kitchen to discover Wendy carrying two huge garbage bags. "What's up?"

"I heard you're adopting a little girl tomorrow. Congratulations!"

My cheeks rise in a genuine smile. "Thanks. We're excited."

"I figured you could use some things. These are all my newborn girl clothes. Charlotte is nine months old now, and after four kids, we are *done*." She plops the bags in the middle of the living room. "You can go through these. If there is anything you don't want, you can donate it. No need to return anything. I also have supplies in the back of my car that you can have. I'll go grab the rest of it."

We walk out with her to help unload. Melvin balances a bouncy seat in one hand and a baby bathtub in the other. I hook my arm around a nursing pillow and clutch the infant sling.

"I can't thank you enough, Wendy. We have nothing. This will really help. Most people have nine months to prepare. We only got forty-eight hours. And the clock is ticking." Tapping my bare wrist, I thank her with a hug.

"I'm happy to help. I remember when we brought Olivia home. It was a little slice of heaven. Enjoy every moment with your new daughter." I watch her climb into her car and drive away. After all the moments I silently resented her, she is quickly growing into a friend.

As we are inside sorting through clothes and equipment and throwing things in the laundry, the doorbell rings again. I pad to the door and find an older woman from church. "Hello, Louise. What are you doing here?"

"I learned that you are adopting a baby girl. I am always crocheting blankets, and I had this pretty pink one waiting in the closet." She holds it out to me. "I thought you could use it for your daughter."

"That is so kind. She will love it." I take the blanket and hug her. The afternoon continues like that. People stop by with blankets and burp cloths, sleepers, bedding, towels, and washcloths. One family even brought us a rocking chair, in perfect condition because their kids have grown too big to be held in their laps. I am overwhelmed by the outpouring of love. I was careful not to share our struggles for so long, but one quick announcement and our church has turned into an extended family.

After dinner, Allie and Powers stop by with Ruby. "She gets bigger every time I see her." I open my arms toward Ruby, and she lurches toward me. "Hey, Ruby! Remember our adventures at the park?" I smile. That was quite a day. "Tomorrow, we're going to get a friend for you."

"Do you have a name picked out?" Allie asks.

I glance at Melvin. "We haven't told anyone yet. Once we hold her and see her, we'll decide, but my gut tells me she's going to be Hope. We had to hold on to hope through all of this. And she will be the manifestation of all our hopes and dreams."

"That's beautiful, Amelia." She strokes her hand down my arm. "It's the perfect name for all you've been through. I'm dying to meet her. And speaking of meeting her, can I bring you guys dinner one day this week? And I want to throw a baby shower for you. You knocked it out of the park with mine. I want a chance to repay the favor."

"That would be awesome." I shift Ruby on my hip. She clutches my necklace. "I don't have any inkling of what our schedule will be like tomorrow, but dinner on Tuesday would be great." I bounce Ruby and hold her chubby hand. "And it would be nice to have the shower in a couple of weeks while my mom is visiting. That would mean a lot to have her here for that."

"Perfect. If you have ideas about what you want, share them. But I don't want you to lift a finger. Let me celebrate you, and you can be the guest of honor, deal?"

"There's a secret Pinterest inspiration board I can send you." I smile and give her a side hug. What would I do without a friend like Allie?

We visit for a while longer before Ruby's eyes start drooping. Allie and Powers buckle her into her car seat and go home. Melvin and I gaze at each other. He draws me into his arms. "You ready for this, Mommy?"

"Ready as I'll ever be." I sigh and rest my head on his chest.

"This time tomorrow, we will finally be a family." He holds me tighter, feelings of hope, excitement, and unity binding us together as one.

# Chapter 26

M y brain slowly awakens, and I turn my head to check the time. 1:10 am. I force my eyes shut. Five more hours. Thoughts of a baby girl fill my mind.

Later, I stir again and open my eyes to darkness. 3:44. It's still not time to be up. I shift and fluff my pillow. Is she up for a nighttime feeding right now?

4:17. It took me forever to fall asleep, but now I can't seem to stay asleep. I mentally run through my morning routine. Did I allow myself enough time?

Finally, at 6:00 a.m., my alarm goes off, and I roll out of bed and onto my knees.

*Heavenly Father, I'm thankful for today. It's been a long time coming. Thank you for blessing us with a new baby. Thank you for the brave birth mother who made this sacrifice. Bless her during this difficult time in her life. Help her recover physically and emotionally from giving birth and giving her away. Bless us with safety on our trip to Madison. Help us*

*be the parents this little girl needs. I have no words to say except—thank*
*you! In Jesus' name I pray, amen.*

We're on the road by 7:30. It's about four and a half hours to Madison. We will grab lunch while we are there and then go to the adoption agency at 1:00 to sign papers and meet our sweet Hope. Melvin
navigates through town to the freeway, and I go through my mental
list. "Okay. We've got the diaper bag in the backseat. It's stocked with
diapers, wipes, three changes of clothes, bottles, and formula. You got
the stroller and the car seat, right?"

Melvin pauses before responding. "Um, did we grab the car seat?
Check in the back. Is it there?"

I glance back at the empty seat. "How could we forget that?" I lift
my hands in disbelief. "You've got to turn around. They won't let us
take her home without a car seat." I run my fingers through my hair.
"Don't say a word about this at the agency; they might change their
minds and not let us have her."

"Everyone forgets things, Amelia. We've never had to remember a
car seat before." He pats my arm. "Don't panic. We're close enough to
go back and get it without being late." We turn around and maneuver
back to the house. The car seat is sitting in the garage. We walked right
past it, but I was worried about the diaper bag, and Melvin was loading
the stroller in. I can't believe we almost showed up without a car seat.

Before long, we are back on the road, about ten minutes behind
schedule. Melvin will make up for that with his lead foot. We pass the
time singing to the radio and talking about our hopes and dreams for
our daughter.

"She'll be about four months old at Christmas. I wonder if she
will be sitting up or rolling over? Next summer, she will probably be
crawling but not walking. We can take stroller walks around the lake."
The vision of the three of us parading through the neighborhood

causes my heart to expand in my chest. "She has a late-August birthday. Do you think we should hold her back a year from kindergarten?"

Melvin shrugs. "I guess we'll have to wait and see."

"I was thinking that since we found out about Hope at the State Fair, we should celebrate her birthday there every year. Wouldn't that be a fun tradition?" I ask.

"I love it. We can get deep-fried cake on a stick for her birthday cake. We can take a picture of her by the entrance every year, along with the picture we took of us this year, and see how she changes as she grows."

A smile spreads across my face imagining a slideshow for her senior party with eighteen pictures at the entrance of the State Fair. A lifetime of memories that all began there. I open my phone, looking over the schedule for the week. We should be back in time for dinner tonight. We can pick up a rotisserie chicken.

I note the airplane icon on Friday afternoon with the words, *Mom arrives.* My heart flutters with excitement at sharing our new baby with her. Next week, Melvin's mom will tag in, bringing her home-made cookies and the collection of baby clothes she's been stocking up on. Two weeks of our moms taking care of us. I feel blessed.

Audrey called earlier. *"Clement and I are thinking Thanksgiving. We want to meet our niece, spoil her rotten, and fight over who gets to hold her first."*

Christmas is still a question mark. Both families have extended warm invitations, but as I anticipate becoming a family, a quiet idea tugs at me. This year, we should stay put—just us, the tree, and new traditions of our own.

I reach for my phone again, scrolling to the shipping confirmation. "I ordered her Halloween costume," I say, showing Melvin the picture. A fuzzy pink pig, complete with floppy ears and a curly tail. "Since we found out at the fair... it just felt right."

"Our chubby little piggy. She's going to be adorable."

The hours fly, and we are approaching Madison. We stop for lunch at Culver's and enjoy a Butterburger and some frozen custard.

"Well, this is our last meal before we're parents. Last chance to back out—you ready?" Melvin grips my hand.

"More than ready. I can't wait." I press his hand in return.

After lunch, we drive to the social work office. It's a nondescript brick building, like any other office building. But this is a place where our dreams will finally come true. Somewhere inside is our daughter. In the movies, having a baby involves a rush to the hospital, careful breathing, and screams of pain. My journey to motherhood involves slow, steady breathing to calm my racing heart and—if I would allow it—squeals of joy. Although I never planned on becoming a mother like this, a palpable, jittery pulse flows through my body—a mix of nerves and anticipation. I sweep my eyes over Melvin in his black-and-white checkered bowling shirt. He bumps me with his shoulder and grabs my hand. We swing our hands, floating our way to the door. He opens the door for me, his brown eyes sparkling.

We wander through the stark hallway until we find the office. Melvin pauses, one hand on the doorknob, gripping me tighter with the other. The door lets out a creak as we walk in, and the receptionist immediately greets us. "You must be the Greathouses. Welcome!"

"That's us," I sing, unable to suppress the smile on my face.

"Have a seat, and I will tell them you are here. They should be out in a minute."

We sit next to each other without letting go. Melvin's clammy palms remind me of when we were dating, and he made the move to hold my hand for the first time. His knee is bouncing involuntarily. The butterflies in my stomach swoop and swirl. Nothing will ever be the same after this. And one day, we probably won't remember what it was like to be only the two of us. I breathe in and slowly let it out.

"Amelia and Melvin?" A matronly woman emerges from down the hall.

"Yes, that's us." Melvin clears his throat, and we stand, still clinging to each other.

"I'm Pam. Jessica told me all about you. I'm glad to meet you." She extends a handshake. "Follow me."

I grasp Melvin's arm as she leads us into a private office. She invites us to have a seat again and proceeds with the formalities.

"We have a couple of papers for you to sign, and then we'll bring your daughter in. She is adorable." She sets the first page in front of us and hands us each a pen. "Here is the first paper. If you will sign in the highlighted spots at the bottom of the page. This form states you have sufficient resources to support the child." We take turns signing, and she exchanges it for the next form. "This next one states you are assuming legal custody of her." Our pens flourish, and she slides the next one across the table. "This one says that the birth mother has ten days to change her mind, and in that case, you will return the baby to the agency."

"Does that happen often?" I pause and cock my head toward her.

"It's simply a formality. We are required to allow ten days for the official termination of parental rights, but usually, once it gets to this point, the birth parents have made their decision."

Once we sign all the papers, Pam pushes herself up. "I'll be right back." And we are alone in her office. My mind races. I try to picture her. Will I be able to distinguish her from other babies? How will I discern what she needs? What will I do when she cries?

The door opens and interrupts my mental musings. Pam appears with a ball of blankets. "Here's your daughter. Who gets her first?"

"She does," Melvin quickly defers, and Pam hands me the bundle. I catch my breath as I take her in for the first time.

I cradle her head in my arms, my heart expanding with overwhelming love. She wriggles and settles. I inhale her sweet baby scent. "She's beautiful," I whisper, tears leaking down my face. I stroke her chubby cheeks and soft, dark hair. She blinks her eyes and peers at me. "Hello, sweetheart. I'm your mommy." Melvin peeks over my shoulder and touches her tiny, dimpled fingers. She grabs hold of his pinky and latches on.

"She's so soft," he says. "And those blue eyes."

"Wrapped around your finger already, isn't she?" I notice, and we exchange a meaningful look.

Melvin's voice cracks. "Maybe it's the other way around."

My heart expands, and goosebumps run up my spine. We sit mesmerized by this tiny being. No words are necessary. We're both smitten with our perfect little girl. And I know we would do anything for her.

"Does she have a name?" Pam asks.

I nod, pulling in my lips. "Hope. Hope Amelia Greathouse."

"That's a perfect name." Pam updates us on when she was last fed and changed. "The foster mom recorded her schedule and some observations over the last couple of days to give you an idea of her schedule." She hands a paper with handwritten notes to Melvin. "But, as you're aware, a newborn doesn't have a schedule. It is ever-changing. You'll figure it out as you go." She turns and grabs a bag. "She has a few belongings here. There are a couple of pacifiers and a bottle, and some clothes."

"What's next?" Melvin turns to her for instructions. "What's the procedure?"

"You are free to go whenever you are ready, but take as much time as you want. Can I take a couple of pictures for you?"

Pam's question breaks the spell. Melvin pulls himself away and turns to his camera bag. "I can't believe I forgot." He busies himself with his equipment, testing the lighting, focusing the lens. I listen to the click of the shutter and focus up at him with a smile.

He turns to Pam. "If I set everything up, can you snap a few of the three of us?"

"Of course." She steps into position, and Melvin slides in next to me. She snaps a few photos to record this moment so we will remember it forever. We soak up the precious occasion and then gather our things. At the car, Melvin tries to put her in the car seat.

"Umm, Mel? I think you have that in there wrong."

"What do you mean? It's all buckled in tight."

"I understand that, but it's backward. The carrier isn't snapping in."

Melvin takes everything out to start over, and we end up with baby supplies strewn all around the vehicle in the parking lot. A kind man walking by asks, "Do you need some help?"

"No, thanks." Melvin shakes his head and clears his throat. "I've got this." Is he trying to convince the man or himself?

The man moves on, and Melvin continues to struggle. As he stretches the seatbelt across to buckle it in, he loses his grip, and it jerks back, smacking him in the face. I'm holding in a laugh when he says, "Where are the instructions for this thing?"

"That guy tried to help you, but you turned him away."

"Point taken." With one last try, he finally has it secure. The carrier pops in with a click, and we are ready to roll.

"Just like that, we're parents!" Melvin announces, brushing off his hands. "It seems somehow wrong that we're sneaking away with her. Like she isn't ours. I realize she is. But it doesn't feel real yet." We open our car doors and climb in.

"I get what you mean. But it's true." We snap our seatbelts in place, and Melvin starts the car. "And I won't ask you to pinch me this time." A chuckle bubbles up from my chest. Melvin pulls out of the parking lot and steers toward the freeway. Four and a half hours went quickly this morning, but I bet we'll have to stop at least once on the way home. "It says she has been eating every two to three hours, and her last bottle was over an hour ago. We should be able to get somewhere between Wisconsin Dells and La Crosse before she needs to be fed again."

We are on the road for a short time when Melvin exits.

"Where are you going?" I ask.

"Our first family picture with a sculpture!" he shares enthusiastically as the giant pink elephant wearing glasses comes into view. Of course, he would think of that. He pulls into the gas station and gets out. "I'll get Hope," he says with a grin.

He takes a few photos of Hope and me, directing me where to stand and how to pose. A family pulls up to the gas station, and the dad offers to take a few pictures of all three of us. We walk into the convenience store and purchase a couple of "Pinkie the Elephant" souvenirs before hitting the road.

"That was fun." I glance at Melvin and bump shoulders with him. "You're a sucker for statues."

"You know me. We've got to get Hope used to it now because I'll be doing this with her for the rest of her life."

We hum along. There isn't much traffic on the open Wisconsin roads, especially on a Monday afternoon in late August. About an hour and a half in, Hope makes noise in the backseat.

"Should I pull over?" Melvin asks.

"I'm not sure." She might be stirring in her sleep. Or is that her hungry cry? I can't tell. "What should we do?"

"Well, she doesn't sound like she's in pain or anything. The farther we get before we stop, the fewer stops we'll have to make and the quicker we'll get home. Let's keep listening. Let's see if we can get a little farther."

We drive another thirty minutes, and she erupts, making us aware of her needs. Probably food.

"Sounds like she's ready for us to stop now," I say.

"I'll get off as soon as I can find a decent place to stop." Melvin drives another ten, another fifteen minutes, and Hope is wailing.

"Listen, we need to stop and help her. It doesn't matter if it's on the side of the road. Pull over someplace, and I will grab the diaper bag and make her a bottle."

Melvin pulls over at the next exit, which is nothing but farmland. There are no cars behind us and none to be seen anywhere. He stops at the stop sign, and I get out. I dig through the supplies and retrieve a bottle and the formula. "One scoop plus two ounces of water." I read the directions on the can. "Wait. We need water to mix the formula. I didn't pack any."

"I have some left in my water bottle, but I've been drinking out of that. It's not sanitary, but I'm not sick or anything. Could we use that?" Melvin asks.

Shoot. I ponder our dilemma. We don't have much of a choice. I suppose we're family now. Sharing germs comes with the territory. "Here, you mix it up, and I'll get her out." I hand him the bottle with the scoop of formula and turn my attention to Hope. "Hey, Hope. It's okay. Mommy's here. We're going to get you something to fill that empty tummy. Here we go. I've got you now." I twist my head toward Melvin. "Do you have it ready?"

"I believe so. Add the water and shake it up?"

"Yeah. That should work." Melvin hands me the bottle, and I put it in her mouth. She takes a couple of sucks and then cries again. "What's wrong, sweetie? Take a drink. It will make your tummy better. You're hungry." Then I grasp the problem. "This bottle is cold. Like ice cold."

"Well, yeah. That's how I like my water," Melvin retorts.

"That may be how you like your water, but our daughter prefers her milk warm. How are we going to warm her bottle in the car?"

"I left my car microwave at home, sorry," Melvin says with an edge of sarcasm.

"You aren't supposed to microwave bottles anyway," I reply, my frustration mounting.

"Listen. Why don't you buckle her back in? GPS says there is a rest stop about five minutes away. We can go there and get warm water from the bathroom sink and mix up a fresh bottle. Hopefully, she will take that."

"Okay," I reply and return my attention to Hope. "Hang in there, sweetheart. We're going to go for a short ride, and we'll get you some warm milk. It's going to be okay."

The five-minute ride seems like five hours when there's an infant siren going off. I didn't expect a small human to make that much noise. While Melvin drives, I stay in the backseat and try to get her to take the cold bottle. Once we arrive at the rest stop, I hand Melvin an empty bottle. "Fill this up with warm water—not too hot. I'll put the formula in another bottle, and we can mix it up when you get back." He dashes into the rest stop. Is rest-stop water sanitary? I don't know. But we don't have a lot of choices. This place doesn't look like it has amenities like vending machines. He returns with *hot* water. "Honey, this is steaming hot. We can't give this to Hope."

"I figured it would cool down a bit when I walked back to the car, so I got hot water to be sure."

I'm about to lose my ever-loving mind. Hope is wailing like an ambulance off to rescue a victim, but I feel like I'm the victim of a prank or some sort of torture device. My patience is wearing thin with Melvin, and I can't bear to see Hope upset. We've only been parents for a couple of hours, and already we are failing miserably. This isn't how I pictured motherhood at all.

"How about this?" Melvin offers. "If we add some of the hot water to the cold bottle, it should even it out."

I don't have any better suggestions, so I hand him the bottle. "Let's try it."

He adds the warm water to the bottle, shakes it up, and has me test it on my wrist. That's what they do in the movies, right? The temperature is exactly right. It's not cold anymore, and it won't burn her, so I pop it in her mouth again. Her siren turns off, and she suckles. Immediately, the car fills with the sound of silence. I let out an enormous sigh of relief and ease back into the seat of the car.

"We did it," I exclaim in a whisper so I don't activate the alarm again.

"We did it," Melvin agrees.

Hope falls asleep as she finishes her bottle. I gently burp her and tuck her into her car seat. Once she is all buckled in, I give Melvin a thumbs up. He starts the car and pulls onto the freeway for home.

# Chapter 27

The days blur together—freshly washed bottles lined up on the counter, the smell of formula and baby powder, the soft click of the rocking chair. Melvin moves beside me in the dark without being asked, lifting Hope with gentle strength, his voice a low hum against her cheek as she settles. She loves Melvin's voice—her head pressed to his chest as he whispers. We're learning her language—the sharp, insistent wail that means hunger, the whimpering fuss that just needs to be held.

One evening, Allie, Powers, and Ruby come by, arms loaded with dinner. While the food warms in the oven, Allie folds a receiving blanket with swift, confident hands. "Like this," she says, tucking Hope in tight. "It'll help her sleep longer." She's right.

We pass around our family photo with Pinkie the Elephant looming in the background. "Let's do an elephant theme," Allie grins, already pulling up a template on her phone. The phrase 'Help us welcome our new little peanut' appears under the image before I can even respond. She schedules the baby shower for a week from Saturday, timed perfectly so both our moms can be there.

I offer a few suggestions—ideas for food and clever favors—but mostly, I step back. Allie's got this. And honestly, it feels good to let her.

When Wendy shows up with dinner on Thursday, it appears she hasn't showered in days. I notice crusty stains on her t-shirt, and her messy bun is a true mess, not a style choice. Now that I have a newborn, I kind of get it. This gesture is a sacrifice, and I appreciate her for it.

"She's precious." Wendy cradles Hope like the pro that she is. "Your house is so calm and organized. I can't believe how peaceful it is here, especially with a newborn disrupting your schedule."

"Well, with us, it's two against one. We are tag-teaming infant and household duties."

"I got an email about a baby shower next Saturday." She smiles. "Can I help with it?"

"That would be wonderful. My college roommate, Allie, is hosting it. She would probably appreciate some help. Her email is on the invitation, or I can give you her cell number."

"Why don't you give me her cell? I'm on my phone all the time, but I rarely check my email." She hands Hope back to me. "I'd better be on my way before there's a mutiny at home," she jokes.

I place Hope in her bouncy seat and walk Wendy to the door. Once the door clicks shut, I go to the kitchen to share Wendy's spaghetti and meatballs with Melvin.

After a quick prayer to bless the food, Melvin takes the first bite. "Hmm. It's kind of gummy. And it could use a bit more sauce."

I take a bite and wrinkle my nose. "The noodles didn't get cooked all the way. We can't save that, but we can eat the meatballs and the bread and salad. It'll be fine."

Melvin cuts into a meatball. "It's still cold on the inside, Amelia."

"She probably threw them in frozen, expecting the pasta would thaw them out." I cross the kitchen. "Nothing a microwave can't fix. We have extra sauce in the fridge."

Melvin separates the pasta and meatballs. I nuke the meatballs while he throws out the pasta and grabs the tomato sauce and salad dressing. We sit down again and dish up our modified meal.

An hour later, my stomach grumbles. Melvin tips his head at me. "Are you still hungry?"

"A bit," I say, guilt gnawing at me because Wendy was trying to be helpful.

"How about if I order a pizza?" Melvin asks. "They can probably deliver it in thirty minutes, and we will have leftovers for lunch to-morrow."

"Sounds perfect."

As we are sitting on the couch watching TV, the doorbell rings. "Pizza's here!" Melvin exclaims, getting up to answer the door. "Hi, Wendy! What's up?" He stretches out his words. "Did you forget something?"

Panic seizes my chest. Why is she back? What if the pizza delivery guy shows up while she's here? She'll know we hated her dinner. I ease up with Hope in my arms and walk to the door. "Hi, Wendy! What are you doing here again so soon?"

"Well, I went home to eat dinner with my family. I made double to share with you guys. It was terrible. I'm mortified. The kids distracted me, and I forgot to set a timer. The pasta was undercooked, and the meatballs weren't even heated through. Olivia, my oldest, was supposed to put together the salad with a bagged salad from the fridge. She didn't mention it was going bad. I had to scrap our meal and start over, so I made some for you guys, too. I couldn't let you eat that garbage."

"Oh, it wasn't that bad," I reassure her with my sweetest smile. "We warmed it up. Anyway, it's the thought that counts. You didn't have to go to all this work for us."

"It's no problem. And if you're not hungry tonight, you can always reheat it tomorrow."

"Thanks, you're too sweet. You'd better hurry home to your family. You've spent way too much time taking care of us today." I try to shoo her away before the pizza guy shows up. We shut the door behind her and bring the new meal to the kitchen. We gape at each other with wide eyes.

"That was a close one," Melvin says with a sigh.

*Ding-dong.* The bell interrupts our conversation, and we go to the entryway, opening the door to find the pizza delivery guy. Over his shoulder, I see Wendy pulling out onto the road. My heart sinks. They must have passed each other in the driveway. I hope it doesn't hurt her feelings. Tomorrow, I'll write her a thank-you note. I do honestly appreciate her efforts.

Melvin takes the pizza, and I place Wendy's new meal in the fridge. I'll save it for tomorrow. I'd rather not take my chances with her cooking twice in one night.

# *Chapter 28*

V ideo calls with our parents and each of our siblings sprinkle throughout the week. They are all thrilled to meet Hope. Friday afternoon, my phone buzzes with a text.

Mom

> Made it through security, and I'm at my gate. It says my flight is on schedule. Can't wait to see you guys and hold my granddaughter!

Me

> We can't wait either! See you soon!

Hope takes a nap, and Melvin and I lie down, too. They say, 'Sleep when the baby sleeps.' She didn't sleep much last night. We both could use a nap. An hour later, she wakes up wailing. Melvin makes a bottle while I change her diaper. The diaper is secured on one side, and my baby is half-dressed when my phone rings. It's our social worker. Since we picked up Hope in Wisconsin, she didn't get to meet her. She's probably eager to see her and congratulate us. Jessica has been a tremendous support and cheerleader for us. She wanted us to be parents almost as much as we did. I answer the phone and put her on speaker so I can have my hands free to finish getting Hope dressed.

"Hi, Amelia, how are you doing?"

"Tired but blissful. It's been a bit of an adjustment, but we couldn't be happier. Would you like to meet Miss Hope?"

"Actually, I'm calling with some news..." Jessica sighs, and a weight falls into my stomach.

"Okay... what's up?"

"There's no easy way to say this, Amelia. The birth mother changed her mind."

The floor drops out from beneath my feet, and a tight hold wraps around my throat. I fumble through the house, clinging to Hope, searching for Melvin. The second he catches my face, his smile fades, and he hurries to take the baby. I must be more off-balance than I realized.

"What's going on?" he mouths. My voice is stuck somewhere on my tongue. The weight of my arm is ten thousand pounds as I lay the phone down in front of us and flop onto the couch.

"Amelia, are you there?"

"Yeah. I'm here. I'm just... What does this mean?"

Melvin sits next to me with Hope in his arms and turns his attention to the phone.

"Well, as you are aware, there is a ten-day waiting period before the parental rights are terminated. It's a big decision, and that allows them the opportunity to change their minds. Hope was born a week ago, so they are still within their rights to take her back. The birth mother has given it a lot of consideration and decided she wants to raise her."

I gawk at Melvin in disbelief. He hands Hope back to me, along with the bottle. "But... doesn't Hope have a better chance with us? We can give her a good life. An *amazing* life." I grasp at anything that will change the result of this phone call.

"It's not about what you or I think. In this situation, the birth mother is entitled to make the decision she believes is best. I'm sorry."

"When do we have to give her back? How does this all work?" Melvin interjects, his hands resting on his knees as he leans toward the phone.

"Since it's Friday afternoon, and our offices will be closed for the weekend, we can wait until Monday. If you bring her to my office, we will take it from there. I understand this is hard and not what we were hoping for. But it happens sometimes. Can you be here on Monday morning? Does 10:00 work for you?"

"I guess so." My voice shakes. Like emptying a bathtub, all the joy has drained from my soul.

"Thanks. I'll see you on Monday. Amelia and Melvin, I'm sorry. It will take some time, but we will find you another child." She hangs up, and sobs erupt from deep inside me. Hope startles, and I gasp to quiet my sorrow. I struggle to keep the bottle still, but my shoulders tremble. My tears paint polka dots on her onesie.

"What in the world..." Melvin shoots up and paces back and forth. "She can't be serious, can she? The birth mother probably said it because she knew the deadline was coming." He curls his arms over his head. "She still has the weekend to consider it. She'll figure out she can't handle being a single mother and change her mind by Monday. Her family will talk some sense into her."

"Do you really believe that?" I consider his suggestion, aching for it to be true. He collapses next to me and holds me. Tears pool in his eyes. We watch Hope suckle her bottle.

"They said she's barely out of high school. She lives with her parents. They have to make her see reason." He rubs my arm, trying to comfort me and himself at the same time. "They'll recognize that if she keeps her infant, they will be supporting both of them. She's probably struggling with hormones and emotions since giving birth. She's not acting rationally. They will clear their heads over the weekend."

"Or they won't." I pause, tentacles of dread reaching through and strangling my dreams. "The grandparents might be heartbroken over losing their granddaughter."

We stay like that long after Hope finishes her bottle and drifts to sleep. Melvin's arms are around me, and mine are around Hope. Tears keep coming, but there is nothing to say. Even though it's been less than a week, she's already a part of me. I anticipate her cries. I'm attuned to her needs. I *am* her mother. Me. God brought her to us; how can He allow her to be taken away?

My phone buzzes to announce a text. I glance down, and my heart drops.

Mom

> My flight barely touched down. I'm still on the plane and need to pick up my bag at baggage claim. It will be a while yet.

"It's my mom." I look to Melvin for support.

"It's better to talk about it in person. We'll tell her when we pick her up."

I lower my gaze in silence. "I can't do it, Melvin. Don't make me say the words out loud to her. I don't want to see her expression. Or for her to see mine. Can you pick her up and break the news?"

He swallows. "I can do that." The words form a weight around his neck.

I text back.

Me

Melvin's going to pick you up. Call or text him when you reach your door. He'll be on his way in a minute.

Mom

Sounds good. Can't wait to meet my grand-daughter!

Her words are like a knife in my chest, but she is completely un-aware.

Melvin kisses me tenderly on the cheek and rubs the side of Hope's face. "Bye, girls. Be back in about an hour." He walks out the door, and a fresh wave of sadness flows over me. I pull Hope closer, my arms shaking, wanting desperately to never let her go. How can this be? I pour out my heart, hoping He is listening.

"Why would you do this to us, God?" I look up toward the ceiling. "We're trying to do what's right. We have good intentions of raising a family of children who believe in you. I believed this was the answer to our prayers. How could you grant us an answer and then take it away? I don't understand."

My heart aches as I try to comprehend the purpose of all of this. I hope it's all a mistake. Certainly, she will rethink it over the weekend and realize that she isn't at a place in life to take care of an infant. She's barely an adult. Taking on the role of a mother at this point in her life will be a challenge. She'll have to put her whole life on hold. I pray she will recognize the odds are better for both of them if Hope remains a Greathouse.

The hour passes, and soon Melvin walks through the door with my mom. In an instant, she is by my side, her blue eyes pooling with tears. "Oh, honey. I'm so sorry." Her honey-blonde hair falls into my face as she holds me. My mother's touch and words crack me wide open once more.

"It's not fair, Mom. How could she do this to us?" I grab a tissue and wipe my nose. "If she wanted to keep the baby, she should have kept her from the start. But this is cruel. Even though Hope is too young to remember, she'll sense something—being shifted back and forth between caregivers. She'll be confused about whom to bond with. If her birth mother truly loved her, she would want what's best for her."

"You're right, honey. It's not fair." She strokes my hair. Here I am trying to be a mother, but my own mother is holding me like she has done since I was a little girl. "I hate this as much as you do. There's nothing I can do or say to change it."

Mom makes a big pot of soup for dinner. We set the bouncy seat on the table so we can admire Hope while we slurp our soup. Mom cleans the kitchen, starts a load of laundry, and prepares a bottle. I watch her snuggle with Hope, and I pretend Monday morning won't come.

My heart plummets to my stomach when Melvin calls his mom. I brace myself for Brenda's response to our news.

"I'm counting down the days until I'll be there next week. Your dad and I are going to drive straight through on Friday. We'll have the car packed full of gifts and treasures for Hope. My friends are sending presents for the baby shower, as well. What's Amelia's mom's schedule?"

"Her mom goes home next Sunday. But, Mom, that's what we wanted to talk to you about. We got some bad news." As Melvin speaks, I curl my arms around my middle, focusing down at my knees bound tightly together.

"Oh no. What's that? Are Amelia's parents okay?"

I rock back and forth, allowing Melvin to be the voice of our conversation. He rests his arm across my shoulders. "Her folks are fine. It's actually about Hope—"

"Hope? What's wrong with Hope? She doesn't have her doctor's appointment until she's two weeks old, does she? Did something happen? Was there an accident?"

"Hope is perfectly healthy. But the social worker called today, and the birth mother has changed her mind. We have to bring her back Monday morning." Melvin's voice cracks as he delivers the news. My throat constricts, and tears pool in my eyes.

"Can they do that? I mean, she already gave her up. Isn't there a rule?"

Melvin pulls at his hair. "The birth parents have the right to change their minds for up to ten days after they give the child up. She is completely within her legal rights."

"Well, that is completely wrong. Who would do that? I mean, she had nine months to decide. Why would she suddenly change it in a week? Can't you guys fight it?"

I lean my head on his shoulder and listen to him explain. "It's out of our hands. The birth parents have all the rights during the grace period. It doesn't matter what we say; the law is on their side."

Melvin finishes the conversation and convinces her to stay home next week. He holds his forehead in his hands, and I slump further onto his shoulder. For once, I agree with my mother-in-law. This situation is completely wrong.

# Chapter 29

On Saturday, I sleep in, and Melvin takes the morning shift with Hope. I wake to a clatter coming from the kitchen. Mom got up early and made us breakfast. As we sit down to eat, I share an idea that came to me when I was up with Hope in the night.

"What if we wrote a letter to the birth mom? We could plead our case and show her how much we love Hope already. If we email it to Jessica and call her, maybe she can forward it. It's worth a try... it might change the birth mom's mind. I can't give up without a fight. "

"I don't know..." Melvin hesitates and looks at my mom expectantly. "What do you think, Bethany?"

"I ache for where you're coming from. But birth parents have more rights. They might not even pass it along to the birth mother because they don't want to pressure her." She takes a sip of orange juice. "You can try. But I don't want you to be disappointed."

"I'm already disappointed." Straightening in my chair, I pause from eating. "Let's do it. It doesn't do any good to sit here and wait." I wave my fork in a battle cry. "We have nothing to lose."

After breakfast, my mom takes care of Hope, and we work on composing our email. Before we begin, Melvin suggests we pray. We kneel together in our bedroom, and he offers the prayer.

"Our Father in Heaven, we are here before thee with heavy hearts. This week, we have experienced such exquisite joy as we brought Hope into our lives. You comprehend how much we have wanted a child and how long we have waited. We were sure this was our answer. Now we found out that the birth mother wants to take her back, and it's breaking our hearts. We love Hope so much. We want to be her parents. Please provide a miracle for us. Change the birth mother's mind. Help her understand what we have to offer Hope. We want to write her a letter and pray that Thou will guide our words to say the right things. Help us accept your will, no matter how things turn out. In Jesus' name, we pray, amen."

Melvin and I compose the letter, trying to be impartial, sharing how much we love her, even though it has only been a week. We share our infertility journey with her–the failed treatments, the miscarriages, the heartache–and how this baby is an answer to our prayers. Our message states the facts and shows the benefits of living in a home with two parents who are both professionals and college graduates, being careful not to judge, trying to show her that Hope's best chance in life would be with us.

Once we finish, we have Mom review it for a more objective perspective. "Beautifully said, guys, I wouldn't change a thing. I pray it makes a difference so we can have Hope in our family permanently."

I put in a call to Jessica.

"How are you guys doing?" she asks softly.

"It's been rough." I drag in a deep breath and plow forward. "We composed a letter to the birth mom. We hope she will change her mind. If I email it to you, can you make sure it gets to her today, so she has time to read it before Monday?"

"I will try, but the birth mother may refuse to accept any communication." Jessica hesitates, choosing her words carefully. "As hard as it is for you, it's also difficult for the birth mother. She's making an impossible decision. Raising a child as a young single mom is hard. But living with regrets because you don't get to see your baby grow up is also hard. No matter what, she has the right to decide for this child because she gave birth to her. We have to respect her decision."

I exhale slowly, trying to steady the storm inside me, but the knot in my stomach twists tighter. My shoulders slump, grief pressing down like a weight I can't lift. When I finally speak, my voice wavers. "You're right. It's just that we love her so much already... Please try."

"Send it over."

We hang up, and I email it to her. I stand and embrace Melvin, clinging to him like a life buoy in rough seas, trying not to drown. Jessica's words echo in my head. *An impossible decision.* Did she decide to put Hope up for adoption in haste? Was she pressured by her family? And now she's having second thoughts. Choosing to keep her baby will change the course of her life forever. She'll have to put everything on hold—her schooling, social life. More than anything, I hope she finds peace with whatever path she chooses. And I hope I can feel peace, too.

"*Trust in the Lord with all thine heart; and lean not unto thine own understanding.*" Melvin's words pull me from the deep.

"*In all thy ways acknowledge him, and he shall direct thy paths,*" I reply, keeping my head above water. For now.

We pass the day silently, going through the motions. My phone rests in my palm like a lifeline, my fingers continuously refreshing the screen, hoping for a text or an email... anything to make this nightmare end. But there is nothing.

Melvin fires up the grill, and Mom grills pork tenderloin. The smoky smell wafts through the air.

"Are you planning to go to church tomorrow?" Mom asks.

"I can't face everyone." I take a sip of water. "We announced our adoption last week, and people were so kind to us. I can't show up with a baby this week and then without one the next."

"Let's have a quiet morning and enjoy the time we have. We'll make the most of every moment, so you'll have no regrets on Monday morning."

"Thanks, Mom." I pat her hand.

Melvin clears the table and does the dishes while Mom and I sit out front with Hope. The little babe observes us, but the soothing rocking of the swing causes her eyes to blink. Soon, gentle sighs slip from her lips as she sleeps in my arms.

Anyone walking by would observe the idyllic picture of us on the porch and assume all was right in the world.

But a blanket of sorrow and unease is tucked around our laps. What lies ahead of us is unspeakable anguish and grief no parent should have to face.

*Am* I a parent? If we lose Hope after only a week, it will be as if I were a babysitter. Like I was pretending or playing house. I might have to cling to this memory for the rest of my life and remember the beauty, no matter how brief.

"Have you noticed how she always sleeps with one arm stretched over her head?" I ask.

"Yes, it's sweet. She's peaceful." Mom strokes her soft, chubby arm.

"Completely unaware of the chaos in our hearts right now," I add.

"I'm sorry, honey. I hate that you are going through this. You are so brave and strong. I couldn't have done this when I was your age. I'm wondering how I can say goodbye to this angel on Monday, and I'm merely her grandma."

***

On Sunday morning, Hope is up with the sunrise. After she is fed and taken care of, Melvin and I put her between us in bed and watch her. She moves her eyes back and forth, following the sound of our voices as we talk.

"This is what I've always dreamed of," I say, my heart clenching in my chest.

"She's perfect. It's amazing to watch her. A tiny body filled with so much potential." Melvin holds his finger out for her to grab.

"And we're going to miss out on all of it," I lament, letting my head fall onto the pillow.

"What should we do today?" Melvin leans on his hand and looks at me expectantly.

"Stop time." I fixate on the ceiling, avoiding his gaze.

"I agree." He reaches across Hope to stroke my arm. "But really, how should we spend the day?"

"I'm not sure. All the plans I had for this weekend with my mom seem hollow." I blow out a breath. "It's like the meaning has been sucked out of life. I feel empty. And powerless."

"Let's get out of the house. It doesn't help our spirits to sit here, staring at these four walls and contemplating what tomorrow will bring. Why don't we take your mom to Minnehaha Falls? We could pack food, hike to the bottom, and have a picnic. How does that sound?" Melvin's enthusiasm gains momentum with each word.

"That sounds fun." I muster a weak smile. "It's better than sitting and sulking."

At breakfast, we present the idea to Mom. She happily accepts our plans. The drive is beautiful, with the trees changing colors, yet it's just the right temperature to drive with our windows down. At the park, the sunshine filters through the trees, dappling the ground around us. I slide Hope into the infant sling, and Melvin grabs the backpack. We begin at the top of the falls, soaking in the view of the rushing water, the sound of it soothing my soul. We make our way down the stairs to the bottom, pausing for a few photos before hiking to where the creek is calmer. There is a ledge where we sit and enjoy the gurgling water, the sunshine warming our backs.

"It's such a beautiful day. Thanks for taking me here. It's so peaceful," Mom says. "It's remarkable that you can find this in a big city like Minneapolis."

"Well, Minnesota is the 'Land of 10,000 Lakes,'" Melvin explains. "There are tons of parks and lots of water around here."

After enjoying the water and sunshine, we hike to the picnic area. The food hits the spot, and it's a great way to spend a fall afternoon. Kids squeal with delight, chasing each other around the playground nearby, and my heart sinks. We may never get to do that with Hope. Never get to watch her run and play. Never hear her laugh or listen to her first words. We won't get to watch her learn to crawl and walk. All the plans we had for her are being stripped away. Despite the sunshine, there is a dark cloud hanging over us. I brush the dread away, along with the crumbs from the table, trying to dismiss it. Even the fall breeze can't blow away the brewing storm. Numbness washes over me, dreading what the next twenty-four hours will bring.

Mom is in the backseat with Hope when she fusses. With tender words and a pacifier in hand, she expertly calms Hope. As much as I want this for myself, I want it for my mom, too. I want her to get to dote on Hope, buy her frilly dresses, and bake cookies with her. The birth mother's decision is going to affect an entire extended family, not only Melvin and me. My heart aches for her, making such a life-altering decision. I wish I could talk to her. But I will never have that opportunity. The letter was my best chance, and she might not even get it or read it.

Back at home, we enjoy a lazy Sunday afternoon. We set Hope on a blanket in the living room, the one Louise gave us. Should we send it with Hope? What about the gifts people have given us? Are they ours or Hope's? Melvin and I stretch out on the floor next to her. She grips Melvin's finger in one hand and mine in the other.

"We love you, sweet girl," I whisper, fighting the tears. "We always will."

Melvin grasps my other hand, and we make a connected circle. My heart is heavy. My spirit wants to cry out, but I can't waste this moment. I'm trying to memorize her face and stuff the impressions into my heart. What if I meet her again someday? Will I recognize her? Will I remember her if I run into her when she's an adult? Probably not. All I will have is a vision of a chubby-faced cherub, not the woman she will become.

My mom is busy in the kitchen, cooking up a storm. Sometimes, she stress-cooks. It's a release for her. Before long, dinner is ready. We sit down to baked chicken, mashed potatoes and gravy, and asparagus. She made chocolate chip cookies, and they are still warm. After dinner, Mom insists on cleaning and lets us enjoy Hope. As bedtime approaches, I dread what tomorrow will bring. There is still a chance something will change. I haven't heard anything, but I couldn't bother

Jessica on the weekend. We can call her in the morning before we go. I won't give Hope up unless there is no other way.

In the quiet of the night, we are all in bed. The lights are out. The house is dark. Through the darkness, I can sense Melvin's breathing hasn't found the rhythm of sleep. "Are you awake?"

"Yeah." He rolls toward me. "The quicker I go to sleep, the sooner we lose Hope. I don't want that."

"Me neither," I croak, stifling my grief. His hand slides across the sheets, tumbling over my shoulder and running up and down my back. Somewhere through the tears, we both drift off. I'm pulled from sleep in the middle of the night by newborn cries. Groggy, I shuffle to her room in the dark. My body moves instinctively, picking her up and walking to the kitchen. The soft glow of the stove light spills across the kitchen counter as I prepare a bottle, rocking her gently, mumbling consoling words to her.

We curl up on the couch, her tiny body pressed against mine. I study her as she gulps down her midnight snack, completely at peace while a battle rages inside me. My spirit wants to fight for her, but in the morning it will be time for surrender.

I glance at the time and mentally count down the hours. Ten hours left to hold her. To love her. In silence, I offer a prayer to the only One who can rescue me.

*Father in Heaven... You have the power to change this. Please send a message to the birth mother and help her change her mind. And if it is not meant to be, please give me the strength I need to give Hope back in the morning. I don't believe I can do it.*

A breeze catches my hair and sends a shiver down my spine. I notice the window open and rise to shut it, being careful not to disturb Hope.

*When the Lord closes a door, somewhere He opens a window.*

The idea fills me from my toes up through the top of my head, and I am flooded with a sense of peace. My heart swells, and I slide the window closed. I stand a little taller and lift my head to the ceiling. A soft smile spreads across my face, and tears trickle down my cheeks.

God has a window for me. I'm certain. He is mindful of me. He has a plan for my life. I want it to include Hope, but maybe that door is closing. I need to have faith that there is something else in store for us. And He will watch over Hope and take care of her. I get Hope to bed, turn out the lights, and settle in my room. I'm still sad, but God is in charge.

# Chapter 30

Hope's cries drag me from a fitful sleep. I lumber across the hall and scoop her up. I absently change her diaper and dress her, trying to detach myself from the connection I've built over the past week. Slogging downstairs, I prepare a bottle and sink into the armchair, staring off into space. My arms are full, but my heart is empty.

Picking up the phone, I make one last call to Jessica, just in case.

"I wondered if the birth mother replied to our letter."

Her voice is gentle through the phone. "I passed the information along to her social worker, but there was no response. I'm sorry. Are you going to make it to the office by 10:00?"

"We'll be there." I blow out a heavy sigh and study Hope's round cheeks, her tiny nose, her long eyelashes splaying over her smooth, pale skin, memorizing every detail. "Thanks for trying."

I turn to my mom and Melvin, shaking my head. "No luck. We're still scheduled to bring her to the office."

"At least you tried," Mom says with a side hug. "Do you want me to go with you, or would you prefer to do this on your own?"

"Melvin and I can do it. We're her par—" A sob cuts off the word before it gets out. Because we aren't anymore. Mom pulls me close, and I rest my head on her shoulder.

I pack her things in the diaper bag, in case she needs anything between now and when we turn her over. Turn her over? It sounds like a police arrest. Give her up? That sounds awful, too.

This whole thing is awful.

"Before we go, let's pray for her," Melvin suggests.

"Of course," I agree. Mom and I gather around, and the three of us surround Hope with love and our combined faith. Melvin offers the prayer.

"Our Father in Heaven, we are heartbroken right now. We love this little girl with all our hearts. Yet you love her more than we do, and you are watching over all of us right now. Please bless Hope with a happy life. Give her protection, health, and strength. Help her grow in her faith as she grows through the years. Let her always know she was loved in the earliest days of her life. Bless Amelia and me so that we can experience peace with the birth mother's decision. Allow us to accept Thy will and trust in Thee. Bring us comfort in the days ahead as we work through the loss of our daughter. We pray for her birth mother, that she will have increased capacity to care for Hope. Bless her with a supportive community that will help her and Hope live their best lives. We ask these things in the name of Jesus Christ, amen."

"Amen," Mom and I say in unison. She gives Hope one last kiss on her forehead before I strap her into the car seat, and we start our journey to Jessica's office. I hug my arms around myself and gaze out the passenger window while Melvin drives. Tears silently trickle down my face. I grab for the tissue box in the cup holder. The car fills with a heavy silence, interrupted by my sniffles. There isn't much to say. This is the worst day of our lives. About thirty minutes later, we pull into the parking lot.

Melvin squeezes my hand. "Do you have the strength for this?"

"Absolutely not."

"Do you want to wait in the car? I can take care of it."

My heart expands at his gesture, but this is something we need to do together. "Absolutely not." I blow my nose and wipe the tears, trying to pull myself together.

I encircle my arms around Hope and lift her from the car seat. Melvin carries the bag of her belongings. We drag our weighed-down souls into the building. The walk stretches before us like miles, but it is over in an instant. Jessica greets us at the door.

"Thanks for coming," she says, placing her hand over her heart.

"It's not like we had a choice," I squeak out.

"I'm sorry. Our hearts are breaking for you. But we need to believe it is what's best for her." Jessica presses her lips together. She isn't even referring to her as Hope anymore. I suppose after today, she won't be Hope Amelia. She will have a different name and have no memories or connection to us. She'll never remember how much we loved her. How we waited for her and wanted her.

"What happens now?" I ask.

"Whenever you're ready, I'll take her. We'll get her to her birth mother today, and your names will remain on the list of available adoptive parents."

"How much longer will it take? Are we at the bottom of the list?" I can't bring myself to look up from the floor as we stand awkwardly in the reception area. I cling to Hope, her warmth spreading as she rests on my shoulder.

"There is no ranking," she explains. "Birth parents have the option to choose who their baby goes to; your bio will be available to all interested birth families. There's no way to predict how long it will take. Keep marketing yourselves and spreading the word through friends, coworkers, and social media channels."

I hold Hope close to my chest and breathe in the newborn smell one last time. My voice comes out in a whisper. "I love you. I always will." Holding her out to Melvin, he takes her in his arms for a final goodbye.

"Here are a few things that belong to her." I bite my lip and swallow. "There are some pacifiers and a change of clothes... She ate barely over an hour ago... she will probably want another bottle... between eleven and noon," I share the facts in broken phrases, interrupted by sniffles. I fight to steady my voice. I can barely get the words out. Melvin gives her one last hug and kiss and hands her to Jessica. Grief wraps itself around my throat, and a whimper escapes. We'll never see her again. I pinch my lips together and wipe away the tears.

"Thanks, guys. I realize how challenging this is. We'll be in touch soon," Jessica says.

As soon as the door closes behind us, Melvin's arm is around my shoulder. He holds me in the hallway of the office building, sobs piercing the quiet. I focus on the gray carpet under my feet. My body shakes violently in his arms. A couple of guys in polo shirts walk through the main entrance, carrying their coffees. I had better get out of this building, and fast. I can't have insurance agents, financial planners, and random office workers watching my breakdown.

"Let's go," I choke out to Melvin. He takes my hand, and we make our way to the parking lot. Back in the privacy of our car, I let it all out. We hold each other across the center console and cry together for what seems like forever. There are no words to describe it. We have lived through a cruel joke. Grant us our wildest dreams and then say, *'I'm kidding!'* It's not funny.

Eventually, we calm down enough to let go of each other and ease back into our seats.

"What would you like to do now, Amelia?"

"I want to march in there and demand they give us Hope back," I proclaim, then breathe out slowly in acceptance. "But we can't do that."

"I wish we could. Would you like to go anywhere? Or back home?"

"I can't be in a public place right now. I want to crawl into my bed and pretend this never happened. Perhaps I will wake up, and Hope will be in the next room crying for her bottle."

"I wish I could make it all go away, Amelia. I really do." He holds my face in his hands and brushes away the tears with his thumbs. "Let's go home. Your mom is waiting for us." Melvin navigates back to our suburban home. I lean my head against the window, and everything goes whirring by, everyone we pass completely unaware of the fact that our world is falling apart.

Mom greets me with a hug when we walk through our front door. I fall into her arms and bawl all over again.

"Oh, honey. I don't know what to say. I'm sorry," she tries to console me. My body trembles, but I can't seem to produce words. Only tears.

"Is there anyone you would like me to call so people don't accidentally contact you to congratulate you?" Mom inquires.

I pull a tissue from the box. "That's probably a good idea. Could you inform our pastor? And I haven't called Allie—" *The baby shower!* She needs to cancel that. "Will you call Allie and have her cancel the shower?"

"Of course, dear. Do you want any lunch? I could make you something."

"I'm going to lie down. Here's my phone. You can scroll through my contacts and make the calls." I hand her the phone and wander to my room. Right across the hall is Hope's room. My chest tightens as I observe the unfinished space. We didn't even get a crib. We were going to do that over the weekend, but then we got the news. It was pointless. I wander in, pulling her blanket from the edge of the pack and play. Crumpling to the floor, I curl on my side, clinging to the reminder of her, inhaling her scent. The sound of footsteps padding down the hall reaches my ears. I feel as if I'm covered by an avalanche, unable to move. Melvin lowers himself to the floor near me, lying on his back. His hand inches across the floor, connecting with mine. We lay there in silence, our fingertips touching, looking vacantly into the emptiness while time disappears.

At some point, sleep must have overtaken me, and Melvin is no longer here. Confusion lingers for a moment before reality rushes into my consciousness. As I roll onto my back, my fingers rub the crust of dried tears on my face. I sit up, resting my arms on my knees. My stomach growls, and I am compelled to fill the emptiness inside me.

Every ounce of effort goes into dragging myself upright and trudging to the doorway. One last glance toward Hope's nursery before pulling the door shut behind me with a click, closing off the pain.

I trudge downstairs and find Melvin in the kitchen. I sit down on the stool, the counter stretching between us.

"Where's Mom?"

"She's running errands... giving us some time to ourselves. She'll be back in a couple of hours. Are you hungry? I could reheat some leftovers."

"Starving. That sounds nice."

We take our food outside and sit at the patio table, sharing a quiet lunch. The sun hangs low in the sky, and bees buzz around the plants. The neighborhood is still. Kids are in school. Parents are at work. All is quiet except for the sound of dead leaves scraping against each other in the wind.

I turn my face toward Melvin. "Last night, I was up with Hope, and I was praying. I wanted God to change the outcome. I wanted a miracle—that He would change the birth mother's mind." A soft, warm breeze blows around me and sends a shiver up my spine. "I had this overwhelming impression enter my mind. It's a quote from *The Sound of Music*. '*When the Lord closes a door, somewhere He opens a window.*' It's not scripture, but it was a message for me. Like we will get a second chance somehow. It might not be with Hope, but with another child who needs a family." I dip my spoon into my soup and bring it to my mouth.

Melvin tips his head toward me, nodding. "I had a similar peace flood through me this morning. I'm still sad about losing Hope, but it's like God was saying, *It's okay. You're going to get through this. And there will be something amazing on the other side.*"

"I hope so. Because... this sucks." I lift the corners of my mouth, trying to smile, but blink back the sting of tears instead. "When are you going back to work?" I ask.

"I was planning to go back tomorrow." He sets his spoon down and wipes his mouth with a napkin. "I mean, I was going to take a week off. I've already extended it by a day. And you have your mom here for the rest of the week. What about you?"

My shoulders lift and I let them drop. "I planned on taking six weeks' maternity leave. I should probably go back to work since I don't have a baby. It's going to be awkward. I can't handle the questions or the pity on people's faces. But I can't sit around here with nothing to do, waiting for a baby to fall into my lap."

"Talk to your boss. Work will probably take your mind off things. Maybe you can return next week after your mom goes back home."

"I'll call and work things out. But not today. I can't face anyone today."

We remain there in the stillness and quiet of the day, numb from the life-altering events of the morning.

"Want to go for a walk?" Melvin asks. "It's quiet with the kids in school. We could go to the park."

I fold my arms across my chest. "Putting one foot in front of the other is like climbing a mountain. Did my mom make those phone calls for me?"

"Yeah. She notified everyone. Pastor Matthew asked if we needed anything. Your mom asked him to pray for us." He moves to pick up our bowls and spoons. "I'm going to watch some TV. Want to join me?"

"Not right now."

Melvin takes our dishes inside, and I sit, my mind blank, my heart hurting. I stare into space. My whole body aches, and my eyes are dry from all the crying I've done. It's surreal. This kind of thing doesn't happen to anyone, does it? And yet, as the brittle leaves crackle in the wind, the breeze blows across my face, and I remember the window from last night. The sun warms me, and I fill my lungs with crisp fall air. The maple trees are on fire, and it is beautiful. I lose all sense of time before I decide to wander back inside. My phone is sitting on the counter. I pick it up and go back to our bedroom. I open a text.

Allie

I'm sorry, Mel. I can't believe this is happening to you. I'll cancel the shower and ex-

> plain to everyone on Evite. We'll have to set a date to go to lunch soon. Ruby would love to snuggle with you.

Tears fill my eyes. Holding Ruby right now would hurt too much. There's another text waiting for me.

Pastor Matthew

> I spoke with your mother today, and she shared your news. I'm sorry for your heartache. I will add you and Melvin to my prayers. Please contact me if there is anything your church family can do to help you through this difficult time.

Lying in bed and gaping at the ceiling, I contemplate the position I am in. Everyone knew we were adopting an infant, and now...there isn't one. I want to rewind and go back to being that young couple with no kids... no one even conscious that we *want* kids. I scroll mindlessly on my phone, watching videos. But even funny videos aren't cracking the slightest smile. Everything that used to make me laugh feels pointless now.

# Chapter 31

On Tuesday morning, I lie in bed listening to Melvin rustling around the room. He gives me a quick kiss goodbye, and I remain in the darkness. Even though I had my first full night's sleep in a week, all I want is more sleep. Closing my eyes is the one escape from the heaviness that fills my soul.

After dozing a little longer, I smell something delicious coming from the kitchen, but that doesn't even entice me to get up. At 9:00, there is a light tap on my bedroom door.

"Good morning, Amelia." Mom pokes her head in. "What would you like to do today?"

"Nothing." I sit up in bed, scooping my arms around my knees.

"I made a pan of baked oatmeal. Would you like to share it with me?"

"Sure." I shake my head, trying to clear the fog. "I'll be down in a minute."

Mom shuts the door, and I pull myself out of bed. I shuffle to the bathroom and grab my robe before padding into the hall. Across the hall, Hope's door is open. I was positive I had closed that. I pull it shut and go downstairs. We sit at the barstools and scoop out the warm baked oatmeal, covering it with sliced bananas and a splash of milk.

"This is good, Mom. Thanks."

"I knew it was one of your favorites. I wanted to cheer you up."

My heart freezes in my chest. It's going to take a miracle to cheer me up.

I drop my spoon in the oatmeal, my appetite gone. My voice chokes on its way out as I whisper one solitary word.

"Why?"

Mom turns to me. "This isn't easy, honey." She rests her hand on my arm. "You need to stop asking, 'Why?' and start asking, 'What's next?'"

I poke at my bowl and lift a questioning brow at her.

"The whys may never get answered. And you'll make yourself crazy trying to arrive at those answers. Your perspective is limited, and the birth mother has a different perspective of what is best for her baby. God has an even bigger perspective, and we should trust that He is in charge of Hope, and He is in charge of you. Your job is not to figure out why everything happened the way it did. You need to ask God, 'What's next?' Only then will you be able to move forward. Trust that He has magnificent plans in store for you."

"You're right, Mom. It hurts so badly right now." A whimper escapes, and I try to hold myself together.

She scoots closer and holds me in her arms. "It's okay to be sad. You lost something precious to you. I wouldn't expect anything less than a time of mourning. But don't get stuck in this place. Give yourself time to grieve and then look forward with eyes of faith."

We cling to each other, tears wetting our shoulders. After several minutes, Mom pats my back, and we return to our oatmeal, which is getting cold.

We venture out for a walk after breakfast. There's a path through a park nearby. I breathe in the fresh air. There are a few moms with their preschoolers gathering at the playground. My head snaps toward them as I hear the distinct cry of an infant. A young mother takes her baby out of the stroller, and immediately, tears spill out of my eyes. Mom grabs my hand, and we keep walking.

"Doing okay?" she asks.

"It sounded like Hope."

She frowns. "Let's keep walking." We follow a trail through a wooded area. There is a small brook flowing along the path and a bench at the top of the hill. We stop to rest.

"When do you plan to go back to work?" Mom asks.

"I need to call Margot today." Gazing across the wooded area, I fold my arms around my stomach. "I'll probably go back on Monday. I hate thinking about facing everyone. Either they won't have a clue what happened, and they will ask about her and want to see pictures, or rumors will have spread that we lost our baby, and they will want to talk about it and throw me pitying glances every time they walk by. I can't talk about it without crying. And I don't want to spend my day buried in a pile of Kleenex."

"Your boss can explain to your coworkers what happened and ask them to respect your privacy. That way, you only have to talk through it once."

"I'll try." We stand up and finish our walk. Back at the house, there's a package on the front step.

"Melvin must have ordered something," I say, picking it up. "Hmm. It's addressed to me." Inside, I grab a pair of scissors and slide them across the packing tape, curiosity niggling in the corners of my mind. *Please don't let this be a gift for Hope*, I pray. My heart is too exhausted to receive well wishes from a friend who didn't get the memo.

But beyond the crinkled bubble wrap, there pokes the brightest shade of pink, and my stomach drops, my hands freezing over the half-open box.

"What is it?" Mom asks, her voice distant in my muffled ears, like I'm suddenly underwater. My lungs fight for air, visions of my sweet little Hope invading my mind. The pink piggy I would've carried in my arms, with an orange jack-o'-lantern bucket hanging from my forefinger. The smiles, laughter... not just from Melvin, but from me, fade into a wisp of black smoke.

I choke on a sob begging to rip its way out of my throat. Mom rushes to my side, peering over my shoulder. I can't bring myself to say it, to tell her the visions that all faded as quickly as I dreamed them. The fabric slides from my fingertips, and I trip my way up the stairs to my bedroom.

The dull ache in my heart thrashes open—the single costume taking a knife to the freshly sewn wound. I curl on the bed, darkness blurring my vision, fighting for every breath I can muster.

I want to ask why. The word ricochets off my vocal cords, trapped behind my teeth. *God, why? Why? Why? Why?*

But I can't ask that. I *won't* ask it. It's a question that may never have an answer.

I stretch along the sheets, searching for something, anything, to stifle the anguish. My fingers wrap around the corner of Melvin's feathery pillow, and I pull it to my face, burying myself inside. The scent of his cologne fills my nostrils, weaving through my head and my heart.

*What's next?*

I can ask that. I can ask God what to do. He's told me millions of times before. Give me lists and tasks, and I manage them. I do them without question, without hesitation.

*Heavenly Father, please... what do I do?*

Nothing. Silence. Ache. Pain.

I grapple for something to hold on to, but the pillow and my grief are all that surround me. I can't do it anymore—this waiting, this aching for something I might never have. If by some miracle, we're blessed with another baby, how could I love it fully when there's nothing left in me to give?

Later in the afternoon, I call my boss and plan to return to work. Margot says she'll inform everyone and ask them to give me space. She tells me to take as much time as I need, and they'll welcome me back whenever I'm ready. I'm grateful to have an intermediary between my coworkers and me so I don't have to relive this nightmare with each of them. Her support means a lot to me. With the entrepreneur conference in a few weeks, there is plenty for me to do.

When I wander downstairs, the pig costume is gone, and Mom is making lasagna for dinner. The entire house smells like an Italian restaurant. Melvin walks in the door with a bouquet. He gives me a hug and a kiss and hands them to me.

"I hope they cheer you up. How was your day?"

"Thanks. They're beautiful. My day had its ups and downs." I press my lips together in a tight smile. He curls one arm around my waist. I recap the day, from the infant in the park to the package I forgot I had ordered.

Melvin pulls me in closer and rubs my back. "I'm sorry, honey. It's going to take time to forget about her."

My heart stops, and I push away from him. "Forget about her? I'll never forget her. What kind of mother would I be?" I glare up at him, my pulse racing. Doesn't he understand what it's like to want something so badly it's hard to breathe? The moment I held Hope in my arms, everything changed. She climbed inside my chest and made a spot for herself in my heart. She will always be a part of me. I pick up the flowers and jerk toward the cupboard to locate a vase. Melvin goes upstairs to change clothes. I fill the vase with water and snip the ends off the flowers with swift, purposeful motions. Pushing down my emotions, I steady myself against the counter and draw a calming breath. I turn to help Mom in the kitchen.

"It smells amazing, Mom. How can I help?" I force a cheerful voice.

"Why don't you mix up a salad? The lasagna should be out of the oven in about fifteen minutes."

"Mom, you have been cooking so much. With only three of us, we will never get through all this food," I say.

"I can freeze the leftovers, and then you won't have to cook much for the next couple of weeks."

"That sounds wonderful. It will be one less thing to do when I go back to work."

"Did you call your boss yet?" Melvin asks when he returns to the dining room.

"Yes, she's thrilled I'll be back." We tuck into our chairs at the table.

Melvin takes my hand. "It will be good for you to have something to fill your time." He tilts his head and peers into my eyes.

"I'm not as quick to move on as you. It's going to take me some time."

His eyes drop. "I'm still hurting, too. This wasn't what anyone expected."

My heart softens, and I brush the back of his hand with my thumb. "I know you are. Sometimes I just feel so alone."

Mom sweeps into the dining room and sets the steaming pan of lasagna in the center.

"That looks delicious, Mom."

"I hope you enjoy it," she says with a smile.

We pause to say grace and then serve steaming, gooey slices. I grab a piece of garlic bread and scoop some salad onto my plate.

The doorbell rings. Melvin hops up to answer it, kissing my forehead on his way.

"Is Amelia here?"

"Sure. Let me get her. Come on in."

Melvin walks to the kitchen and whispers, "It's Wendy."

My eyes widen toward him. I don't feel like talking to anyone right now, but I force myself to stand from the table and walk toward the front door.

"Hi, Wendy. What's up?" I clear my throat and try to act normally, but my voice sounds unusually bright and cheery.

"I heard something happened with your adoption. Allie canceled the shower, and I wasn't sure what to do, so I brought you chocolate. Here." She shoves a gift bag filled with chocolate into my hands. Lots of chocolate.

"Thanks," I squeak out, my fake cheeriness suddenly gone. I fixate on my feet, trying to find the words to explain. "The birth mother changed her mind, and we had to give her back."

"Amelia, that's awful." She presses her hand to her mouth. "Can they do that?"

I scuff my foot on the floor. "I guess occasionally, the birth mother has second thoughts, and she is legally within her rights to change her mind. It sucks," I shrug and wipe at a tear. *I won't bawl like a baby in front of her.* She holds her arms out for a hug, and I'm done for. I try to give her a quick one, but she draws me in. I suck air into my lungs and let it out in a staccato rhythm, trembling in her embrace. Despair bubbles over like a witch's cauldron, spilling all over the floor and filling the room around us.

She strokes my back and whispers, "I'm sorry." My sobs recede slowly, as if someone turned down the heat on the boiling pot.

I pull away, my face forming a tight smile, but no words form in my mouth.

"Nothing will make it better, but chocolate can soften the pain for a little while."

We stand there awkwardly, and she asks questions I don't have answers to. I put on a brave face and answer the best I can. But out there, the future is out of focus now. A few days ago, I assumed I knew what it held. I was making plans for holidays and visitors. All of those plans included Hope. But now that she's gone, the plans are, too.

"My mom leaves on Sunday, and I'll go back to work on Monday. It's probably best to get back to normal." *And forget the nightmare I'm going through.*

"Listen, I'm here for you if you need to talk or cry or whatever." She runs her hand down my arm and clasps my hand. "And tell me when you're coming to church so I can watch for you."

"Thanks, Wendy." Shutting the door, I lean against it, peek in the bag, and pull out a Lindor truffle. I open it, pop it in my mouth, and let the soft chocolate center melt on my tongue. Closing my eyes, I fill my lungs with air before turning to the kitchen, where my mom and Melvin are cleaning up.

"Who wants dessert?" I hold up the bag of chocolates, pressing my lips together and raising my eyebrows.

"Oh, you keep that for yourself, honey. I was planning to make chocolate mousse in a bit," Mom says.

*I didn't want to share anyway.*

"That was nice of Wendy to stop by," Melvin says.

"Yeah."

"Is she a friend from church?" Mom asks.

"Honestly, I didn't like her at first. Her life is chaotic with four small kids. But as I have gotten to know her and understand her, she's becoming a friend."

"Sounds like she's got a lot on her plate," Mom says.

"Yeah. Four kids are a lot. I'd be happy to have one."

"That's tough, sweetheart. It isn't easy seeing other people get the blessings you pray for. We need to trust God's plan for each one of us."

"I want a different plan," I jest, but the humor somehow doesn't make it into my tone.

# Chapter 32

Allie suggests a girls' outing with my mom and me that weekend. By Saturday, I've stopped crying in my bed for hours at a time. I'm feeling more like myself. Planning our day out gives me something fun to anticipate. After pampering ourselves with pedicures, we settle in for lunch at Yuzu, Chef Lee's Asian place. As we eat, the conversation turns to work.

"What events do you have coming up?"

"The first week of October is an entrepreneur conference. It's going to be held at the conference center downtown. We are having a special event the night before for women in business with a local keynote speaker, dinner, and break-out sessions."

"That sounds cool. I've been thinking about starting a business." Allie glances at me out of the corners of her eyes.

"Really?" I tilt my head at her. "I could get you a comp ticket for Wednesday night if you'd like. Aren't you enjoying being a mom and hanging out with Ruby?"

"That would be amazing. I love being home with Ruby. That's why I want to have my own business, so I can have the flexibility to be with her but also bring in a little money."

"What kind of business are you considering?"

"I haven't decided yet. I thought about opening a daycare. Bring in a couple of other kids to play with Ruby. But I'm worried that would tie me down more. I contemplated giving piano lessons. Ruby naps in the afternoon, and I could teach kids after school while she's napping and in the evenings when Powers can watch her. I'm still exploring my options, getting ideas."

"I'll get you a ticket, and you get Powers to watch Ruby. You can spend some time figuring out what sort of business you would like and then attend the breakout session about starting a business to determine what to do next."

"Thank you so much. That's a huge blessing to me. Bonus that I get an evening away with you."

The server drops off our bill, and Mom grabs it to pay.

"You don't need to do that," says Allie. "It was my suggestion. Besides, you already paid for the pedicures."

"It's my treat. You need to save your money to get that new business off the ground," Mom says with a warm smile.

"Thanks, Bethany. You're the best."

"Yeah, Mom. Thank you. It's been amazing having you here this week."

"I wouldn't have missed it for the world."

We hug Allie before getting in the car and driving home. "I can't believe you have to fly back tomorrow. What am I going to do without you?" I ask.

"You'll be busy with work. It'll be good for you and Melvin to get back into your routine. He'll be there for you. Besides, Audrey is already asking when I'll be home. She needs a babysitter."

"I guess you are always taking care of someone, aren't you, Mom?"

"I wouldn't have it any other way." She extends her arm and pats my hand.

Back home, Melvin is at the kitchen table, his gray hands kneading a hunk of clay.

"Hi, Hon." I rest my hand on his shoulder, peering over his head at his whimsical creation. The precarious sculpture appears to be straight out of a Dr. Seuss book. What appear to be wings jut up from the base, covered in three-dimensional polka dots.

"Hey, did you guys have fun?" he asks, without taking his eyes off his handiwork.

"Yeah. It was great. First, we—"

"Oh, shoot!" A ball of clay falls off his artwork with a squishy splat onto the plastic-covered table.

He glances over at me. "Sorry. What were you saying?" His eyes quickly dart back to the project. I want to share every detail of our outing—showing off my new pedicure and telling him about the sticky mango rice we had for dessert. But his attention is not on me.

"We had a nice time."

"That's great."

Mom and I walk through to the kitchen and set down our purses.

"I'm going to straighten up and pack my suitcase for tomorrow," Mom says.

"Okay. I'm ready to take a nap anyway." We part ways, and I go upstairs and sink into my bed. Melvin was so preoccupied that he barely noticed me. I could have dyed my hair pink while we were out, and he wouldn't have seen it. It would be nice if he could multitask like me, but he zones out when he's deep in an art project, and I feel like I don't exist. I scroll through my phone, wanting something to entertain me mindlessly for a few minutes, but when all it shows are baby ads and videos, I click it off and force my brain to rest.

My nap lasts longer than I intended, and I'm groggy. I stumble downstairs, bleary-eyed. I can hear Melvin in the living room on the phone with his mother. My mom is in the kitchen again, cooking for us. I bypass the living room and head straight into the kitchen.

"Hello, Amelia. Did you have a good rest?" Mom is busy at the stove. I smell beef and onions sizzling in the pan.

"Yes. What are you working on?"

"I ran to the grocery store while you were asleep and started more freezer meals for you." She smiles, pushing the meat and onions around with a wooden spoon. "Tonight, we'll have stroganoff, and by the time I'm done, your freezer will be packed. You should be able to go the next two weeks simply reheating food from your freezer."

I help Mom in the kitchen, and Melvin joins us. "Smells good in here."

"Stroganoff and green beans," Mom says.

"Yum. I'll set the table." He gathers plates and silverware.

"What did your mom have to say?" I turn in his direction, tossing the beans in the skillet.

"Just checking on us. She wants us to visit. I told her we might come for Christmas this year. She's going to find out if Celeste and Elise will be home."

"That would be fun. I love spending time with your sisters."

As we spend our final evening together, I feel like I'm about to cross a threshold. My mom will leave in the morning, and I will go back to work on Monday. I'm stepping back into my old life, but I'm carrying a new load of unexpected baggage. There is an invisible backpack on my back, weighed down with rocks. It changes everything, but no one else can see or understand it.

# Chapter 33

W hen my alarm goes off Monday morning, I slide my hands
across the sheets to find Melvin's spot empty. I push back
the covers and sink my knees into the thick carpet beside the bed.
Surrounded by darkness, I plead with the Lord to help me through the
day. The churning in my stomach quiets to a flutter, the Spirit settling
over me like a warm blanket.

After my shower, I pull on my favorite pair of black dress pants.
They're awfully snug. It seems I overdid it on those chocolates from
Wendy. I ditch them for a more forgiving pair, and apply my makeup,
adding a little extra concealer for the dark, puffy circles under my
eyes. I step back to inspect myself. On the outside, nothing significant
has changed in the last two weeks. Blonde hair, blue eyes. But inside,
everything is different.

Melvin enters the bathroom to brush his teeth. My mind runs
through scenarios. What will my coworkers say, and how will I respond? If I have sound bites at the ready, then I won't break down and
cry. I feel almost as nervous as I did on my first day on the job. Because

today, I'm starting over. It's the same job, but I'm not the same. We silently ebb and flow around each other like tides, my heart brooding with concern. I want to be the first one in, so I don't have to walk past everyone and catch their awkward glances.

Melvin pauses, holding the door open for me as we leave. "You've got this, Melly."

I tuck my arm around his waist in a side hug and stretch up on my toes for a kiss. "Thanks."

The office is still and quiet when I arrive. I flip on the lights and wander to my desk. A card and a gift basket await me. Everyone signed it, giving me their support. Tears pool in my eyes reading their sweet messages. Breaking open the chocolate, I take a couple to soothe my spirit. I'm not going to fit back into my favorite pants anytime soon. I dab my eyes with a tissue and blow my nose. *Compose yourself! You've got this!*

I log on to my computer and tackle my inbox. Margot emailed a to-do list for the conference. Most of it, I was already working on before I left. There are two more weeks for participants to register, and then we will be busy printing name badges and putting together conference materials. I make a checklist for this week.

*Send the final emails.*

*Finalize the headcount.*

*Create the programs.*

At 9:30, we have our team meeting to go over the tasks for the next few weeks. I get to the conference room early to avoid making an entrance. My coworkers filter in, greeting me with enthusiasm instead of pity. That helps. I can't take pity without the waterworks starting. Enthusiasm, I can handle.

Margot opens the meeting by welcoming me back. *'Don't start,'* I silently pray.

"We missed you and are glad you are here." Thank goodness she keeps it simple.

"Thanks. I'm glad to be back." I turn up the corners of my mouth and smooth the papers on the table.

She outlines the plans for the entrepreneur conference, pointing out staffing needs. I jump back into my assignment to head up the marketing and communications. This is my time to shine. It's the last big event before Margot decides on her successor. I quickly volunteer for the Wednesday evening women's session besides my regular responsibilities. I might as well take the shift. The more I have to keep me busy, the less time I will have to wallow in my sadness. This will get me back in the zone and give me purpose again.

"That would be great." Margot continues to get all the slots filled and moves on. "We have comp tickets available. If any of you have a potential client who might like this, you can offer them up. Then, after experiencing what a great job we do with the conference, they may be more likely to hire us for their events."

"Could I get a comp ticket for the Wednesday evening portion?" I ask. "I have a friend who is contemplating starting her own business."

"Sure. You can get it from my office later."

I plod through the week. Each day, I cling to my to-do list like a life raft. But checking things off doesn't give me that spark like it used to. Below the surface, there is a dull ache that I can't seem to shake. I make it through without breaking down, but I don't care about the details the way I used to. I used to light up designing programs and materials. But the spark is gone now. My light has dimmed. There's no magic when all the logistics line up. It's all so... pointless. Just like my favorite pair of pants that no longer fit me, I don't seem to fit back into the life I created for myself.

Evenings are the hardest of all. The silence drowns me. No baby cries to respond to. No bottles to prepare. Losing Hope stripped away my sense of purpose. Every evening, I sit alone on the couch, mindlessly binge-watching something I don't care about to fill the space in my mind, my heart, my hands, and my home. Melvin withdraws to the dining room table, playing with clay in solitude. So I end up working late more often. It makes sense to put in more hours to make up for the time I was off. Plus, if Margot sees my extra effort, I can earn the promotion.

Friday night, I come home late and find Melvin deep in his art supplies again. "There's some leftover pizza in the fridge," he says without looking up from his project.

I flop my purse onto the counter. "I had food delivered so I could eat while I worked." There are dirty dishes in the sink, so I rinse them and fill the dishwasher. Melvin is still pinching and plying a blob of grey clay. "I think I'll head up."

"Okay. I'll be up soon," he mumbles.

My feet take me on autopilot up the stairs. Hope's door is open, and I pull it shut again. Why does he keep opening the door? I want to block it out. It's like it doesn't even bother him.

I change into my pajamas and burrow under the covers until I doze off.

When I wake up Saturday morning, the sun is reaching through the curtains and brightening the room. Melvin lies beside me, his chest rising with each breath. I reach for my phone and scroll through my social media feed.

Melvin rouses and stretches, pushing himself up to sit. "Morning." His lips smack together.

"Morning." I drop my phone and turn my head toward him. "What are you up to today?"

He lifts his shoulders. "Probably do some yardwork." He stands with his back to me and stretches, his shoulder muscles filling out his t-shirt. "Might as well get started." He changes clothes and slips downstairs in silence.

I stare blankly at my screen, scanning without seeing, looking for something to distract my brain. Eventually, I climb out of bed and shuffle to the bathroom. I toss my hair into a ponytail and take a nice, warm shower. On my way downstairs to get something to eat, my body stiffens when I find Hope's bedroom door open. My jaw clenches, and I pull the door shut with a loud thud.

I march downstairs and shove a bagel into the toaster. Jerking the refrigerator door open, I pour a glass of juice. As I sip my juice, I narrow my eyes and notice Melvin outside raking leaves.

After I finish my bagel and juice, I do a quick survey of the fridge and cupboards, consult my menu for the upcoming week, make a grocery list, and head to the store. As I'm unloading the groceries, Melvin slides in the door from his yard work, sweaty and disheveled. That used to be attractive to me. But right now, I'm indifferent toward him and everything in my life.

"I'm going to go take a shower before I go to the hardware store," he says.

"Okay. I'll put this stuff away, and then I'm going to vacuum."

Melvin bounds upstairs and then pops back down. "Hey. I've been meaning to ask you—why do you keep closing the door to the nursery? The airflow is much better if we leave the door open. It helps keep the temperature even in the house."

My heart pounds in my chest. Airflow? This is about *airflow?* "I don't care about airflow, Melvin." I spin around from the groceries, my hands shaking slightly, and fold my arms across my chest, trying to protect myself from the cold, heartless words. Blinking back the stinging in my eyes, I blow out a sharp huff. "What difference does it make if we maintain a pleasant temperature? No one uses it anymore. Every time I see her room, I want to cry all over again. I can't... I can't fall apart every day."

"Oh." His voice is flat, distant. "I didn't realize. She's been gone longer than we had her." He drops his shoulders and rubs his neck. "We could change it back into an office, but I figured we should leave it so we're ready when we get another baby."

Doesn't he care? Doesn't he have this constant ache like I do that floods my heart? I presumed he loved her the same way I did, that this pain would be something we shared... but it's like I'm drowning alone. Maybe his silence is his way of trying to hold it together for both of us.

"I'm not certain I want another child." My voice cracks, but I force myself to continue. I turn back to the groceries, desperate to do something, anything, to stop this emptiness from taking over me. I pace back and forth, shoving things into kitchen cabinets with more force than necessary. Each movement is a battle against the weight pressing down on my chest. "We should have stuck with fertility treatments. Even if we stay on the adoption list, only time will tell how long it will take. What if we lost our chance? And what if we get another infant and the birth mother changes her mind, too? Have you considered that?" My breath catches, and I try to keep my voice steady, but the reality of those words tears through my heart like shards of glass, sharp and cutting.

"Melly, the odds of that happening are next to nothing." He shoves his hands in his pockets, his eyes avoiding mine.

"The odds weren't likely that the birth mother would take Hope back either, but it still happened," I snap, my voice rising against my will, my emotions spilling out like a dam breaking open. His indifference puts a distance between us, like he's standing on the shore watching me get swept away in the flood.

"You can't dwell on the negative. You need to have hope."

"I *had* Hope. She was taken away from me!" I storm out of the kitchen and grab my jacket. "I'm going for a walk."

# Chapter 34

I turn down the street, replaying everything from the moment we found out about her until we handed her over to the social worker. Our entire experience lasted less than two weeks, but my whole life revolves around those two weeks. Who was I before? Who am I now? It changed me. But I'm not sure it was a change for the better. I was happier before this happened.

A beautiful yellow and orange canopy crowns the neighborhood. But on the ground, what remains is brown, dry, and withered. The autumn trees mimic my time with Hope. Melvin and I were on fire like those brilliant colors. Being parents changed us from our everyday green into something so beautiful. But then our lives changed again, and we lost Hope like the trees lose their leaves. I'm grateful for our time with Hope. I still have a deep, unbreakable love for her. But how much happier would I be if that week had never happened? I would still be enthusiastically plugging along at my job. Melvin and I would probably be blissfully planning our next adventure. I don't understand why this happened to us.

I pause to catch my breath, resting my hands on my hips. My eyes survey the barren trees. Even with their foliage stripped from them and trampled on the ground, they stand tall and wait. Although they have lost everything, spring will awaken them, and they can start fresh with new growth. Perhaps I will get a second chance, too. Can I survive this winter season of my life, not knowing when spring will arrive for me?

I pull my jacket tighter to guard against the chill and turn toward home.

Melvin pops up from the couch when I enter the house. With his arms clasped behind his back, his brown eyes peer at me expectantly. "Are you okay?"

I shrug. "Yeah. I'm a little better now."

"Do you want to talk about it?"

The few feet between us is like a giant chasm, and I'm not ready to cross it. I'm afraid that if I try, I will fall down the ravine and hurt more than I already am. "Not right now." I pass through the living room and ascend to our bedroom. Perhaps I can lose myself in Saturday chores.

I strip the bed and pull out clean sheets. The top sheet floats down after I shake it out. In the midst of tucking, straightening, and fluffing pillows, my phone dings in my pocket. Pausing to retrieve it, I see Allie's name. She hasn't ceased reaching out.

Allie

> How are you doing? I'm praying for you. God has a plan. He is aware of you and loves you.

My heart pinches. I appreciate her kindness, but I don't have it in me to respond right now. *What* is *your plan, God?* I gaze up at the ceiling, searching my soul for answers, but there are none.

\*\*\*

The next morning, a deafening silence surrounds us as we awkwardly get ready for church. We take turns in the bathroom to avoid being too close to each other.

Melvin leans on the doorjamb of our room, straightening his bright yellow tie. "Ready to go?"

"Just about; I'll be right down." I clasp my necklace and scoot to the closet, scanning for a pair of shoes. Slipping into a shiny pair of black pumps, I scurry down the stairs, grabbing my purse on my way out the door.

Melvin turns on worship music on our drive to church. I lean back and close my eyes as the familiar strain of *It Is Well with My Soul* fills the car. I breathe in, and the tension releases with my exhale. Peace washes over me. My heart swells, and I feel like I'm floating, lifted up by the love of God. Melvin pulls into the parking lot, and I close my eyes, relishing the swelling feeling in my chest. He offers his hand as we walk in, and I accept the gesture.

Across the foyer, I catch Wendy's eye. She makes a beeline for me. She gives me a half-hug with Charlotte on one hip. I brace myself, fighting back the tightening of my throat and the tears threatening to slip from my eyes. We pull apart, and I stare down at my shiny black shoes.

"How are you doing? I'm glad you're here."

I lift my head and notice the concern in her eyes. "Thanks. We're doing okay."

"But really. How *are* you?" She places her hand on my arm.

My heart melts at her sincerity, how she can see through my polite "fines" and "how do you do's."

The corner of my mouth twitches, and I swallow. "It's been rough."

She nods. "Is there anything I can do for you?"

"Pray?" That's really all I need. All I want.

Her back straightens, a sparkle in her determined eyes. "Absolutely."

Melvin and I maneuver to our usual spot and situate ourselves while the prelude music plays. He puts his arm over my shoulder and pulls me close.

After church, I traipse upstairs to change clothes. I pause at Hope's door and run my hand along the grain of the wood. Maybe it wouldn't hurt to keep the door open. I turn the handle and crack it open, noticing the rocker next to the window. My heart clenches, remembering the moments I cradled her there in my arms. I turn back to our room, kicking off my heels into the closet. I sit on the bed, slipping into a comfortable pair of yoga pants, and notice my Bible on my nightstand. Picking it up, I venture across the hall and nestle into the chair. In automatic movements, the seat sways rhythmically back and forth, soothing my spirit. The sunlight streams in, illuminating the words on the page.

The pages open to the 113th Psalm. I read and am reminded to praise the Lord. Pausing, I bow my head. God is good. I continue reading and am surprised by verse nine: "He maketh the barren woman to keep house, and to be a joyful mother of children. Praise ye the Lord." How have I never noticed this verse before? The words pierce through my soul. Do I dare hope for such a blessing? A flutter fills my chest. It's as if He is speaking to me. I acknowledge the promise in my heart. I will be a joyful mother of children. *Children.*

Tears spill down my cheeks, and I rock back and forth, my scriptures resting in my lap. I turn to find Melvin standing in the doorway.

"Are you okay?"

I pull in my lips and nod my head. He strides across the room and kneels in front of me, grasping my face in his hands. His thumbs brush the tears from my face. "Are you ready to talk about it?"

My heart clenches, searching for the words. "I guess so. It's been hard." Sniffling, I blink away more tears. "I'm devastated about losing Hope. I'm 'Hope-less.'" The corner of my mouth quirks up.

Melvin eases onto the floor, resting his arms on his knees. "I miss her, too. But I keep leaning back to the peace I experienced the night before we brought her to Jessica's office. I knew it would be challenging, but I also knew we would get through it." He stretches his arm and rests his hand on my knee. "And I remember the impression you had about the Lord closing a door? We can't keep focusing on the closed door, Amelia. We have to search for the window."

I press my lips into a thin line. "And I keep closing the door. Literally. To Hope's room." I gesture to our surroundings.

Melvin pulls me down to sit next to him. "Sorry for opening it; I wasn't trying to cause you more pain. I didn't understand how difficult it was for you to even see her room."

As I lean into his shoulder, I allow the silence to speak for a moment. "It's okay. I'm ready to leave her door open. I think God gave me a glimpse of His window today."

"How so?" He strokes his hand over my hair.

"A sense of peace came over me today." I reach for my Bible and place it in my lap, pointing to Psalm 113:9. "This verse jumped out at me today. God can make something good out of the pain we have gone through. For now, our job is to live our lives the best we can. We need to get back to enjoying being a couple and be ready for when God brings us a child that can be part of our family permanently." I rub my hand over his leg.

"I like that." With a gentle kiss on the cheek, he pulls me in closer. "I love you so much, Amelia. I want a family, too. But if we never have one, you are enough for me."

I squeeze his thigh. "And you will always be enough for me."

Melvin jumps up and holds his hand out to me. "I want to show you something."

He pulls me to my feet and leads me downstairs. In the corner of the dining room, plastic drapes over his clay project. He carefully unwraps it and sets it on the table to reveal what he's been working on.

The sight takes my breath away, and my hand flies to my mouth. "Oh, Melvin. That's amazing. I didn't know this is what you were working on." Before me is a sculpture of a tiny cradle. Emerging from it are three butterflies precariously perched on the edges.

"Do you like it?" He searches my face for a reaction.

"It's amazing." I turn it around on its base to observe it from every angle.

"I needed to work through my grief." He stuffs his hands in his pockets. "Butterflies are a symbol of infant loss. And we lost three this year."

My heart swells with understanding. I throw my arms around his neck and bury my head in his shoulder. He folds his arms around me.

Pulling back slightly, I look him in the eyes. "I'm sorry I've been so angry lately. I thought you were ignoring me, but you were creating beauty from your sorrow."

He smiles and leans forward, kissing me firmly. My eyes flutter closed, and I lean into him, the warmth of his lips spreading through my body and quieting my ever-swirling thoughts. In this moment, there's no past, no future, just the two of us here, now. In the hush between us, our grief and love grow together. Knowing he has been hurting too makes me feel a little less alone.

# Chapter 35

The following weekend, Allie invites us to play cards. We gladly agree, and with a spring in our steps, we go over after dinner with a bag of potato chips and a package of Oreos.

"Hey, guys," Powers answers the door. "Mmm. Oreos. I hope they're double-stuffed."

"It's the only kind we buy." Melvin jabs him in the arm.

"Hi, guys." Allie pops out from the kitchen with Ruby in her arms.

"Hello, Miss Ruby!" I exclaim and hold out my arms. She leans over to me, and I balance her on my hip. "Are you going to play cards with us tonight?" She smiles at me and then holds her arms out for Allie. "You want your mama?"

"She's a mama's girl lately." Allie motions for me to follow her into the kitchen. "How have you been?"

"I've finally turned a corner."

"What made the difference?" She opens the fridge and pulls out a veggie tray.

I grab the tray from her and arrange the snacks on the kitchen counter. "Pouring out my heart to God and trying to decide what's next."

"Have you figured that out yet?" She moves Ruby to her other hip and watches me.

"Make the most of our lives as they are. Since we can't predict when we will get chosen, we need to keep moving forward one day at a time."

Allie puts her hand on my shoulder. "I admire you so much. I don't know if I could go through what you are going through with such courage and grace. You're amazing." She stretches her arm around me and gives me a side hug.

I turn and hug her back. "How are things with you? I have your ticket to the conference. Have you decided what you want to do?"

"Not yet, but I'm leaning toward virtual office work—something I can do from my computer at home while Ruby naps. A job like copywriting or social media management. I'm hoping they will have suggestions at the conference."

"You'll get plenty of inspiration there." I ponder my career. The possibility of taking over Turn of Events when Margot retires was so exciting. I felt so capable of having it all and doing it all. But one week as a mother changed me. It made me reevaluate my priorities. I still want a career, but I want to make sure it gives me the flexibility to prioritize my family.

We sit at the dining room table and play a couple of rounds of Skipbo before Ruby fusses. Allie takes her upstairs and gets her tucked in for the night. The evening continues with laughter and connection. A joy-filled outing with my best friend is the lift that my spirit needed.

\*\*\*

The days leading up to the entrepreneur conference are a whirlwind. Wednesday night attendees are streaming in for the Women's Session. I line up the registration list, nametags, and programs in neat rows on the table like soldiers. Once everyone is seated in the banquet hall and the dinner is served, I slip in to prepare for the keynote presenter while the team readies the breakout rooms.

Allie is sitting at a table of women, making small talk and meeting people. Networking 101. The keynote's message is "We Rise by Lifting Others." Too often, women tear each other down to build themselves up. The speaker is pointing out that we need each other. We need to encourage and help other women, but also allow others to help us. That's good advice. I should probably take it.

After the keynote, everyone disperses to the breakout sessions. Once I confirm everything is running smoothly, I pop into the Start Your Business seminar to check on Allie. They have a panel that includes a lawyer, an accountant, a marketing professional, and a sales coach, giving attendees an overview of the basics. Allie is furiously taking notes. She spots me, and we share a smile across the room. I'm excited to find out where this takes her.

I wander over to the Passive Income class to see how things are going. From the back of the room, I hear the presenter sharing how you can combine digital products and affiliate marketing to produce income. "Find the intersection of what you know and what you love. Then, create unique content that will help people solve a problem." A zing runs through my spine, and I pay attention. A fuzzy idea forms, but I can't quite capture it. Could I do something like that?

For the last session, everyone returns to the banquet room. They serve dessert shooters while our keynote speaker wraps everything up and motivates the women to take the "Next Right Step." The evening is a great success. Allie catches me before she leaves.

"That was great. Thank you, Amelia!" She folds me in a big hug.

"My pleasure. I'm glad you could be here. Did you get lots of good information?"

"Yes. My mind is spinning right now. I have enough to keep me busy for weeks, if not months. But as the speaker said, I need to take the next right step."

"Good for you," I say, resting my hand on her arm. "Keep me in the loop; I'll catch up with you again soon." I proceed to the end-of-evening duties, cleaning up and verifying that the venue is ready for tomorrow morning. As I work, I ponder the messages from this evening. Help others and allow them to help you. *I'll work on that.* Solve people's problems with what you know and what you love. *I know so much about event planning, and I love birthday parties.* Take the next right step. *Could I create my own business?* I thought the next thing for me was taking over for Margot and running an event planning business. It would mean so much to be recognized by her. When I consider that, it feels big and important. And yet, something is calling me to go smaller so I can balance work and family.

# Chapter 36

S omehow, Melvin and I have found our way back to our rhythm.
Work. Home. Repeat.

We cram in all the projects and errands we can on the weekends.
Today we are painting the baby's room. I tie a bandana around my
head to protect my hair from paint splatters. Stepping into the nursery,
I find Melvin crouched in the corner, taping the baseboards. We may
not know what the future holds, but we want to be more prepared
next time around.

Melvin's old t-shirt hangs down to the middle of my thighs. I lean
against the doorjamb, my hand on my hip. "Ready for action?"

"Almost. Can you open the paint can and pour it into the trays?"

I drop to one knee and grab a screwdriver. The lid pops, releasing
its suction. We chose a pale green that we can add accessories to for
either a boy or a girl. If it is a girl, I will add pink floral wall stickers
with green stems and vines. If it is a boy, we will add earth tones and a
woodland animal theme. I can picture either in my head, but I refrain
from spending money on bedding.

The smooth liquid flows into the tray. My mind goes back to the thoughts I had at the entrepreneur conference. I wanted to have it all. But now I'm not so sure.

We work together like a well-oiled machine. Melvin cuts in while I roll over the white space. He looks down at me from the ladder, dipping into the paint. "When do you find out about the promotion with Margot?"

My heart races forward, then settles into its regular beat. "I meet with her in a couple of weeks. But I'm thinking of withdrawing my name from consideration."

Melvin twists around suddenly, paint flinging from his brush and splatting on the drop cloth. "Really? How come?"

I pause mid-roll. "Ever since we had Hope, it hasn't been the same. The loss has made me reevaluate." I coat the roller with more paint and return to spreading color. "Margot mentioned to me months ago that it's hard to balance family in this industry. When you're in charge of an event, you have to be fully present. When I'm a mom, I want to be fully present with my kids, not with my job."

"Do you want to stay home? Because we can make that work."

My insides go soft. His support means the world to me. "Actually, I overheard some things at the entrepreneur conference that gave me a better idea."

"What's that?"

I take a deep breath, gathering courage to speak out loud the ideas that have been forming in my head. "I'm thinking of creating a website filled with birthday party plans. Birthday parties aren't very profitable in the event space, but I can take my knowledge and create resources for people to host their own parties."

"How would you make any money at that?"

"At the conference, they were talking about affiliate marketing and information marketing. I could create some paid products, and I can get affiliate links for all the resources I share."

Melvin climbs down from the ladder. "That sounds pretty cool. I think you should do it." He crosses the room, kisses my cheek, and dabs my nose with his paintbrush.

\*\*\*

Clutching my notebook to my chest, I knock on Margot's office door for my end-of-year review. She invites me in, and I shut the door behind me with a click.

"Have a seat." Margot waves to the chair across from her desk. "It's been quite a year, hasn't it?"

I nod my head in agreement. "You can say that again."

"How are you adjusting back to work after losing the baby?"

Dropping my shoulders, I breathe a deep sigh. "It's been hard to feel normal again." I search her face for validation. "How do you think I've been doing?"

"Well, that's why we're here, isn't it? Let's go back through the entire year and each area of focus."

"Sounds good."

"Way back in January was the Restaurant Convention. You were in charge of content and program management. How do you feel it went?"

I sit up straighter in my chair with a smile. "That one had good food! It went well. I enjoyed interacting with Chef Lee and coordinating all the classes and speakers."

"I agree. We received a lot of compliments about that event." She flips through her notes. "For the Leadership Summit, your responsibility was operations and logistics. That event had a few snafus."

I pull my hand through my hair and rest it on the back of my head, looking up at the ceiling. "You're right. We had some hiccups. There was an abrasive vendor. The caterer didn't deliver all the lunches, and we had a spelling error on the programs."

"Most important is what you learned from those mistakes."

"First, I need to screen the vendors better and have a written policy about their interaction with guests. When the caterers deliver food, inventory it, and verify that we got what we ordered. And as far as the program goes—proofread, proofread, proofread."

"Those are all wonderful insights. If you were the operations coordinator, you shouldn't have been in charge of the programs. That job belongs to the marketing department. How did it end up as your responsibility?"

Leaning forward in my chair, I explain. "I volunteered. It's easy for me, and I wanted to make sure it was done right."

"And yet, it wasn't done right, was it?"

I turn my head from side to side. "No."

"Amelia, you are capable. It can be tempting to take on too much. That's when problems occur. It's one thing to help a member of the team. It's another to overstep. I think you overstepped in this situation."

"Understood."

"You were in charge of marketing and communications for the Entrepreneur Conference. I know that was right after you lost the baby. How did that go?"

I cock my head to the side. "The timing wasn't ideal, but the programs turned out better."

"They did." She leans her arms on the desk in front of her. "You suffered a major personal loss. How are you doing?"

I look down at my shoes, gathering my courage. "It changed me. That's for sure." Lifting my head, my heart thuds inside my chest. "It caused me to reevaluate some things. I want to remove my name from consideration as your successor."

"What led to this decision?" She speaks without judgment, but only with genuine concern.

"After you found out we were planning on adopting, you warned me that it's hard to balance a family within the industry." I cross my arms across my abdomen, holding myself together. "Having a child for only one week taught me how fleeting things can be. I don't want to regret a moment of motherhood whenever it comes. New seeds have taken root in my heart, guiding me to a different purpose."

"I'd love to hear about it if you're willing to share."

The words tumble out of my mouth, excitement building, sharing my vision for an online resource for parties.

"That's a great pivot, Amelia. Does that mean you're leaving us soon?"

I shake my head. "No. Not yet. I want to stick with you if you'll have me. It will be a while before I'm ready to branch out."

"I'm glad to hear it."

As I leave Margot's office, relief washes over me. She believes in me. I still have my job. But my future holds a new sense of promise.

# Chapter 37

We made the trip to Ohio for Christmas, and arrive on the afternoon of the twenty-third at Melvin's parents' house. We shuffle in, dragging our suitcases. Brenda greets us with awkward hugs. Melvin and Marcus unload the presents from the car and bring them in while I visit with Brenda and Elise in the kitchen.

"How was the drive?" Brenda asks.

"Good. There was traffic in Chicago, but there's always traffic in the Windy City. Melvin took that leg of the trip."

"I hate driving through that area." Brenda puts her hands on her hips. "I can't believe people deal with that every day."

"How are the newlyweds?" I ask Elise.

"Life is good. Working and saving for a house." She waves her arm and takes a sip from her water glass.

"If you girls want to set the table, I'll finish getting dinner ready," Brenda says. Elise and I set the table for six. Her husband, Paul, will be over soon.

"It smells delicious," I say to Brenda, breathing in the tangy sweetness paired with a touch of garlic in the air. "Is there anything else I can do?"

"Sit down and relax. I'm making cranberry chicken and garlic mashed potatoes."

In the living room, I help Melvin arrange the gifts under the tree. He places his hands on my round hips and gives me a peck on the cheek. "Brace yourself—ready for another Greathouse Christmas?"

"We'll see." I inhale the scent of the food cooking in the kitchen. "I remember last Christmas when we announced our short-lived pregnancy. A lot has happened since then." I drop my head in sadness, reflecting on all we have lost. Three babies in one year. I wonder how Hope's first Christmas will be. Are they managing okay? I hope the grandparents are helping. She needs a lot of support. Most of all, I hope she is well and happy.

"A lot *has* happened in the last year." He rests his hands on my shoulders and pulls me back to fully take me in. "And we have a lot of good things to anticipate. It's possible that next Christmas we'll have a baby to celebrate with. The next year is bound to have amazing surprises in store for us."

"I can get on board with that." I push onto my tiptoes and kiss him.

"Ooh! Watch out, lovebirds! There isn't even any mistletoe in here," Elise exclaims. Paul sneaks in behind her, sweeps her off her feet, dipping her into a kiss and embrace.

"I guess you don't need mistletoe, either." I laugh, and we wander to the dining room for dinner. After dinner, we nibble on Christmas cookies in the living room while Brenda and Marcus go to the airport to pick up Celeste and Tim.

"We haven't seen each other since the wedding. You've been through a lot this fall. How are you guys doing? It must have been hard," Elise inquires.

I lean into Melvin, his arm stretched across the back of the couch. "It was. But things are getting better."

We answer the same questions that have been posed hundreds of times by people who care. Sometimes, it's as if I'm a Hollywood star on tour. Same questions, different talk show. When Brenda and Marcus return with Celeste and Tim, the house fills with hugs and exuberant greetings. Tim takes the bags to their room while I help Celeste and Elise set the gifts under the tree. Afterward, the conversation continues until exhaustion demands we retreat for the night.

No one sets their alarm the next morning, and the smell of sausage wafts up the stairs, creeps under the door, and gradually rouses us from our slumber. Two by two, couples groggily emerge and make their way downstairs in their jammies. Today's spread includes pumpkin pancakes, sausage, hash browns, and fried cinnamon apples. We indulge in the assortment of flavors, allowing our gaze to settle on the winter wonderland outside the sliding glass window. The snowstorm has started in earnest, and it is beautiful, white, and fluffy. Although we are all adults now, with the fresh snow and being on vacation, it's the perfect time to play. Sledding and ice skating are a must today. Brenda has a big Christmas Eve meal planned, but until then, we have the day to ourselves.

We take turns with the bathrooms and don layers of warm winter clothing to prepare for stepping out into the snow-covered world. Celeste, Elise, and I wrangle our sock-laden feet into ice skates and side-step down the hill to the pond. A loud "Whoop!" interrupts my concentration. I turn to see Paul barreling down the hill on a sled, with Melvin and Tim not far behind.

I glide across the ice, my skates cutting tracks on the glassy surface. The cool air fills my lungs and blows out in fluffy white clouds. Celeste and Elise flank me on either side, and the three of us link arms as we make a lap. Melvin disappears and reappears with his camera, capturing the scene as if we are figurines encased in a snow globe.

Warmed from the exercise, I unzip my coat. Celeste attempts a twirl and lands with a thud. Unable to stop in time, I fall in a heap on top of her, and Elise swerves around us, giggling.

She reaches out to us. "Need some help?" Her eyes sparkle, and she smiles down at us.

Celeste gives me a subtle wink. "Sure!" She grabs Elise's hand and gives a sudden tug, pulling her down with us.

I rub my palms together, trying to take the chill off my tingling fingers.

"What do you say we head inside? My toes are freezing." Elise taps the tips of her skates together.

We skate to the edge and tiptoe up the hill when there is a thud behind us. The guys let out a war cry, and suddenly, pelt us with snowballs. Cold powder slides down my back, and I hightail it to the door. I scoop up a handful of snow just as Melvin catches up to me, and I smash it against his face.

He tips his head forward and shakes the frozen powder from his eyes, nose, and mouth. "I deserved that." His eyes twinkle with delight.

We all pile into the house and peel off our winter gear. The fire crackles in the fireplace, and we draw closer, rubbing our hands together. Brenda hands out hot cocoa. Warmth seeps back into our fingers and toes, steaming mugs cradled in our hands. Thoroughly thawed, we venture into the kitchen.

Brenda stands at attention, a wooden spoon in her hand. She doles out assignments like a military taskmaster, and Celeste, Elise, and I eagerly enlist.

"Elise, I need you to whip up the topping for the Jell-O salad." She points her spoon at me. "Amelia, cheesy potatoes." She turns to Celeste. "And you can set the table and mix up the punch—China's in the hutch."

"Yes, chef!" We reply in unison before bursting into giggles.

"Oh, stop it, you girls!" She swats her hand in our direction.

We move with precision. The whir of the mixer in Elise's confident hands drowns out the clink of dishes in the dining room. The rhythm of measuring, dumping, and stirring leaves me alone with my thoughts. Despite the losses this year, celebrating the birth of a babe in Bethlehem is cause for joy. Brenda slides the ham into the oven with a practiced motion.

Outside, the crunch of boots on snow and the scrape of shovels echo as the men attack the icy driveway—loud shouts, then bursts of laughter, like boys let loose.

Soon, the air is thick with both sweet and savory scents. Celeste ladles out punch. We perch on stools, cups in our hands, fizz spritzing our faces. My breath slows. The house fills with the quiet anticipation that always comes before a holiday celebration.

# Chapter 38

We all sit down for Christmas Eve dinner, the glow of candles giving warmth to the room. Breathing in the salty scent of the ham, my mouth waters. Marcus offers a blessing on the food, and I lift my goblet of Christmas punch to my lips.

Brenda clears her throat. "I have an announcement to make." Everyone turns their attention to her. She sits tall in her chair and, with a huge smile, spreads her arms and announces, "I'm giving away the family jewels!"

I inhale my bubbly punch, and it fizzes up my nose. Celeste screeches and howls with laughter. Elise coughs and sputters, trying not to expel her mouthful of mashed potatoes. Paul and Tim fixate on their plates.

Melvin's eyes go wide. "Mom!"

Marcus and Brenda glance at each other in confusion.

"What? What's so funny? Is this one of those inside jokes you kids leave me out of?" Brenda asks, focusing on Marcus.

"Don't ask me. I don't know what's going on here," Marcus says, holding up his arms.

None of us can speak because we are all in different fits of laughter. Tears stream down my face. Paul pats Elise on the back. Celeste is hyperventilating. The guys hold their heads in their hands and shake them back and forth softly without making eye contact with Brenda.

"Will someone please tell me what's going on?" Brenda asks after several minutes of howling laughter. "I have lots of diamond earrings and nice jewelry I want to share with you girls. They're family treasures."

Finally, Celeste takes a settling breath, wipes her eyes, and explains the term to her.

Brenda gasps. "What? Why would they call it that? That's not what I was referring to. I'm talking about actual jewelry from my jewelry box that I'm not using anymore."

Marcus shifts uncomfortably in his seat, staring down, along with the other men at the table. He clears his throat. "Well, let's never mind about that. Pass the food. It's getting cold."

We dish up food and pass it around the table. Everyone is silent, except for soft chuckles we all try to hold back, Brenda's announcement replaying in our minds. We gradually fall into small talk about jobs and hobbies as we stuff ourselves with dinner. Once we clear the table and do the dishes, we gather around the fireplace. Marcus pulls out the Bible, flipping through the thin pages to Luke 2. Mary and Joseph's journey to parenthood was not what they had planned. But God had bigger plans for them. I try to believe in God's plan for us as parents, too.

Brenda serves chocolate peppermint pie. I bite into the sweet, creamy slice, Christmas carols playing in the background.

***

In the morning, the smell of cinnamon fills my nose. I roll over and snuggle up to Melvin.

"Merry Christmas."

"Merry Christmas, Amelia."

Suddenly, a retching sound comes from the bathroom that shares a wall with our room. We gawk at each other.

"Someone has a stomach bug," Melvin whispers. "If that spreads, this could be a miserable holiday."

"Either that or someone has morning sickness. One of your sisters might be pregnant."

"Nah. Elise and Paul are still newlyweds. And I don't think Celeste and Tim are ready for that. Besides, I'm the oldest. I always figured we would be first, like I have been with everything else in life."

"It's not like we haven't tried. Your sisters won't wait for you if the maternal instinct kicks in. When they're ready, they'll start their family regardless of your being the oldest."

"I suppose you're right. We'll see."

Like the day before, we progress downstairs in our jammies and gather around the table to begin our day. Fresh cinnamon rolls, sausage links, and orange juice extend across the table. We say grace and dig in.

"After Mom's announcement last night, I would like to make an announcement this morning," Celeste ventures. I raise my eyebrows at Melvin.

"Wait. I have an announcement to make, too," interrupts Elise. "But you go first."

Celeste takes Tim's hand and, with a huge smile, says, "We're pregnant!"

"What?" Brenda exclaims, rushing to Celeste for a hug. "I can't believe this. I'm going to be a grandma! This is fantastic! Wait until I tell Ruth and Charisse. When are you due?"

Melvin clasps my hand under the table and presses gently. My heart clenches for a moment, wishing it were us. I knew this could happen eventually. Warmth radiates through my chest. Paul and Celeste will be great parents. And Melvin and I get to be an uncle and auntie. I smile at the image. I'm truly happy for them.

"June. I'm about three months along. But we heard the heartbeat a couple of weeks ago, and things are good so far," says Celeste, catching Tim's eyes with a soft smile filled with hope for their future child. Brenda settles in her seat, absolutely beaming.

"Congratulations, guys. That's awesome," I say. As I cut into a sausage link, I notice Elise glancing at Paul. "Elise, what's your announcement?"

Elise takes a deep breath and locks eyes with Paul. "Well... We're expecting, too."

"You're kidding me?" Brenda exclaims and almost knocks the table over attempting to get to Elise. "Two grandbabies in one year? This is amazing! When are you due?"

"Early July. We weren't planning on starting our family yet, but I guess God has other plans." Elise shrugs.

Even though Melvin and I have moved on to adoption, part of me still wishes for a miracle. I mean, it could happen, right? And Elise and Paul getting pregnant before their first anniversary? Without even trying? Why is having a family easy for some people but so challenging for others? Even among siblings.

Celeste turns to Melvin and me. "We know this has been a frustrating journey for the two of you. We so wish you were pregnant with us."

Elise nods. "We love you both and hope this isn't too hard for you."

"Thanks," I say, smoothing my napkin on my lap. "We're happy for you. It's been a rough couple of years for us, but we have peace about our decision to adopt." I smile at Melvin. "It's like Elise said, 'God has other plans for us.' Speaking of that, Melvin and I would like to ask a favor of you."

"Of course," Brenda volunteers.

"We have realized we need help to get matched with a birth mother. They say matches often happen through mutual connections. We set up a website and social media pages for our adoption. Melvin designed adoption cards with our picture and a QR code to lead to our profile online. Can we give you each some cards so you can share and spread the word?"

"We would love to." Elise stretches over and touches my arm.

"We are also planning a social media blast in January. We will post graphics and links. If you could all share them, it would help."

"Absolutely. This is such a great idea. Thanks for letting us be a part of it." Celeste smiles from across the table.

Melvin rubs his hand along my back. "Thank you for your support. It means the world to us." He pauses and smirks. "And which one of you did we hear puking in the bathroom this morning?"

"Morning sickness got the best of me," Elise confesses.

"Oh, you poor dear," Brenda begins. "We should have ginger ale out in the garage. Do you want me to get you some? How about you, Celeste? Are you sick too? Goodness, I remember when I was pregnant with you kids. Sometimes, the slightest smell would set me off. I hope this breakfast isn't bothering you."

"I'm okay now, Mom. It usually hits me first thing in the morning, and if I can get past that, I'm fine for the day," says Elise.

"I was sick at first, but once I hit three months, things got better," Celeste shares.

We finish breakfast and clean up the table. As the family gets ready to open presents, Melvin pulls me aside privately while all the chaos is going on in the other room.

"Are you doing okay?" he asks.

"Yeah." I encircle my arms around him. "I'm super excited to have some nieces or nephews on your side of the family. It's going to be fun playing Auntie. And hopefully with their help in spreading the word, we can be parents, too. God has a plan for us."

"I agree. I'm ready to be a dad, but I'm willing to wait on the Lord. Heck, we could still be parents before either of them. Hope came quickly to us."

"So true. It's her first Christmas today. I hope it's a good one for her and her family."

"I hope so, too. God is watching over her." He hugs me and plants a kiss on my forehead. "Wait right here a minute. I have something for you.

He darts back to the bedroom and returns with a shoebox wrapped in Christmas paper, holding it out to me. Pushing aside Styrofoam peanuts, I gasp at the sight. Carefully, I pull out the finished sculpture that Melvin was working on. He painted it in bright, whimsical colors and fired it to a glossy sheen. Three butterflies perch on the edge of the empty cradle, each one unique in color and design.

I trace the curve of the cradle with my finger. "This is beautiful, Melvin, I love it!"

"I thought we could put it on the mantle so our three butterflies will always be in our sight."

Hooking my arms around his waist, I place my head on his chest. "That's perfect. We'll never forget them."

# Chapter 39

January is a never-ending pattern of snowfall, freezing temperatures, bundling up, and going back and forth to work. Day after day of leaving in the dark and coming home in the dark. It is truly the doldrums of winter. Cloudy days mimic my cloudy heart. Waiting is like that. Everything moves slowly and repetitively.

We sent out a hundred and fifty holiday greetings on December thirty-first with an adoption card tucked in each one. Today is the day we've set to flood the internet with our adoption dreams—January eleventh. My mouse hovers over the share button. All I have to do is push it, and the post will be live. My heart flutters. There is no turning back after this. It will all be out in the open. I click, shut my eyes and breathe in. Then I walk away.

My phone pings all day long with notifications of my posts being shared and commented on.

*This is so exciting!*

*You guys will be great parents!*

*I hope it goes smoothly for you!*

Each new comment lifts my heart higher until I feel like a bird soaring high above the trees. I feel free with my heartache out in the open. It's the opposite of what I expected. I carefully guarded my struggles, shoving them down inside of me to deal with alone. Yet all around me was a community ready and willing to support and encourage me.

***

Our lives continue in a familiar pattern. We keep getting updates on the family group chat about Celeste and Elise's pregnancies. Their babies are growing, and so are their tummies. My heart is happy for them and still disappointed that motherhood won't come in the traditional way for me. I picked up some baby gifts. While I can't say when a birth mother will choose us, I'm counting down the days to my new auntie responsibilities.

Waiting is the hardest part of anything. We waited so long to get pregnant and then felt disappointed by our loss. We felt confident about adoption, but that failed us once already. It's hard to have faith that sharing our private struggles publicly will be the answer to our prayers. And in the quiet moments of waiting, we vacillate between trust and doubt.

Two months after our social media announcement, when the clouds of uncertainty are growing darker, a glimmer of possibility shines light in our lives. After seeing our post shared online, a birth mother wants to interview us. My heart soars at the possibility, but then I remind myself it's only a conversation. I push my emotions into a safe corner of my heart and try to approach the meeting objectively.

On the evening of the video call, we inhale our dinner. Melvin paces back and forth, clearing the table. I busy myself wiping down the counters. When there is nothing left to clean, I rub my hands down my thighs. "Should we set up the computer?"

Melvin busies himself at the dining room table, flipping open the laptop and checking connections. He perches on the edge of his chair, his leg quivering. I scoot into the seat next to him, rubbing my hands together. There is so much riding on this meeting. I don't know how many other couples she is talking to, but our interaction with her tonight could make or break our opportunity to adopt her child. It's like I'm a finalist in the Miss America pageant. I'm dressed well. My makeup and hair are on point. I advanced from the earlier rounds, but now it's time to step out on the stage for the interview portion of the competition. I can either make a fool out of myself or win the heart of the judge—the birth mother.

My heart skips a beat as we join the call. A beautiful blonde-haired, blue-eyed young woman peers at us through the screen, her mother close beside her. We navigate through awkward introductions and nervous chitchat. Zoe glances down at a piece of paper and then back at the screen. "I wanted to ask you guys a few questions."

My stomach flutters. The interview questions. A spotlight is shining on us, exposing all our flaws. I push down my nerves and spread a broad smile across my face. I lean on Melvin for a boost of confidence. We can do this together. "We would be happy to tell you anything you want to know."

"First, tell me about how you guys met and how long you've been married." She takes a pen and makes a mark on her paper. Ooh, I like this girl already. She's checking off her list. We could be fast friends.

"Of course. It's a funny story." I gaze at Melvin, and we smile. "We were both attending a party in college. My friend Allie called out,

'Hey, Mel!' and we both turned to her." I chuckle, pointing at myself. "I'm Amelia—some people call me Mel." Gesturing toward Melvin, he finishes our story.

"And I'm Melvin, so I also go by Mel. That was our introduction, and then we dated a while and got engaged. We've been married six years now."

After responding to her inquiries, we ask her to share her story. She glances down at her lap and draws in a deep breath, then focuses on us through the computer screen. "My parents warned of the dangers of premarital sex growing up. I heard it from my church youth leaders, too. But I knew in my heart we would get married one day, so I made an exception." Her shoulders sag under the weight of her predicament.

"He went off to college. And then I was late." She pulls her lips together in a thin line, and her mom rubs her back. "When I told him, he freaked out. He said he wasn't ready to be a dad. He couldn't afford to raise a family. And he wasn't about to drop out of college. He actually asked if I had been cheating on him after he left because he knew we used protection." A tear trickles down her cheek, and she quickly wipes it away.

"So it was all up to me. There was no way I could abort this child. I was so scared to tell my parents, but when I did, they said they would help me if I wanted to keep it. When I really prayed about what was best for the baby, I knew I wanted it to grow up like I did—with two parents who loved it."

I want to reach through the screen and give her a big hug. "Thanks for sharing your story. I'm sorry for everything you are going through. You're a courageous young woman."

Before the call ends, we learn she had enough credits to graduate after the fall semester, so now she's working part time at Target. Next fall, she plans to go to college. When we shut the laptop, Melvin and

I are hopeful. After the initial awkwardness, we connected with her. Conversation flowed between us, and we felt like we had known each other for much longer than an hour. We put it in God's hands and try to trust.

A week after our call, Jessica contacts us to say that Zoe and her parents want to meet with us in person. We agree to exchange contact information and plan to meet Friday night at a restaurant in Minneapolis. Melvin and I arrive a few minutes early and secure a table.

"Ready to meet them?" I ask.

"Yeah. I liked her when we met on the call last week. She's such a mature, faithful girl who is trying to make the best of a tricky situation."

"I thought so, too. I hope this goes well." Zoe and her parents enter the restaurant, and I wave at them to join us. Her black leggings and oversized sweatshirt camouflage the roundness of her midsection. Zoe tucks her long blonde hair behind her ear and nods at me. She leads her parents to the back corner of the restaurant, twisting and turning strategically through the maze of tables and chairs, trying to fit her growing shape between them.

Her mom glides through the space in a pair of dark-wash fitted jeans. Her terracotta blouse complements her warm blonde hair. A rich olive-green wrap drapes artfully around her shoulders. Just behind her mom, her dad's head bobs a few inches above. As they approach, I can see specks of grey appearing in the sideburns of his short, dark-brown hair. His light blue golf shirt and blue athletic pants make him look like he came straight from playing a round. Zoe introduces her parents, Nicole and Tom, and they slide into the booth while we peruse the menu.

"We've never eaten here before. What's good?" I ask, trying to break the ice.

"You can't go wrong with their burgers. They also have great wall-eye bites," Tom says.

I tip my head toward Zoe. "How's work going?" We are all here because of the baby, but Zoe isn't a commodity. I figure it's best to talk about her, not her pregnancy.

"Not bad. I love getting dressed in my red shirt and khaki pants," Zoe proclaims with sarcasm. "I'm just glad to be done with high school. It's the pits. Especially when you're pregnant." She fiddles with her silverware.

"How are you feeling?" I ask.

"Much better now that the morning sickness has worn off. I'm packing on the pounds, growing out of my clothes, and getting more and more uncomfortable every day." She waves her hand in the air and chuckles.

The server brings us water and takes our order. In his absence, we survey each other, grasping for things to say.

Nicole breaks the awkwardness. "Tell us more about the two of you. We would love to hear your story."

"We aren't all that exciting." I smile over at Melvin. "We met in college. Got married while Melvin was working on his MFA. He's a curator at an art museum. I work as an event planner. We tried to have kids. When things didn't work, we went to specialists and tried fertility treatments. That was a series of further disappointments." I roll my eyes toward the ceiling. "Ultimately, we felt led by God to adopt."

"It sounds like it's been a difficult journey." Nicole smiles and rubs Zoe's arm. "A difficult journey for all of us."

"I'd love to learn more about your family."

"Tom and I have been married for twenty-five years. We have three kids. Iris is a sophomore in college. Then Zoe. Our youngest, Liam, is a freshman in high school."

"What do you do for work?" Melvin directs his question to Tom.

"I'm a mechanical engineer, but Nicole's the one with the impressive resume. She's a professional speaker, jet-setting around doing keynotes all over the country."

"That's amazing." I turn my attention back to Zoe. "What about your college plans? Do you have a major picked out?"

"I'm considering art. But everyone says I'll end up being a starving artist. So, I'm torn."

"Art gets a poor reputation. Believe me. My dad had that reaction when I told him I wanted to major in art." Melvin shifts in his seat. "But there are ways to make a career out of your love for art. What medium are you interested in?"

She hesitates, glancing over at her parents. "I love to paint."

"My emphasis was photography, but I had to take my share of painting classes. I'd love to see some of your work."

Zoe brightens as she opens her phone, scrolling through pictures. Soon, they are passing it back and forth, discussing techniques and favorite artists.

The server brings our food. I dip a walleye bite in tartar sauce and crunch into the crisp coating.

"When are you due?" I take a sip of water.

"May. I'm hoping she arrives on time so I can walk with my class at graduation in June." Zoe grabs the bottle of ketchup and shakes it up.

"It's a girl?" I ask.

"Yeah. I wasn't sure if I wanted to find out since I'm giving her up for adoption. I wondered if that might make it more challenging. But I'm glad I did. I love knowing she's a girl and imagining her future," Zoe says.

"Do you think you might change your mind? Since you have that attachment to her already, won't it be hard?" I can't go through that again. I want to confirm how committed they are to adoption.

"It won't be easy, but I'm not ready to raise a child. My aunt is a single mother, and it's been rough for my cousins their whole lives. I don't want that for my baby."

"What's your opinion of her decision?" I turn to Tom and Nicole. They are giving up a grandchild, too.

"It's been a stressful few months for all of us. We have given this a lot of prayer, and God has led us to adoption." Nicole pauses, her spoon hovering over her bowl of soup. "We want what's best for Zoe and her baby. Zoe ultimately decided, but we support her one hundred percent."

Zoe glances down and swirls her French fry in ketchup. "I want my baby to have the best possible start to her life. And I can't give her that."

"I admire your faith and courage. This must be an especially daunting decision, and I love the way you are seeking God's will to make the best out of an agonizing situation," I say.

Nicole places her arm around Zoe. "Zoe is hoping for an open adoption. Have you considered that?" Nicole turns to us.

"An open adoption is great for everyone involved," Melvin says, wiping his mouth with a napkin. "So many adopted people feel like a part of them is missing all their lives. Being open and honest from the start seems like it would help the child understand their identity." We've discussed this at length, and it's what we have been hoping for, too. "What level of involvement do you picture for yourselves after you put your baby up for adoption?"

Tom studies Zoe. "We don't want to intrude on the adoptive family, but we would like her to be acquainted with us. We hope to get together from time to time and stay in communication."

"I want to watch her grow up and be able to send birthday cards and stuff like that," Zoe shrugs.

I imagine raising a child surrounded by a village of adoptive and birth families. While I want that for my baby, the possessive three-year-old part of me is screaming, *"Mine!"* After losing Hope, I fear the birth family will change their minds.

Dinner ends, and we split the bill. In the parking lot, we part ways and wish them the best. I wonder what the proper protocol is here. I'd love to volunteer to stay in touch, but that would probably cross a boundary. In this situation, the ball is in their court. We will have to wait and let them make the next move.

On the way home, we share our hopes and fears.

"I really like them. We formed a bond," I say.

"Me too. It was great meeting them in person."

"Is it dumb of me to get my hopes up? We've had two meetings with them now, and we hit it off. It's not a competition, but I hope they choose us."

"I get it. It seems like a good match. But we can't count on it. It's their decision." He glances my way and turns his eyes back to the road.

"I kind of wanted to ask how many adoptive parents they've been talking to. Are we in the top five or ten? But I figured that wasn't appropriate to ask. I'll see if Jessica can tell us."

*Ding.* I glance down at my phone.

I read the text from Zoe aloud to Melvin.

Zoe

> Thanks for meeting us for dinner. You guys are awesome. We had such fun tonight!

"That's a good sign. What should I say back?"

"Say we had fun, too. But respect their boundaries. Even though we have their numbers, it doesn't mean we should text them. We need to wait and go through the proper channels." Melvin steers the car down the dark highway toward home.

"You're right. I'll reply and then leave them alone unless they contact me."

# Chapter 40

It's a rare warm Saturday in March for Minnesota, and it's perfect for some spring cleaning. Hope's closet creaks as I open it. She's been gone for six months, and it has turned into a stashing place for things that don't have a home.

We pull out Melvin's photography portfolio and flip through the prints.

"We should create a gallery wall in the hallway," I suggest. "Pick your favorites and I'll get them framed."

A smile tugs at his lips. "Thanks." He sets a few against the wall for me. Melvin digs deeper into the depths of the disarray and pulls out my desk treadmill. "Do you still want this?"

My failed fitness aspirations haunt my mind. "Heaven knows I could stand to put in some time on that thing, but if I haven't used it in the past year, I'm probably not going to." Pulling down a bin from the top shelf, I discover the shirt Melvin gave me. 'Not a Food Baby.' I hold it up and show Melvin.

"I won't be wearing this. Should we give it to one of your sisters?"

"That would be funny. But then we would need to get another one. I can't show any favoritism."

"True. Who else is expecting?" I ask.

"Zoe is."

"We should probably donate it. We aren't exchanging gifts yet." I toss the shirt onto a pile in the corner of the room. We continue sorting, keeping the few baby supplies we have. I tuck everything neatly into the dresser, and we call it a day.

***

Sunday at church, I run into Wendy, or rather, I run into Wendy's belly. She's rounder than I remember. Could she be pregnant again? After four kids, I don't expect her to be as thin as a model, but this is more than putting on some pounds.

"Hey, Wendy! What's new?" I direct my gaze at her eyes, willing myself not to stare at her tummy.

She bites her bottom lip, hesitating. "I've been meaning to tell you...but I wasn't sure how to say it." She pulls in a deep breath. "I'm pregnant." She plasters a fake smile on her face, her eyes wide.

I swallow and fumble for an appropriate response. "Wow... Congratulations!" I allow my eyes to fully take in her midsection, a knot forming in my own. Charlotte is about a year old.

"Honestly, I was sure I was done. This is a complete surprise." She waves her hands over her stomach. "I bet this is hard for you. We have more than enough, and you've been waiting for so long. I hope God answers your prayers soon." She grips my arm, kindness filling her eyes.

I force out a polite chuckle. "That's quite a surprise. You're going to have your hands full. We can get your baby supplies back to you. I guess you'll need it before we do."

"I hope it happens soon for you. You and Melvin will be great parents. I mean, you're so organized."

"Thanks. I appreciate that. Reach out if you need anything." I grasp her hand and turn in retreat, trying to locate Melvin. Quickly grabbing his arm, I steer him toward the parking lot, Wendy's news swirling inside me.

"I found someone to give the 'Not a Food Baby' shirt to," I blurt out as Melvin starts the car.

"Oh yeah? Who's pregnant?"

"Wendy." I lean forward, watching for his response.

"Again?" He raises his eyebrows and tips his head.

"Yeah. She said it's a surprise. If there's something in their water, I want a drink." I slump back in my seat.

Melvin rubs his hand on my thigh. "Good things come to those who wait, Melly. It'll be our turn soon."

***

I read my email while I stir-fry vegetables on the stove. Multi-tasking at its best.

One message grabs my attention and sends my heart racing. I drop the wooden spoon and glance over my shoulder for Melvin. "Mel! There's an email from Jessica! She says Zoe has chosen us!"

Melvin wraps his arms around my stomach, reading the email over my shoulder. He kisses my neck and says, "Congratulations, Mommy!"

"She says the next steps are to meet with them and their social worker to talk through their birth and adoption plan. They want to get together soon. Oh, hon. I'm so excited!" My chest expands with gratitude. Could it really be possible? Our journey to becoming parents is finally going to be achieved?

Melvin spins me around to face him, his brown eyes sparkling. "Alexa. Play Big Band music." As "In the Mood" by Glenn Miller plays, he clasps my hand, intertwining our fingers. I float as he bounces and swings me around the kitchen. A spark of connection pulls us together. The kitchen is alive with energy, and I giggle with delight. I spin under his arm. The smell of something burning reaches my nose. The stir-fry! I abandon our dance party and rescue the vegetables before it's too late.

Melvin comes up behind me, placing his hands on my hips and swaying to the music. "I knew God would answer our prayers. And I had a good feeling about Zoe."

"Me too. We should give her the 'Not a Food Baby' t-shirt." I twist and clasp my hands around his neck, pulling him into a kiss.

Melvin chuckles. "I think that's perfect."

Seated at the table with our hands joined, Melvin offers a prayer before we eat. "Our Father in Heaven, we come to Thee in gratitude for bringing Zoe into our lives. We thank you for her courageous decision. Please bless her and the baby with health. Give her an extra measure of peace with her decision. And help us trust that all will work out as planned. Thank you for the food. We acknowledge Thy hand in all things. In the name of Jesus Christ, amen."

"Amen." I open my eyes and reach for a napkin to wipe away my tears, only to see Melvin doing the same.

After dinner, we load the dishwasher. "Let's celebrate our good news, Amelia. I'll pop the popcorn. You go pick a movie."

"Sounds good to me." I give him a quick smooch before I stride toward the living room.

Ten minutes later, we snuggle on the couch under a blanket with a bowl of popcorn balancing on our legs. I crunch into the buttery, salty goodness, my heart wanting to pop out of my chest.

*** 

A couple of weeks later, we meet Zoe and Nicole at their social worker's office to talk through their expectations and desires. This is completely different from the last time. With Hope, we had no warning and no communication with the birth mom. We got the call after she was already born. This time, we can plan and prepare.

With Zoe and Nicole across the conference table and Melvin by my side, my heart is pounding like a warrior's drum call. I fiddle with my wedding ring under the table, trying not to view this as a high-stakes negotiation.

Zoe brushes her blonde hair over her shoulder. "My mom will be in the delivery room, but we want you to be at the hospital so you can meet her soon after she's born."

"We would love that." I smile and nod at Melvin.

"We want to have the rest of the hospital stay to ourselves. Then, you can pick her up from the hospital and take her home."

My stomach flips at Zoe's announcement. What if she changes her mind in those few short days? She will have time to bond with the baby and might not want to give her away.

Nicole places her arm around Zoe. "Tom and I want to give Zoe and the baby lots of love. We want her to have time to say her goodbyes and feel at peace with her decision."

Melvin rests his hand on my leg and turns to them. "We respect that. We want you to know we are all in on this adoption, and we hope you are, too. You might not know, but last fall, we adopted a baby girl. A week later, the birth mom changed her mind. It devastated us. I'm not sure we could go through that again."

Nicole's eyes widen, and she covers her mouth with her hand. "I'm so sorry. That must have been awful."

I swallow. "It really was."

Zoe shakes her head. "I don't want to be a mom right now. But I want to be involved in her life. I'd like to stay connected on social media, and I'd love to see her in person once in a while."

My heart settles a little. They seem committed to the adoption. But plans can change.

On our way out, I hand Zoe a gift bag. "Here's something for you. You mentioned you were growing out of all your clothes, so I thought you might like this."

She peeks in the bag and pulls out the t-shirt and holds it up. "Oh, my gosh! This is hilarious. I love it! Thank you!" She gives me a big hug.

"We have something for you, too." Nicole goes to their car and grabs an envelope. We follow her, and she hands it to us. "Open it."

I open the envelope to discover ultrasound pictures. My heart swells with joy, and there is an instant connection to the grainy images. "Oh... This is wonderful."

"Her first pictures," Zoe beams. They point out foggy blobs and explain what the pictures are. Arms, legs, and her profile come into focus like one of those optical illusion pictures.

"We will treasure these. Thank you." I press them to my chest.

We part ways, and as Melvin drives, I study the pictures.

"This is really happening, isn't it?" I ask, my hand resting over my heart.

# Chapter 41

After a miscarriage, expectant parents are much more cautious about announcing the next pregnancy. It's like announcing a new job before receiving the official offer or sharing your optimism that you won a competition before the judges' final scores. No matter how certain you are, things don't always go as planned. After meeting with Zoe and her mom, our confidence has grown, but we still feel a little gun-shy. We decide to share the news with our family because we want their support no matter what happens. I call my mom over the weekend to share the good news.

"We're having a baby!" I exclaim, my enthusiasm bubbling over like a shaken bottle of soda.

"You're pregnant?"

"Not exactly. A birth mom has chosen us. She's expecting, but she's planning on adoption and wants us to be the adoptive parents."

"That's amazing, honey. When is she due?"

"Zoe is due in May."

"Is that what you are going to name the baby?"

"No. The birth mom's name is Zoe."

"Is this the girl that you and Melvin went to dinner with a while back?"

"Yes. We met her and her parents. She's a high-school student. They live here in Minnesota, so we will go to the hospital right after she's born."

"It's a girl?"

"Yep! Another girl. Hopefully, this one is for keeps." We make plans for my mom to visit after the baby is born.

"I wouldn't miss it for the world. I have been praying for this for you and Melvin since you put in your adoption papers. And even more fervently since you lost sweet Hope."

Warmth fills me, and I rest my hand on my heart. "Thanks, Mom. That means a lot. I'm glad we have you on our side."

We talk through dates so she can search for flights. Later, Melvin calls Brenda to give her the good news. I can only hear one side of the conversation while I work in the kitchen, but I can envision her response.

"Hey, Ma."

"We're good. How about you?"

"Yup. That's great."

"I bet they are."

"We have some good news, too."

"A birth mom has chosen us to adopt her child."

"We still have a few months before the baby is born, but yes, three grandbabies in one year."

"Yes, it's hard to believe."

"May."

"It's a girl."

"Yes, we're thrilled."

"Okay. I'll let you go make your phone calls. You can tell Celeste and Elise."

He hangs up and gapes at me with wide eyes, shaking his head.

"I take it she's excited?"

"That's an understatement. She will alert all of Northeast Ohio before sundown," he jokes.

We spend our Saturday working on our daughter's room. Our daughter's room! I line the top drawer with diapers stacked with care. I neatly fold soft pastel sleepers and tiny onesies, tucking them away. My heart swells with joy, picturing a new morning routine of wiping a tiny bottom and sliding socks over dimpled toes. Melvin assembles the crib, and we stretch a pale pink sheet over the mattress, smiling across at each other. I hold the crocheted blanket from Louise close to my heart before draping it over the side. As we finish up, Melvin sits in the rocking chair, and I climb into his lap, resting my head on his chest. Giant pink flower wall stickers that are five feet high cover one wall. My heart is as oversized as those flowers. Everything is perfect. I can't wait for our daughter to arrive.

After dinner, we sit shoulder to shoulder in the living room with bowls of ice cream.

"Do you have any name ideas?" Melvin asks.

"That's a silly question. You know me; I'm a planner. I always have lists." Turning my phone toward him, I share my top five girl names.

"How about you? Do you have any names you've been considering?" I ask.

"Well, I've always loved Isabella. Or we could stick with the 'Mel' theme and name her Melanie." He grins.

"We probably have enough Mels in this house already." I bump my shoulder against his.

"What about Faith?" He points to the name on my screen.

"That one has been jumping out at me, too. It has been such an act of faith for us, especially when we lost Hope. And watching the faith Zoe has in making this decision... This baby girl is a product of much faith."

"Let's sleep on it and pray about it. We don't have to decide yet." Melvin pulls me close into a hug.

*** 

*We sit in the hallway at the hospital, the fluorescent lights buzzing in my ears. The smell of antiseptic burns my nostrils. Zoe is in the next room, but it's as if she is miles away. The waiting has stretched for hours, or is it days? Time is fuzzy. Muted footsteps and hushed whispers drift down the hall. I cling to Melvin's hand in anticipation and worry, counting the tiles between us and the door. Suddenly, it opens, and Nicole walks out, shaking her head. The click of the door echoes in the hallway.*

*"Is everything okay? Are Zoe and the baby all right?" I ask, jumping up.*

*"I'm sorry. We can't go through with it." She stands stiffly, staring straight ahead.*

*My heart plummets like a brick into a swimming pool. My limbs tremble. "What? I don't understand." My voice sounds like it is far away, like it isn't coming from me.*

*Nicole's voice sounds robotic. "Zoe wants to keep the baby. We can't let her go. She's ours."*

*I crumple to the floor, wanting to scream, but no sound escapes my lips. This can't be happening again. It seems like I'm falling through a hole, and I reach for Melvin to pull me to safety, but his hands are barely beyond my grasp.*

I wake with a start and jolt upright in bed. The tears and the panic are the only things that are real. The rest was simply a dream. A terrible dream.

Melvin rolls over, swallowing and clicking his tongue. "Are you okay, sweetie?"

"Nightmare," I say, my voice thick, the words sticking in my throat. "Zoe changed her mind. I... I..." Sobs wrack my body, and Melvin sits up, tucking me into his side.

"It's just a dream. They haven't changed their minds."

"How can you be certain? I think we should call them and check in with them tomorrow."

"We can't call them every time we have doubts. They won't change their minds." He runs his hands through my sweaty hair. "You've talked with them. They have prayed about this. Lie down, and I'll rub your back until you fall asleep. You'll feel better in the morning."

We both lie back down, but Melvin is the only one who drifts off as he strokes my back. That dream spooked me. What if it was a warning? A premonition? Zoe has supportive parents. She could keep the baby, and her parents would help her out. I lie on my side, curled in a ball, peering into the inky blackness, imagining everything that could go wrong. When we got the call about Hope, it never occurred to me that a birth mother could change her mind. But now I'm wiser than that. I've lived through the heartache of a failed adoption. It's all too real to me.

As the day wears on, I still can't get that dream out of my mind. I don't want her to think I'm crazy, but it would calm my fears if I heard from Zoe, so I text her to find out how she's doing.

Hearing from her settles me. She's the same as before. I'm sure nothing has changed...

I'm *almost* sure nothing has changed...

I'm *kind of* sure nothing has changed...

Oh, who am I kidding? I'm still worried.

After work, I'm slumped on the couch in a baggy sweatshirt and joggers when Melvin saunters in the door, whistling "Don't Worry Be Happy," his Monet tie loose around his neck. "Hey, babe. How was your day?"

"Fine," I mumble.

"That doesn't sound like someone who's about to be a mommy. My countdown calendar says thirty days."

"I can't stop thinking about that dream from last night." I bite my bottom lip and sink deeper into the sofa. That dream opened the portal to the trauma I went through when we lost Hope, and I've spent the day reliving it.

"Oh, Melly." Melvin pulls me up to stand in front of him. "It was just a dream." He grabs my hands and leads me in a dance around the living room. I resist and push him away.

"I'm serious, Melvin. We can't dance our troubles away. What if the dream was a premonition?"

"Even though it happened to us once doesn't mean it will happen again. We've met them, made plans, signed papers. You've got to stop obsessing over this."

"I'm not obsessing, Melvin. I'm trying to protect my heart. You're not taking me seriously." I turn and storm up to the bedroom. But that's no good. He'll be up here to change clothes. I need a place where I can be alone. Where am I going to go? I go back downstairs and grab the keys.

"I'll be back later," I spit the words out.

"Where are you going?" He follows me as I storm to the door.

"Away from here." The door slams behind me, and I climb into the car. I drive aimlessly through neighborhoods, with no plan for where

I'm going, and unconsciously steer out to the highway. Fleeing from the cities, I end up on a country road. I follow a sign for a state park and turn into the parking lot.

I zip up my jacket and stuff my hands in my pockets to combat the coolness of spring. This park is new to me. The parking lot borders a wooded area, with the trees showing their buds. A paved path parts the grove, directing my way. I walk silently, avoiding puddles of melting snow. Although I'm quiet on the outside, the voices in my head are working overtime. What if Zoe changes her mind? I've worked so hard to achieve motherhood, but somehow, it's always barely out of my grasp.

I pause, put my hands on my hips, and take a deep breath. The cool air pierces my lungs. Even the pain of not being able to have children was less painful than having one and losing her. I can't face that again.

*Even Jesus suffered and asked that the cup be removed from him. But He was willing to suffer because it was the Father's will.*

Was that God's will? *Why, God?* My eyes sting, and I walk again, slowly. Why would you want me to suffer this?

*All things work together for good to them that love God.*

I glance at the clear blue sky. But how can that experience be good for me? It hasn't improved my life. I pick up speed and pass a couple taking a leisurely walk.

*All these things will give you experience.*

That wasn't an experience I wanted. What good did it do? Beads of sweat form on my forehead. The pounding in my ears echoes the pounding of my feet on the pavement.

*Not your will, but mine be done.*

I want to do Your will. But I'm afraid. What if your will isn't for me to be a mother? Can I accept that? I sniffle and dab my nose with my sleeve.

*For I know the plans I have for you. Plans to prosper you, and not to harm you.*

Losing Hope did not cause my life to flourish. It still hurts. Where is the 'prosper' in that? And if Zoe changes her mind... I can't survive another loss. I pull off my jacket and tie it around my waist while I walk.

*Trust in the Lord with all thine heart and lean not unto thine own understanding.*

I'm trying. But why, Lord?

*Don't ask, 'Why?' ask, 'What's next?'*

I round the corner and freeze at the sight before me—a beautiful waterfall. The water crashes into a blue pool, the waves smoothing out as they move to the edge. I inch to the nearby bench and ease onto it, wiping the moisture from under my eyes. My heartbeat slows, and I'm overcome by the scene. This unexpected beauty was right around the corner. I had to keep moving to discover it. I ponder the ideas and impressions in my mind, peace washing over me.

Yes, God has a plan for me. And it seems like that means adopting Zoe's baby. But I will try to trust Him. I need to accept that God had a reason for putting Hope in our lives, even if it was for only a week.

What did I learn from that week?

I learned that I am capable of being a mother, even if my body cannot produce a child.

I learned that Melvin is a great dad, and we make a great team.

And I learned great loss results from great love.

I have never gone through that kind of loss before. It changed me. Now, I will have a new level of compassion for others who have lost someone they love.

The steady sound of rushing water soothes my soul. The noise drowns out my sorrows, and the view brings peace to my spirit. Looking around, I notice new buds forming on the trees and flower shoots poking through the ground. After the deadness of winter, there is new birth. The plants don't force themselves to bloom each year. There is work below the surface, but each flower allows itself to be what God created it to be. A tree can't stop growing. And I have an epiphany that God has been in charge all along.

I lose track of time sitting here. A few families and couples walk past me on the path. I breathe deeply and smell the fresh air.

*What's next?*

I can't control the result. Zoe may change her mind. All I can do is trust. I trust that Zoe will do what is best for her and her baby. And I trust that God is in charge. Whether or not we get to adopt this baby, I will trust in Him.

It's dark by the time I arrive home. I walk in the door, and Melvin approaches. "Are you okay?"

Stretching my arms toward him, I nod. "I'm better."

"I ordered pizza. Are you hungry?" He grabs the cardboard box and some napkins, and we sit on the couch. We hold hands and pray over the food.

"Talk to me." He grabs a slice.

"That nightmare scared me. It brought back all the trials of the past few years." I glance up and see the sculpture he made sitting on the mantle. My chest tightens, remembering each shattered dream. "I can't face another loss. And I kind of freaked out. I'm sorry."

"I forgive you. And I'm sorry, too. I was trying to lighten the mood. I'm ready to listen."

My struggles and concerns pour out of me like the waterfall, but I also share the peace that came over me when I was there. "Despite the work I put in, I can't control the result. I'm ready to trust God. He has our best interests at heart, whether that means adopting Zoe's baby or remaining childless. Either way, He will take care of us. 'All things work together for good to them that love God.' Right?"

"Right." He pulls me toward him, runs his hands through my hair, and kisses the crown of my head.

# Chapter 42

Zoe, Nicole, and Tom arrive at our house for dinner and a game night. We keep things relaxed since she is weeks away from her due date. After we finish dinner, I put homemade chocolate lava cakes in the oven for dessert, and we play a quick round of cards.

Zoe is adorable with her long blonde curls and cute pregnancy bump. Her belly is all baby. She is thin and petite everywhere else. After dessert, I take her and Nicole upstairs to show them the nursery.

"It's adorable." Zoe sighs, slowly turning around and taking it all in. "She's going to love it here."

"It's been fun getting it ready for her. How are you managing? What does the doctor say?"

"Well, the last time I went in, she said I'm measuring right on track, and her heartbeat is strong."

"That's great."

"Ooh! She's moving. Want to feel her?"

"Of course," I exclaim. Zoe grabs my hand and places it on her stomach. Gentle pokes come from inside. "That is incredible. I suppose it's uncomfortable for you, though."

"It's not that bad. Mostly, it's amazing to imagine a tiny human inside, moving around. I love it."

"Actually, Zoe has a doctor's appointment next week," Nicole says. "You should join us. Then you could hear the heartbeat."

"Is that okay? I mean, I would love to, but I don't want to overstep."

Zoe grasps my hand. "I *want* you to be there. You're going to be her mom."

We get out our phones and share information about the appointment. I schedule it on my calendar. Inside, I'm tingling with excitement, but I play it cool. These small gestures from Zoe and her parents calm my concerns and doubts. Part of me is afraid to get my hopes up, but another part of me has faith in the Lord that He will make all things work out for my good.

***

The following week, I join Zoe and her mom for her appointment. I chuckle when I see she's wearing the 'Not a Food Baby' shirt.

"Nice shirt." I duck into the chair beside Zoe in the waiting room and twirl my wedding ring while we wait. The nurse calls us back, and they go through the formalities before settling us into an exam room. We chat briefly about her job before the doctor taps on the door and enters.

"Hello, Zoe." A kind woman in a lab coat smiles at me. "Oh, we have an extra guest today."

"This is Amelia. She is going to adopt the baby," Zoe explains, her face glowing with a smile. I was curious about how open she was about the adoption with her doctor. I'm glad she made the introduction.

"Nice to meet you, Amelia. Congratulations."

"Thanks. We're excited." I smile, smoothing my hands over my lap.

The doctor examines the chart and helps Zoe onto the table. She measures her stomach and makes a note of it.

"Let's take a quick listen to the heartbeat." She grabs the Doppler and jelly.

*Whoosh, whoosh, whoosh, whoosh,* echoes from the machine. Butterflies take over my heart at the sound.

"A nice strong heartbeat. Everything looks and sounds great, Zoe."

That was my daughter. I've seen her ultrasound pictures. I've felt her move. And now I've heard her. It's for real. My little girl.

Faith.

We haven't talked about her name with Zoe. I wonder whether she will like it. But I keep it close to my heart and ponder it.

After Zoe schedules her next appointment, we part with a hug and leave for our cars. On my drive to work, I'm humming with excitement. I'm going to be a mom. I bop in my seat to the music on the radio. At the stoplight, the guy in the car next to mine gapes at me and shakes his head. But I don't care. I'm filled with joy and hope for the future.

After work, I tell Melvin all about it.

"The heartbeat was amazing. It makes a fast whooshing sound. The doctor says everything is good. Zoe even introduced me as the adoptive mom. It was awesome."

Melvin's eyes crinkle in joy as he listens to my exuberant chattering. He holds out his hand. I take it, and he twirls me into his embrace. "I wish I could have heard it. It's good to see you excited again. Did it help calm your fears after that nightmare?"

I cling to him and nod my head. "Yeah. It did."

***

Each week progresses like I'm living in slow motion. As I sit at my desk at work, every second ticks off on the clock. *Tick, tick, tick*. It's a waiting sound. A slow-moving sound. That's how my life is right now. The nursery is ready. I'm caught up with work responsibilities. The freezer is filled with meals to make dinnertime easier after we bring Faith home. All that's left is the waiting. Every time my phone buzzes, I jump. Could this be the news? And then it isn't.

We keep in regular contact with Zoe and her parents. I put together a gift to give Zoe after the birth. Some lotion, bath salts, and chocolates. I imagine the days after we take Faith home will be painful for her physically and emotionally. Not to mention her hormones will take a toll.

The chance to get to know Zoe and her family has given me more compassion and understanding for Hope's birth mother. When she changed her mind, my entire world fell apart. But now I recognize the depth of the decision she had to make, and I respect her for it. Hope should be about nine months old now. I send up a silent prayer for the two of them, that God will watch over and protect them.

At her last appointment, Zoe's doctor said it could happen any day now. We're on high alert. Every morning, I wonder if this will be the day I become a mom. Each night, I go to bed expecting a middle-of-the-night call. And so here I sit, listening to the clock tick down the seconds.

On Tuesday evening, my phone rings. I flip it over to see Nicole's name. "Melvin! It's Nicole!"

Melvin joins me in the living room. I answer quickly and put it on speakerphone so he can hear.

"I'm at the hospital with Zoe. She started having contractions this afternoon. We headed over when they got within five minutes of each other. They admitted her and are monitoring her."

My stomach flips like a gymnast performing the floor exercise. "Should we head over right now?"

"It's her first child, so they expect it to be hours before the baby's here. Possibly not until morning. I wanted to give you a heads-up. I'll call when it gets closer."

"Okay. I'll keep my phone on and next to my bed. Let Zoe know we'll be praying for her." I end the call, clap my hands and let out a squeal of delight.

Melvin pushes me back on the couch and hovers over me. "Looks like we're having a baby, Melly." He dips in for a kiss.

I kiss him back and then pull out my phone. "I have a checklist so we don't forget anything."

A rumble emits from Melvin's chest. "Of course you do. One of the many reasons I love you." He twists and sits back up, pulling me up next to him.

"First, we need to contact our bosses to let them know we won't be in tomorrow."

"Got it."

"Then, let's set everything out. You'll need your camera bag. We should set our clothes out in case they call while we're still asleep, so we don't waste any time getting out the door. I'll let everyone know in the family group chats." I check the time. "We should probably get to bed soon."

"Do you really think you're going to be able to sleep?"

"Probably not, but I'll try." I smile up at him.

After getting ready, we pause on our knees at the side of our bed, hands clasped together. We offer a prayer for Zoe and our daughter, praising God for giving us this opportunity and answering our prayers. It's a restless sleep. The anticipation keeps waking me, my fingers itching for my phone every few minutes.

At 3:15, when I've finally drifted off, my phone rings.

"Hello?" I put it on speaker and roll toward Melvin.

"Hi, Amelia. It's Nicole. Sorry to wake you. You should probably come to the hospital now. She's dilated to a nine, and they said she could start pushing soon. It might still be a while, but we don't want you to miss it."

"Thank you. How is Zoe doing?"

"She's good. Tired, but she got an epidural, and that has helped."

"We'll say another prayer for her, and we'll be there in about an hour."

We hang up and hop out of bed. I tie my hair into a ponytail and put on deodorant before slipping into jeans and a sweatshirt. Melvin gets dressed and wets down his hair. We brush our teeth quickly and rush out the door.

The roads are empty at 3:30 in the morning. We make it to the hospital in record time and arrive on the maternity floor. The nurses are expecting us, and they direct us to the family waiting area. Tom greets us. He's been holding vigil all night. The nurse says she will inform them we are here, and we wait again.

We sit on those plastic upholstered chairs forever, holding hands, watching the clock. At about 4:45, we hear the music that plays throughout the halls every time a baby is born in the hospital. We glance at each other. That might mean our daughter has been born.

In another ten minutes, Nicole is standing at the door, beaming. It's the opposite of what happened in the nightmare I had.

"It's a girl," she exclaims.

Tom folds Nicole in a hug. "How are they doing?"

"Zoe and the baby are doing great. She needed a few stitches, but they are ready for you now. You can meet your daughter."

"Is it okay if we take pictures?" Melvin asks, patting his camera bag.

"Of course," Nicole says, grabbing Tom's hand.

Tom and Nicole lead the way down the hall. We follow them, my limbs pulsing with an electrical current. Melvin and I lock our hands together, warmth spreading between us. We've waited so long for this moment. It's hard to believe it's finally here. On the other side of the door is the answer to years of effort and prayers. Nicole quietly opens the door.

For a moment as big as this is, I expect a choir of angels to be singing from heaven and a shaft of light illuminating the scene from clouds above. Although the heavens are probably rejoicing right now, there is a hush in this sacred place.

Zoe is sitting up in bed with a bundle in her arms. She appears exhausted but happy. I hold back, allowing her dad to approach first. She catches my eye from across the room. "This is your new daughter. Would you like to hold her?"

"Can I?"

"Of course. She's *your* daughter."

"Are you positive?" I hesitate, rubbing my hands together.

"Yes, she's yours," Zoe says confidently.

I stride across the room, take her in my arms, and suck in a breath. A little over a year ago, I held Ruby right after she was born. My daughter is soft and dimpled like she was. The hospital bed, the blanket, the lights are all the same, but this is... different. My chest expands with love and awe. I'm fascinated by her and want to memorize every detail. She has a fuzz of blonde hair on her head and light blue eyes. I swallow and search for words. "She's beautiful." I peer up at Zoe, my eyes suddenly stinging. "Thank you. This is an amazing gift." I didn't even notice it, but Melvin has his camera out and has been capturing this moment. He tucks into my side and admires our daughter. Her eyes blink as she wriggles and stretches under the blanket. Melvin takes her tiny hand, and she grasps his finger. We both fall immediately and hopelessly in love.

After a few minutes, the photographer in him goes back into action. He sets up different combinations of Zoe, the baby, and her parents. Then Zoe and me with the baby. He sets up a photo of both of us with her and asks Tom to push the button.

"Do you guys have a name for her?" Zoe asks.

"We were thinking of Faith." I glance at her for a reaction.

"That's perfect," Zoe says, tears in her eyes.

"This has been an act of faith for us and for you and your parents. It seemed like an appropriate name." I pause and fix my gaze on Zoe. "And we'd like her middle name to be Zoe, if that's okay with you."

"Oh, Amelia! That means the world to me. Yes. Of course. I'm honored I will still be a part of her."

"It's settled then." Melvin nods.

The nurse enters and says they need to bring Faith to the nursery for a few tests, but we can go with her. Melvin and I accompany her, and Nicole and Tom stay with Zoe. After about an hour of tests and observation, they return her to Zoe's room. Zoe has fallen asleep, so we quietly take a seat and take turns passing Faith around, letting Nicole and Tom hold her too.

Somewhere around 7:00 a.m., Faith fusses, and that wakes Zoe. She wants to give Faith her bottle. As much as we hate to go, it's time. We promised them space while they are in the hospital. We say our goodbyes and make plans to return on Friday when they will be released.

On the ride home, we are sleepy but blissful. Melvin grabs my hand, navigating rush hour traffic. We're in no hurry, though. We stop for breakfast on the way home. He pulls out the camera while we wait for our food, and we flip through the pictures he took. She resembles Zoe in her blonde hair and the shape of her eyes.

"I love that one... She's so precious. Look at that little crooked mouth when she was yawning," I say.

"Bringing her home can't come soon enough."

"Two days. Let's run to the store and grab some formula and diapers."

"Can we go home and nap first?" he asks.

"Definitely. There's nothing else I want after breakfast. Just a nice long nap."

"We probably had better call the grandparents, though."

"True. Breakfast. Phone calls. Then a nap." I smile across the table at him. Our breakfast is served, and we scarf it down. I didn't realize how hungry I was. Melvin pays the bill, and we hop into the car. As he drives, Melvin calls his mom over Bluetooth.

"Hey, Mom!"

"Did the birth mom have the baby yet? Am I a grandma?" Brenda asks. She's been waiting by the phone for this call.

Melvin rattles off the stats like a pro. "Yes. She was seven pounds, thirteen ounces, twenty-one inches long. She was born at 4:42 this morning."

"Does she have a name? Did you get to meet her yet?"

"Yes, and yes," he chuckles. "Her name is Faith Zoe Greathouse. We saw her when she was only about fifteen minutes old. She is adorable. You are going to love her."

"When do you get to take her home?"

"They will be released from the hospital on Friday, and we will take her home from there."

"When can I meet my granddaughter? I can pack up the car and help next week."

"We appreciate that, Mom. Bethany will be here next week. Why don't you visit a couple of weeks after that to spread out the help?"

"If that's what you want. You'd better at least send pictures. Can we have a video call so I can see her?"

"Of course, Mom. We will do that this weekend."

"Should I call your sisters? And my friends Charisse and Ruth have been dying to hear. I can't wait to give them the news."

"Of course, call everyone. Tell your friends. Well, I'd better get going. We've been up half the night. We're going to get some rest."

"Sounds good. Don't forget to send me pictures before you fall asleep."

"I'll do that, Mom." They say goodbye and disconnect the call right as we pull into the garage. I feel like I'm moving through a thick fog. My body is weary and heavy. I make a quick call to give my mom the good news about Faith, but I do it from my bed and fight to keep my eyes open before slumber pulls me under like a wave.

# Chapter 43

Two days drag on like forever.

We arrive at the hospital around 10:00 on Friday morning. I bounce into the hospital, one hand holding Melvin's, the other holding the gift bag for Zoe. We printed and framed some photos Melvin took and slipped them into the bag. Hopefully, that will bring her peace in the days ahead. With the diaper bag slung over his shoulder, Melvin carries the car seat, his arm muscles bulging underneath his shirt. Fatherhood looks good on him. We proceed to Zoe's room and knock lightly.

"Come in," Zoe's voice calls from the other side of the door.

We enter to find Zoe holding Faith, with Nicole and Tom on either side of the hospital bed. They are dressed, and their things are all packed up. Faith is wearing a beautiful smocked gown. It is pale pink with a big white bow on the front.

"Hey guys, how are you?" I ask in hushed tones, not wanting to disturb the reverent scene. Zoe's cheeks glisten with fresh tears. Even though this is such a happy day for us, I imagine it's bittersweet for them. I hand Zoe the gift. "This is for you."

"Thanks. We're doing okay. It's hard, but we know it is right." Zoe reassures me and calms my fears, even in her pain.

"That dress is beautiful," I say.

"Thanks. My grandma made it for her. We wanted to send her off with lots of love from our family. We have gifts here, too."

"Thank you. Tell your grandma we love it," I say, accepting the gifts. The nurse walks in to go over everything for discharge. We sign papers and collect her records and newborn care instructions, and the nurse leaves us again.

Zoe nuzzles Faith and kisses her forehead. "It's time to go to your mommy now, Faith." She sniffles out the words and hands her to me. I put her in the car seat and strap her in. Turning back, I pull Zoe into a long hug.

"Thank you for what you've done for us. This is the greatest gift, and we acknowledge what a sacrifice it is. We love you so much." Now we're both crying. We promise to keep in touch and have them over in a few months before Zoe heads to college.

"We'd better get out of here," Melvin says. He secures Faith in her car seat. We gather all her things and wave goodbye. Melvin sneaks a kiss during our ride down the elevator. My heart is full of incredible love for Melvin and Faith, and I am in awe of the gift Zoe has given us.

***

As we enter the house, Melvin sets the car seat down on the coffee table. Sleepy sighs emerge from beneath the canopy. I push it back and stare at her round cheeks and closed eyes. We slip onto the sofa, perched on the edge, watching her in awe.

"Should we move her?" Melvin asks.

"I know you aren't supposed to disturb a sleeping baby, but I just want to hold her."

Melvin leans over and unbuckles Faith. His firm hands slip underneath her as he gently lifts her out, supporting her neck. He hands her to me. "Here you go, Mommy. If you want to hold your baby, then I think you should."

She squeaks and wiggles as he places her in the crook of my arm. I pat her bottom with my spare hand to settle her. Melvin rests his arm across my back, peering down at our precious bundle. I try to memorize this moment. The three of us snuggled together. The disappointments of the past couple of years seem insignificant now. This right here is all I need.

***

Newborn cries rouse me from sleep. I glance at the time. Six a.m. Melvin stirs in the bed next to me.

"I've got her. Go back to sleep." I brush my lips across his cheek and shuffle across the hall. Melvin was up with her a few short hours ago, and I'm happy to take my turn. He has been a godsend. The perfect father. He jumps in and helps with diapers and feedings, a true partner in this new attempt at parenthood. There's a soft glow in Faith's room from the day breaking outside. My hands scoop under her, and a chilly dampness greets them.

"Good morning, sweetheart. Somebody needs a change." I rotate to the changing table, and set her down, finding the pacifier to subdue her while I work. She's been home for a week, and already I've found a comfortable routine. I strip off the sleeper and onesie, tossing them in the hamper. She wails louder. "I know you're cold. Just a minute, and I'll get you washed up." I reinsert the pacifier and reach for a fresh diaper from the drawer. I give her a wet wipe sponge bath and make quick work of the diaper change. Soon I have her clean, dry, and dressed.

My bare feet slap against the hardwood floors, Faith resting on my forearm. I pull a clean bottle from the drying rack, methodically preparing her liquid breakfast, using only one arm. Slurps replace her cries, and I head back upstairs to her room.

The soft creak of the rocking chair gives rhythm to my thoughts. A contented sigh escapes me while I gaze at her round cheeks, her mouth working overtime to inhale the formula. A part of me was on edge that first week, recalling the horrible phone call that stole our joy when we had Hope. But this time we received only calls of congratulations. We will finalize the adoption in court months from now, but a reassuring gratitude fills my heart that we made it through that first week.

***

I pull into Allie's driveway and turn off the ignition. Keys. Phone. Purse. I step out and turn to collect Faith from the back seat. "Hello, baby! We're here!" I grab the car seat and diaper bag and carry my load up the front steps.

"Hey, guys. I'm glad you're here." Allie holds the door open and allows me to maneuver my way through. Faith is three weeks old. Our first official playdate. We decided it would be easier for Ruby to do it here. I set the car seat next to the chair and strip the bundles from my arms.

Ruby toddles over and peeks in at Faith. She thrusts her hand in, attempting to touch her, and Allie is right behind her, guiding her. "Gentle... Gentle... See?" Ruby toddles away, searching for toys, and Allie gives me a side-hug, keeping her eyes on her daughter.

"How's it going?"

"She acts like an angel now, but it was a different story at two this morning." I run my hands through my hair, letting the honey-colored strands fall where they may, and stifle a yawn.

"I get it. Ruby was six months old before I could count on a full night's sleep. Can I grab you something to drink?"

"I brought my water bottle." Holding it up as proof, I sink into the seat. "How's the social media marketing business?"

"Pretty good. I could use another client or two, but it's nice that I can work while Ruby naps. I schedule all the social media posts for my clients, so I don't have to be tied to my computer all the time. How about you? What's your plan for work?"

"I have maternity leave, but I decided I'm not going back. When we had to give Hope back to her birth mother, it changed my perspective. Hearing the speakers at the entrepreneur conference last fall and watching you has inspired me."

"Oh yeah? What are you going to do?"

"I'm going to launch a website for birthday parties. It will have themed plans for sale, complete with activities, decorations, and food suggestions. I will create affiliate links for all the products I recommend. I can blog and make videos to review recommended products and show ideas."

Allie claps her hands together, startling Faith. "Sorry... You're a genius! I love that idea. And we can be 'mom-preneurs' together."

My arms and legs tingle with excitement. "Someday soon, I can hire you to do my social media marketing. But right now, I'm trying to wrap my head around how to get started."

"You'll figure it out. You've always been a great problem solver."

"If there's one thing I've learned over the past few years, it's that I'm not in charge. No matter how much I work to fix things, ultimately I must trust God. His will and His timing are often different from mine."

# Chapter 44

F aith is six weeks old already. I can't believe it. I bustle around during our morning routine. She wakes up earlier than usual, so I miss the window for my shower. Deodorant and dry shampoo will hold me over. I grab the diaper bag and load Faith up into the car. We head to the park, where Wendy and her kids are meeting us.

I wave from the parking lot at Wendy. She's planted herself at a picnic table under the shade of a maple tree. Her kids are crawling all over the playground like ants on a piece of watermelon. The lawn mower buzzes in the background as the park maintenance crew tends to the grounds. I wheel the stroller over and position myself next to her.

"How are you holding up?" I cock my head toward her.

"I'm as big as a house. The doctor says I could go any day now." She rubs her hand across her swollen belly. "How are you doing?"

"I'm tired. She's usually up twice a night, and this morning, she woke up with the sun. Didn't you, little one?" I grab Faith's hand and coo at her. Her eyes focus on me in recognition, and she gives a half smile.

Wendy peers into the stroller. "It's amazing how something so small and innocent can turn your world upside down and change everything."

"Are you ready to have your world turned upside down again?"

Finn hops over. "Mommy, there's something in my shoe!"

Wendy quickly slips off his shoe, shakes out a woodchip, and returns the shoe to his foot. She pats his head, and he races to the playground. "My world is already upside down. I lost all semblance of control ten years ago. It will be another adjustment, but we'll make it work." She gives a little shrug.

"Wendy, you amaze me. You're about to have your fifth child, and here you are at the park with your kids, just going with the flow." A breeze blows through the park, and we inhale the scent of freshly cut grass.

"I learned a long time ago to let go of my expectations. Each of these humans depends on me, and right now, this is a season where they are my top priority. Someday down the road, I can worry about a clean, organized house and take up hobbies. But for now, God has entrusted me with them, and I'm grateful."

"I have a confession to make, Wendy."

She observes me out of the corner of her eye. "Go on..."

"When we first met, I didn't like you. But I realize it wasn't that I didn't like you. I was jealous of what you had. I was so ready to have kids, and you had everything I wanted and more. My heart was full of bitterness about my situation and jealousy that you had the life I was dreaming of. And it seemed so easy for you."

"I did kind of get a vibe from you." She winks. "But I get it. And yes, the getting pregnant part has been 'easy' for me. But the rest of it? It's definitely *not* easy."

"I'm figuring that out now. Thanks for being so kind to me when I was struggling. And thanks for being such a friend this past month and helping me learn how to be a mom." I put my arm around her and pull her into a side hug.

"Oh, please." She waves her hand toward me. "Amazing Amelia. You didn't need any help. You're doing great. I'm glad for your friendship, too."

\*\*\*

"Say cheese!" The kind stranger points our phone at us and snaps a few pictures in front of the State Fair sign. It's the end of August, and we are starting our family tradition. Faith is three months old, so she'll never remember this. But we will.

"Where should we go first?" I look up at Melvin.

"Let's go see the baby animals." We steer our way through the crowds and enter the 'Miracle of Birth' exhibit. The smell of hay, manure, and animals hits us as we near the entrance. We wander around and find a crowd gathered by the pigpen. A chorus of grunts and oinks greets us. There must be a dozen piglets suckling from their momma.

"She's got her hands full, doesn't she?" I joke with Melvin.

"Sure does."

We stand and watch in awe at the pink squirming bundles. "Whatever happened to that Halloween costume I got last year? Is that still around?" I turn toward Melvin quizzically.

He drapes his arm around my shoulders and pulls me in close. "I hid it at the back of the closet. Will it fit Faith this year?"

"It might. Let's take a picture of her with these piggies. It would go great with a photo of her dressed as a pig." I pull her out of the stroller and hold her up next to the pen. Melvin scoots back and frames us with the pigs.

We wander around the exhibits, pausing for food and to give Faith a bottle when she fusses. By mid-afternoon, we are back at the All You Can Drink Milk Booth, enjoying our Sweet Martha's cookies.

"It was a year ago we sat here." Melvin studies me, remembering.

"Can you believe that? I was completely unaware of what we were in for. If you had told me how the year would play out, I probably wouldn't have agreed to it." I grab another cookie and bite into it, the soft, warm chocolate dripping down my lip.

"It was tough. I was worried about you for a while. And us." He leans his shoulder into me as he holds Faith. She drinks her milk, too. But no cookies for her this year.

"Thanks for being patient with me. I'm glad we made it through."

"I love you even more now than I did when we got married. You are so resilient and tenacious. We've gone through so much to be a family. I admire how you submitted to God's will and let Him lead in our lives. You're amazing, Amelia." He kisses the top of my head.

Faith finishes her bottle, and Melvin burps her. Wendy called me Amazing Amelia last month. I spent so much time trying to make myself amazing. I tried to earn the title and get what I wanted in life through sheer will and grit. This journey has taught me that I need to depend on others. I needed my team at work to pull off events. I needed Zoe to give me the gift of motherhood. And most of all, I continue to need God every day to lead and guide my life.

# Author's Note

Infertility and infant loss are typically very private, painful struggles. There are many paths to parenthood, and some will never be parents despite the desires of their hearts.

Although I have not struggled to the extent that many people do, I had a miscarriage after my second child. I remember how heartbroken I was. We hadn't told anyone we were expecting yet because it was still early in the pregnancy. That made it even lonelier as I worked through my loss.

If this is a challenge you face, I honor you. Your decisions will be different from Amelia and Melvin's, but with God's guidance, they will be the right choices for you. I pray that this fictional story gives you hope and renews your faith as you wade through your unique journey.

*Scan the QR code to listen.*

Forever Yours by Sara Cenatiempo

https://youtu.be/JldV2KLXGhI

May this song about the pain of losing a child help you feel a little less

alone.

# Acknowledgements

"If there is a book you want to read, but it hasn't been
written yet, then you must write it."
~Toni Morrison

That is how this book began. It took hold of my heart and would not
let go. I thank my Heavenly Father for planting this idea and allowing
me the privilege of partnering with Him to create this story. Any good
you find is because of Him. All flaws are because of my humanness.

When I decided that the next chapter in my life was to write fiction,
I reached out to the only author I knew personally—Annmarie Boyle.
I appreciate her for always steering me in the right direction and an-
swering my questions.

Writing a book about the struggle with infertility when you haven't
experienced it yourself is challenging. I'm grateful to Ken and Janet
Friday and Craig and Anthea Wilson for opening up and sharing their
experiences. Pieces of their stories inspired this story.

Thank you to early readers: Kaylee Baldwin, Kris Bermel, Teresa Denkers, Helen Lapakko, Jennifer Nunes, and Linda Peshina. I appreciate the time they took to read a very unpolished work and give their suggestions to a newbie author.

The input I received from critique partners Cathryn Lyon and Aleah Donald was an invaluable part of the journey.

The Women's Fiction Writers Association's daily writing dates gave me space and community to work through the daunting task of writing, revising, and editing this novel.

Without professional editors, this book would not be what it is today. Thank you to KaTrina Jackson of Eschler Editing. Her insights helped shape the story, but her encouragement helped me recognize how much this story needed to be told. Cassie Mae of CookieLynn Publishing Services showed me how to make my prose more beautiful, and she did it with a gentle hand.

At the eleventh hour, Ali Cross came into my life with her magic wand and helped take this book to the finish line. I'm grateful for her guidance at just the right time.

Thank you also to every person who took the time to ask about my book, encourage me, and believe in me. I couldn't give up when I knew others were waiting for this story to be completed.

And finally, thank you, dear reader. For reading, for reviewing, for recommending this book to others. A story becomes something more when it is read. I appreciate you for spending your precious time with me in this book.

# About the author

*Photograph by Fernanda Felix
Peña.*

Deb L. Brown had her first piece of writing published in the second grade. The high school newspaper picked up her poem about the color pink. Deb has never been to "the gym" and believes the best thing to eat is chocolate-covered chocolate.

Her hobbies include binge-watching home improvement shows but never DIYing anything, reading until midnight, and sleeping in the next morning. She is magnetically drawn to the clearance section of every store she enters and can't resist a pretty dress.

Deb has a heart for entrepreneurs, and once upon a time, she published her first book, *Lifelong Loyal Clients*.

Deb is a member of The Church of Jesus Christ of Latter-day Saints and volunteers in her congregation. Hailing from the land of 10,000 lakes, she and her husband are the parents of five adult children, two daughters-in-love, and are Graham Cracker and Pop Tart to their delightful grandchildren.

To download your free prayer journal, ***Waiting Upon the Lord: A Prayer Journal for Seasons of Waiting***, go to: https://debbrownau thor.com/

www.ingramcontent.com/pod-product-compliance
Lightning Source LLC
Chambersburg PA
CBHW050025120726
47903CB00006B/1917